Praise for
Kingdom in the Redwoods

Kingdom in the Redwoods is a must-read for families, delivering an engaging plot and diving into profound themes. Reminiscent of the captivating storytelling of C.S. Lewis, this book is both enjoyable and insightful. Aaron, Benji, and Hannah have to complete a mission bigger than any I've done as a Navy SEAL, offering a journey that resonates spiritual truths with readers of all ages.
—**Chad Williams,** *Former Navy SEAL, Best-selling author of SEAL of God, Youth Pastor*

***

Kingdom in the Redwoods is a modern-day allegory that addresses today's societal issues that young readers need to know how to navigate. Keven does an excellent job through his writing, plot, setting, and use of allegory to bring the reader to a place where he or she draws his or her own conclusions, inevitably seeing that there needs to be an absolute truth and the anarchy and chaos that comes when everyone makes him or herself the most significant and important being. The book is truly multi-generational illustrating the significance of family-- both parents and grandparents-- and the influence that they have in their children's lives. It would make for an amazing family read-aloud and open up many important and needed conversations to address the modern-day challenges that children face and how to overcome them all through one's identity in Jesus Christ, and the place of God's infallible word in our life. I am thankful to Keven for writing this novel and excited for the impact it will have on our next generation of children who will be blessed to read it.

—Lesley Russell, *Founder and President of EQUIP 210*
www.equip210.com

***

As a homeschool mom of 2 children, 11 and 13 years old, I'm always looking for literature that both stimulates their mind and soul. *Kingdom in the Redwoods* was a fast read for my kids that was engaging in adventure and theological topics that my kids enjoyed. If your child is looking for a safe enjoyable fantasy fiction novel this one is an excellent choice.

—Wendy, *Homeschool Mother*

***

Kingdom in the Redwoods is a fun adventure story set in a fantasy world that's a real page-turner. It uses allegory to explore real life issues, but more importantly, the story shines a light on Christ and what it means to be made in his image. As a homeschooling parent of four, I highly recommend this book. Even my daughter who doesn't tend to pick fantasy books as her preferred genre loved it and finished it in a couple of days!

—Brooke, *Homeschool Mother*

KINGDOM IN THE REDWOODS

by

Keven Baxter

Published by KHARIS PUBLISHING, an imprint of KHARIS MEDIA LLC.

Copyright © 2024 Keven Baxter

ISBN-13: 978-1-63746-244-7

ISBN-10: 1-63746-244-1

Library of Congress Control Number: 2024930534

Map Illustration *by* **David Leahey**

Developmental editing *by* **Laura Edge**

All KHARIS PUBLISHING products are available at special quantity discounts for bulk purchase for sales promotions, premiums, fund-raising, and educational needs. For details, contact:

Kharis Media LLC
Tel: 1-630-909-3405
support@kharispublishing.com
www.kharispublishing.com

First, to the King of Kings, whose name is above every name, who has extended His grace upon me beyond anything I could hope or imagine.

To my wife, Claire, who inspires me to make every day special. To Daria and Lindsay, who are our priceless masterpieces in this world. To Bo, through whom I see hope in the next generation. Finally, to Baxter and Arlo, who remind me of the abundant goodness and beauty in the world through a child's eyes.

Acknowledgements

Thanks to Dane, Piper, and Tatum who read early drafts of my story and supplied fantastic insights to bring the story and characters to life.

Join Me in the Kingdom in the Redwoods

I invite you to step into this amazing fantasy world to join Aaron, Benji, and Hannah on their adventure. My highest aim as a storyteller is to serve you by delivering an outrageously fun story that not only captivates you, but also delivers light and hope. I have designed multiple ways for you to enjoy *Kingdom in the Redwoods*.

First, you can enjoy the book in one or more of the many available formats: *Paperback, Hardcover, Audio book, and eBook*.

Second, please tell your family and friends about *Kingdom in the Redwoods*. If you would like to enjoy the story with others, or simply reflect on the themes presented in the story on your own, **ask for a free copy of the Discussion Guide at: www.kevenbaxter.com**.

Thank you for joining me on the adventure, *Kingdom in the Redwoods*. I am dedicated to creating captivating stories for you that deliver light and hope, so I would love to hear from you. I value your feedback and what to hear from you. You can email me at: bax@kevenbaxter.com.

Beauty is the brilliance of truth.

Augustine

Table of Contents

Introduction xi

Chapter 1: Last Day of School 13

Chapter 2: The Ranch 33

Chapter 3: The Redwood Grove 45

Chapter 4: Christmas Tree in the Forest 55

Chapter 5: A Climb into the Fog 65

Chapter 6: Mr. Wigglebottom 77

Chapter 7: Shadowlands 85

Chapter 8: King for a Day 95

Chapter 9: An Adventure Awaits 109

Chapter 10: Aspen Meadows 121

Chapter 11: City of Light 133

Chapter 12: An Audience with the King 145

Chapter 13: A Royal Banquet 159

Chapter 14: Kingdom Tour 171

Chapter 15: A Secret War 183

Chapter 16: Spy Craft 193

Chapter 17: Counter Espionage 203

Chapter 18: The Himmel Games 215

Chapter 19: The Battle Begins 229

Chapter 20: Prisoners in Enemy Territory 237

Chapter 21: Attack Against the King 247

Chapter 22: Kingdom Restored 259

Chapter 23: Christmas at the Ranch.................................... 273

Chapter 24: White Christmas... 287

Epilogue: The War is not Over... 297

    Attribution 299

    Continue the Adventure 300

Introduction

This is the story of the Parsons family's adventure one Christmas season. Peter and Sarah Parsons had three children, 12-year-old Aaron, his 10-year-old brother Benji, and their 8-year-old sister Hannah. Peter's parents, Sam and Chloe – Papa and Grandma to the children – lived high in the mountains in a place called Parsons' Ranch, or the Ranch for short. The Ranch was an extraordinary place, as Aaron, Benji, and Hannah would soon discover...

Chapter One

Last Day of School

Aaron's eyes flicked back and forth as his dream took him to a familiar place of terror. He was laying on a high mountain ledge and extending his arm over the edge, desperately grasping for a man's hand. He didn't know the man, but he seemed strangely familiar. The man was crying for Aaron to save him as he clung to an outcropping of rocks. The man's eyes were locked on Aaron, and he silently screamed that Aaron was his only hope. The ledge was giving way under Aaron as he repeatedly reached for the man's hand. The measly inch that separated them could just as well have been a mile. Exhausted and hopeless, Aaron pulled his arm away in the realization he couldn't save this man. As he attempted to stand up, the ledge gave way beneath him, and they both started falling into the dark abyss below. Suddenly, the man began to ascend and extended his arm to embrace Aaron. Safely in the man's grip, Aaron and he soared skyward, gently landing on the mountain top. Aaron opened his eyes and sat up in bed; he shook with the horror that accompanied this dream.

Aaron's mom, Sarah, walked in and saw Aaron getting dressed and his brother Benji still sleeping soundly. She sensed Aaron's agitation and wrapped her arms around him. "How'd you sleep? Have that mountain dream again?"

"Yeah, I'm OK." Aaron's face was flushed, and his heart raced as he wondered if it was just his vivid imagination or something more ominous.

"I'm sorry, Aaron," replied Sarah as she kissed his forehead and ran her fingers through his thick wavy brown hair. "Wake up your brother and make sure he gets ready for school."

She walked over to Hannah's room and softly kissed her cheek. "Wake up, it's time for school."

"Agh," groaned Hannah as she rubbed her eyes. Her stomach was doing somersaults again at the thought of going to school all day. She searched her closet hoping the right outfit would make the ooky feeling go away.

With the children awake, Sarah swiftly maneuvered like a fine-tuned machine picking up a dirty towel evidencing Benji had actually taken a shower last night and tossing it in the laundry room on her way downstairs to prepare breakfast. She scooped out three bowls of oatmeal and set them on the table along with a canister of brown sugar and a carton of milk. She heard the ruckus as Aaron and Benji lumbered downstairs.

"Stop telling me what to do," shouted Benji as he swiped his sun-bleached blond hair out of his face. His bright green eyes glared at Aaron. They provided a sparkling contrast against his tanned face that came from many hours of boogieboarding in the ocean.

"I wouldn't have to if you'd do what you're supposed to. We're going to be late for school again," said Aaron, as he shoved Benji's shoulder and stared him down with his piercing blue eyes. "I'm not going to be late again because of you."

The family's lovable golden retriever, Bailey, bounded down the stairs barking after Aaron and Benji. Bailey was a glass half-full kind of dog; he always saw the best in others. He interpreted the boys' fighting as an invitation to play, so he jumped up on Aaron as he sat down to eat.

"Down boy," said Aaron as he chuckled at Bailey's unbridled enthusiasm.

Sarah pushed aside the strands of hair hanging in her face and shot her "don't mess with me" glare at her sons. "Boys, enough. Eat your oatmeal."

Sarah was petite but as fit as a fiddle, so the boys knew not to mess with her. Daily neighborhood jogs with Bailey, along with managing her veterinary practice and the Parsons household served as her mom workout regimen. Her smooth complexion and silky straight mahogany brown hair gave her the same youthful beautiful appearance as on her wedding day with Peter, the children's father.

"Mom, you're coming to my game this afternoon, right?" asked Aaron as he scooped brown sugar into his oatmeal. "It's the championship game."

"Absolutely, I wouldn't miss it for the world." Sarah pretended to throw an imaginary football at Aaron. "I can't wait to see you beat the Ravens. Lions are going to be the city flag football champions."

"That's what I'm talking about," replied Aaron as he caught the imaginary ball and spiked it. He raised his hand to high five his mom. "I've been practicing with Matt after school this week. We're both super pumped. It's going to be awesome!"

"Benji, are you ready for your math test?" asked Sarah as she watched him vacuum up his bowl of oatmeal.

"Yeah, I'm ready," Benji smirked confidently with the firm conviction that he had no use for math because he was going to be an artist. Unchained from the burden of studying, he had spent the night working on his painting.

"Go brush your teeth and tell Hannah to hurry down," said Sarah as she grabbed the boys' bowls and placed them in the sink.

Aaron ran upstairs and heard soft whimpering. He poked his head in Hannah's room to find her sitting on her bed quietly weeping. He silently backed out of her room and returned to the kitchen. The frown on his face told Sarah what she already suspected.

"Thanks, Aaron. Go get ready with your brother. I'll talk to her."

Sarah rushed upstairs, sat next to Hannah, and gently rubbed her back. "Hannah, what's wrong?"

"My stomach hurts. Can I stay home from school?" Hannah gave Sarah a long look with her big brown eyes that would melt the heart of any mother.

Sarah pulled Hannah closer to her. "Don't you want to see your friends? It's the last day of school before Christmas break?"

"I know, but some of the kids are mean." Hannah stiffened up at the thought of her less than hospitable schoolmates. "They tease me about the way I wear my hair and call me teacher's pet."

"I'm sorry, honey. People can be very nasty at times," replied Sarah as she stroked Hannah's hair. "Some more than others. But staying home won't make those kids go away, honey."

School loomed in Hannah's mind like a dark prison where she would be trapped and tormented. Some of her classmates were bullies who said and did heartless things to her just because she was obedient and respectful to the teacher. It didn't help that she beat them like a drum in handball. She refused to stoop to their level, but she also wished she could avoid them altogether. But her mom's face revealed that she wasn't getting out of school today. She missed her dad. He understood and knew just how to comfort her in these moments. "Did you hear from Dad?" asked Hannah.

"No, honey." Sarah hesitated to firm up her resolve that forcing Hannah to go to school was the right thing to do. The thing Peter would do as well. "I know it's hard, but this is the last day of school."

"I miss Dad," Hannah whispered, wiping her glistening brown eyes in the hopes of preventing a flood of tears.

"Me too. He's the best at what he does. I'm sure we'll hear soon." Sarah's calm expression conveyed a reassuring confidence, but inside, she was anything but. She too was concerned about Peter.

Bringing the focus back to the day, Sarah asked, "How do you want your hair?"

Hannah stood up and walked to the mirror running her hand through her hair. "Braid please."

Sarah smiled at Hannah in the mirror as she brushed Hannah's long silky brown hair into a ponytail. "I thought you liked a top pony. You told me it's better for handball at recess."

"It is, but all the other girls wear braids. The mean boys tease me since I'm the only girl who wears a top pony."

"I think they're jealous because you beat them. You shouldn't worry about what those boys say. If you want a top pony, that's what you should wear." Hannah's face crinkled at the thought of confronting the bullies at school. "But if you want a braid, I'll do one lickety-split."

Sarah began weaving Hannah's hair into an elaborate French braid. "You're an incredibly beautiful and smart little girl, Hannah. Look in that mirror." Hannah was the spitting image of her mom, just the pint sized version. The same beautiful skin, big brown eyes and mahogany brown hair. But Sarah was referring to a deeper image. Sarah wanted Hannah to see herself clearly, which she wasn't doing at the moment. Her self-image had been blurred by fear and doubt in who she was.

Hannah scrunched her nose. "I don't feel that way."

"A girl would be a fool not to be your friend." Sarah held up a small mirror to show Hannah the lovely French braid. "You're smart, nice, and fun to be with. Maybe you can invite one of your classmates over to our house to play after school sometime."

"Yeah, maybe," Hannah said, but frowned as her thoughts moved back to her dad. "It's going to be sad this Christmas without Dad."

"I know, honey, but we have some more time before Christmas." Sarah's heart ached, not only for Hannah but for the whole family. Christmas without Peter would be devastating for them all, and there was nothing she could do about it. "Finish getting dressed and come down for breakfast. I have to get ready." Hannah sighed, gathered her books, and went downstairs to stare down her oatmeal and sip her milk.

Sarah glanced into the boys' room on her way downstairs and was distracted by her thoughts. *How could Peter and I have produced two boys so different?*

The boys were only a year and a half apart, but their bedroom reflected the Grand Canyon sized divide between their personalities. Aaron's fastidious nature would have impressed the strictest military drill sergeant. His desk was immaculate, with labeled files for each class and his pens, pencils, and erasers neatly organized in his drawer. The clothes in his closet looked like a high-end retailer's display. All the long-sleeve button-down shirts first, followed by short-sleeve shirts, then jackets, and finally his pants, neatly creased and folded. Each pair of shoes was carefully stowed on the floor of his closet starting with tennis shoes on one side moving to dress shoes on the other. The books on his shelf were ordered by topic like a library. Atop the shelf was the collection of his many trophies from various sports teams, academic competitions, and other achievements. This meticulous order could never be disturbed. Dirty clothes were immediately placed in the clothes hamper, and he made his bed first thing every morning.

On the other hand, Benji had a markedly less rigid approach to his half of the bedroom. His primary organization system consisted of dropping his clothes on the floor at the end of the day where they would stay until his mom either scooped them up or escalated the matter to threats of grave consequences: If he did not pick up his clothes, they would be donated to children who would be happy to have them. His desk was littered with random papers, old wrappers, and dirty dishes. Every now and then, he would rummage through his desk to look for a particular item and create even more havoc. His closet was typically half empty of hanging shirts and pants, with the remainder of his clothes lying somewhere on the floor. The only thing that had any semblance of order was his painting easel in the corner of their room.

Aaron had gotten so peeved by his brother's utter contempt for order, he had laid masking tape down the middle of the room to officially demarcate his sovereign territory. Today, after breakfast, like many other mornings, Aaron found a pile of Benji's dirty clothes on his side of the room. He picked up the clothes, dumped them in Benji's closet, and yelled, "Get your clothes out of here."

Benji continued working on his painting of a Navy boat speeding over ocean waters. "Easy, bro, I don't hear the floor complaining."

Aaron shook his head in frustration. "Did you brush your teeth? Stop painting; we've got to go."

"What are you, the teeth police? You're not my boss," yelled Benji.

Sarah could hear the commotion and knew they were at risk of another "late to arrive" notice. She grabbed her purse and headed for the car yelling, "Aaron, Benji, Hannah, we're leaving now. Your lunches are on the table. In the car. Everybody. Now." Bailey was unphased by the typical morning commotion in the Parsons house and settled into his bed for a morning nap. His day included a trip through the doggy-door to explore the backyard and several barking sessions with the neighborhood dogs. Aaron often wondered if Bailey was giving some kind of code to his nearby compatriots. Something like, *OK, the coast is clear, time for dogs to rule.*

Benji sensed his mom's annoyance, so on the drive to school he silently skimmed through his repertoire of jokes. When people were disappointed with him, which was more often than he cared to admit, Benji found that a well-timed joke could turn things around. "Hey Mom, how does a veterinarian total a customer's bill?"

"I don't know, Benji. How?" replied Sarah as she navigated through traffic.

"She uses a cow-culator ... that's c.o.w, get it?" Benji chuckled. He cracked himself up with his jokes. Rarely did they have that effect on his family.

Sarah strained a laugh and looked at Benji in the rear-view mirror. "Very funny, mister. Get your things ready; we're almost there."

Even though it was still early in the day, Aaron had reached the end of his rope with his brother. "That's so lame. Mom doesn't even see cows in her office, Benji."

Sarah flashed her mom-glare at the boys through the rearview mirror. "Boys, that's enough."

They pulled up to the school and stopped by the curb. Sarah offered the children the Parsons family symbol and code words to encourage them to 'take on the day.' She raised her hand with two fingers extended and crossed. "Have a great day, Parsons Cord," said Sarah. The children gave the sign back to her and jumped out of the car.

Sarah watched as they strode off toward their classrooms. Hannah looked back at her mom with an expression of quiet desperation.

Aaron noticed Hannah's anguish and draped his arm around her neck. He whispered something in her ear, and Hannah broke into a smile. Benji was throwing rocks at the school sign and Aaron yelled at him to stop.

Sarah turned off the engine and sat silently for several minutes. She felt a deep sorrow welling up inside and began weeping uncontrollably. Her thoughts drifted back over the past several weeks without Peter. *Aaron and Benji's constant bickering, managing Hannah's many fears, the housework, the bills, my veterinary practice.* On top of that, not hearing from Peter was tearing at her heart. She was broken and her mind was spinning out of control. *I don't know if I can do this alone. Is he safe? Why haven't I heard anything?* She took a deep breath and wiped her face with a tissue as she looked in the rearview mirror.

Sarah muttered to herself, "I need family." She pulled out her phone and punched the number of Peter's father.

"Hi, Sarah. What's up?" said Sam.

"I needed to hear a friendly voice. It's been a tough morning," Sarah said as she wiped her tears with a tissue.

"I'm so sorry, Sarah. Have you heard anything?"

Sarah stared blankly into the rearview mirror searching for something to say. "No. Christmas feels empty this year, Sam. Without Peter."

"Hey, why don't you and the kids come up to the Ranch for Christmas?" offered Sam.

"We'd love that." Sarah began to call up memories of the Ranch. "This is their last day of school."

"Great, pack your bags and drive up tomorrow."

"Thank you, Sam. This will mean a lot to the kids," replied Sarah. She knew she wasn't fooling Sam, but she didn't want him to think she was a basket case without Peter. Spending Christmas at the Ranch would mean as much to her as it would to the children. Peter had grown up on the Ranch and they had so many wonderful memories together there during their marriage. She was hoping it would bring

Peter closer to her, even though he was away. With her spirits slightly buoyed, she headed off to the office.

***

Benji strolled into his class unfazed by the impending math test. As always, he had a "can't fail" genius plan. He figured he'd study during the morning reading time – borrow some reading time to catch up on math. As he made his way to his seat, he saw a large box of chocolate bars on Mr. Jacobson's desk. Benji loved chocolate like Bailey loved a juicy bone.

"Good morning, Benji. How're you this morning?" said Mr. Jacobson.

"Fine. I slept like a log last night … and woke up in the fireplace." Benji waited for Mr. Jacobson's cackle, but it never came. All he got was a sarcastic smirk. Most days Benji tried a joke on Mr. Jacobson hoping to get a rise out of him but hitting the target of Mr. Jacobson's funny bone proved elusive. Benji decided to move on to a more pressing matter. "Are you giving out chocolate bars today, Mr. Jacobson?" Mr. Jacobson broke into a wide grin and replied, "Sure am. Better get settled. We have a lot to do today."

Mr. Jacobson stood and cleared his throat to get the attention of the students and picked up the box of chocolate bars, "Good morning, everyone. Since it's the last day before Christmas break, I have a surprise for you. Whoever gets a 95% or better on the math test will win a prize – two chocolate bars. We're going to move the math test up, so I'll have time to grade the tests during lunch hour. Clear your desks and I'll hand out the test."

Alarms blared in Benji's head. His face turned pale as he listened to Mr. Jacobson. The genius plan to study during the reading hour had blown up in his face. To make matters worse, chocolate was on the line. Benji had a habit of doing what was fun in the moment and letting the future worry about itself. This was not the first time this strategy had backfired. He felt beads of sweat on his forehead as he considered his situation. *There's no way I can get a 95%, I didn't study at all. Maybe I can guess. That will never work. Why didn't I study last night!*

Mr. Jacobson walked down the rows and handed out the test. "You have one hour to finish the test. Remember, show your work."

Benji stared at the test and was consumed by a feeling of dread. He didn't know how to do any of the problems on the test. His jaw clenched as he considered the epic disaster staring back at him. He was going to fail the test. His mom and dad would be furious. He grasped at his memory in vain for any tidbit Mr. Jacobson had taught that might help him. Suddenly, he saw a ray of hope shining down from above. He played it out in his mind. *Jeremy's the smartest kid in the class. He's a math wizard. There must be a reason he's sitting right in front of me. If I can get a glimpse of his answers, I just might be able to salvage this catastrophe.*

Benji shifted in his seat to get a better view and was soon writing down the answers directly as he saw them on Jeremy's test. He tried to make it as subtle as possible, taking quick glances and then focusing on his own paper with his head down. Soon he got into a rhythm with his eyes swiveling between Mr. Jacobson's desk, his own paper, and then a quick peek at Jeremy's test. His plan was working like a charm. *I just might get those chocolate bars after all.*

At the end of the hour, Mr. Jacobson called out, "Time's up. Please pass your tests up to the front. I'll grade them at lunch, and we'll announce the winners this afternoon."

The rest of the morning went by quickly. Benji tried to put the test out of his mind. He was simply happy it was over. Benji and the other students made their way back into the classroom after lunch. The students' eyes were fixated on the box of chocolate bars as they passed Mr. Jacobson's desk and took their seats.

Mr. Jacobson stood up and sauntered over to Benji's desk. He asked, "Benji, can I talk to you outside please?"

Benji could feel his heart beating out of his chest as he walked outside with Mr. Jacobson. He avoided making eye contact and decided to butter up Mr. Jacobson, saying, "Sure, Mr. Jacobson. I've got a joke: why's the math book so unhappy?" Benji scanned the hallway to see if there would be any witnesses to this trainwreck. "Because it's full of problems."

Mr. Jacobson gave Benji a stern look. "Benji, I don't know about the math book, but we do have a problem. Can you tell me what it is?" Mr. Jacobson's eyes were like laser beams burning a hole in Benji's conscience.

Benji fidgeted with his shirt buttons as he desperately searched for a response. "Uh... no. It was a pretty hard test. I studied a lot, so it wasn't as hard as I thought it'd be."

"Is that so? When I graded your test, you only got one wrong. That gives you 95%, much higher than your normal score. It was quite a coincidence that you and Jeremy got the exact same score." Mr. Jacobson smirked at Benji with raised eyebrows. "What's even more amazing is that you both missed the same question and you both had the same incorrect answer. What are the odds, Benji? Isn't that strange?"

Benji's eyes widened, and his expression froze as he quickly fashioned a reply. "That's weird, Mr. Jacobson. We must have studied the same way." One thing he'd learned from watching crooked people on the news: deny, deny, deny.

"I don't have proof of anything, so I have to go with your word. You wouldn't cheat would you, Benji?"
Benji stuffed his hands in his pockets to hide his fidgeting. "No, never sir." "OK, thank you, Benji. I'm going to trust you on your honor."

They walked back into the classroom and Mr. Jacobson picked up the box of chocolate bars. "I graded all the tests, and we have three winners. Olivia who got 100%, and Jeremy and Benji who each got 95%. Congratulations to all of you. Come on up to get your two chocolate bars."

Benji walked up with Jeremy and Olivia, and each plucked two bars as their winnings. Despite his underhanded methods, Benji relished the sweet taste of victory. With a grin on his face, he bit a corner off one of his bars as he strolled back to his seat.

Despite a sugar high from gobbling one of the chocolate bars, Benji's pesky conscience gnawed at him the entire afternoon. His mind kept raising unpleasant conversations despite his best efforts to paint his actions with a noble brush. *I had no choice. It was a one-time thing. I had to do it. For my parents' sake. Next time, I'll study.* Finally, the school bell rang, and Benji put his things in his backpack. As he stood up, he took a quick peek at Mr. Jacobson. His eyes were fixed on Benji with a glare that penetrated Benji's heart.

"Goodbye, Mr. Jacobson. Have a nice vacation," said Benji as he walked by his teacher's desk.

"Goodbye, Benji. Enjoy your chocolate," replied Mr. Jacobson. He peered into Benji's eyes for an uncomfortably long time. Benji turned away with his head down. He rushed toward the football field, hoping to escape his guilt.

***

Aaron raced out of his class toward the football field looking for Coach Miller.

Coach Miller saw Aaron out of the corner of his eye and looked up from his clipboard to call out, "Hey Aaron, come on over. Get your jersey and flags. Game starts in a few minutes."

Aaron joined the other players who were adjusting their jerseys and putting on their flags as Coach Miller began his pep talk. Coach Miller was a rugged man with a tight crew cut and rough voice. He was a little too generous with his application of cologne, making his presence unmistakable.

"Who are we?" said Coach Miller in a low coarse voice.

The players shouted, "The Lions" in unison like a roar thundering across the field.

Coach Miller continued raising his gruff voice with each statement. "We're going to play this game just like every other game we've played this year. Keep your mind on the game, no mistakes, and play as a team. You guys are playing for the championship, so enjoy every minute of it."

Coach Miller raised his hands, and all the players lifted their arms to join hands with his. "Lions on three, 1-2-3 LIONS."

The game went by quickly and the teams were evenly matched. Aaron was a wide receiver and was defended by a boy who was called

Reaper by his Raven teammates. On every play, Reaper shoved Aaron as he started his route and knocked him one step off his normal pattern. Reaper's plan worked well as Lions quarterback Matt and Aaron had a tough time hooking up in the first half.

The Lions scored first on a long run by Matt. A quarterback sweep around the right side. The Ravens scored on a long run in the second quarter to tie the game 7 – 7 at halftime. Aaron caught a screen pass in stride before Reaper could get to him and ran past the entire defense for a score in the third quarter. The Ravens countered with a long drive and a run into the end zone to tie the score at 14 – 14 at the end of the third quarter.

As time was winding down in the fourth quarter, Coach Miller called a long pass play to Aaron. Aaron broke free of Reaper, sprinted down the field, and beat Reaper by several yards. Matt stepped up and unloaded a long pass. Aaron's eyes were locked on the ball as it glided into his hands. Suddenly, dirt flew into Aaron's eyes, and he lost sight of the ball for a split second. It slipped through his hands and bounced on the ground. As Aaron turned to return to the huddle, Reaper gave him an evil grin as he wiped dirt from his hands and mocked Aaron with a fumble-fingers gesture.

Aaron felt a wave of panic as he replayed his dropped pass and Reaper's shenanigans. He scanned the sideline for his dad, but quickly remembered he wasn't there. And wouldn't be there. Peter had taught Aaron everything he knew about football and usually warmed him up before games. It was a tradition Aaron loved, probably even more than the game itself. This time with his dad was precious to Aaron, and carrying on without him in the championship game was racking him. His dad would know what to do about Reaper. Aaron turned back to the field and joined his teammates in the huddle.

"Sorry guys, I should have had that." Aaron scanned across the huddle ending with an apologetic look to his quarterback. "Good pass, Matt."

"Don't worry, bud, we got this," said Matt as he patted Aaron on the head.

Coach Miller called timeout, walked slowly towards the huddle, and smiled at the boys. "It's go-time boys!" he said. "We have time for one more play."

Coach Miller looked at Jason and Matt. "Let's try a slant to Jason on one. Reaper's been clamping down on Aaron all game. Jason has been all alone; I think we can sneak one to him."

They broke the huddle and the players jogged to their places on the line of scrimmage. Aaron hung back and whispered to Matt, "Look for me on the slant, I'll be open."

Matt was under center with Aaron lined up on the right side and Jason wide out on the left side. Matt called out, "Omaha, 32, 32, hut, hut… One" and Jason and Aaron both shot off the line like racehorses. After three steps, they both broke hard inside for the slant play, placing them on a collision course at full speed. Matt threw a perfect spiral just as they turned inside, but Reaper shoved Aaron and threw dirt in his eyes. Aaron hesitated, and in the commotion, Jason looked away from the ball. Reaper stepped in and intercepted the pass. He turned up field, ran past all the Lions players, and danced into the end zone for the winning touchdown as time expired.

The entire Raven's team rushed the field and dogpiled on Reaper to celebrate the amazing last-minute win. The Ravens were league champions. As Aaron's team walked the line to congratulate the Ravens, Reaper grinned at Aaron while pounding his own chest. Reaper's whisper stabbed Aaron as they walked past each other, "Ravens are champions – winners do whatever it takes, loser."

Aaron ripped off his jersey and stormed off the field to look for the family's car. Sarah gathered up Benji and Hannah to hustle after Aaron. "Great game, Aaron, I'm really proud of you," said Sarah. She patted him on the back, not knowing what else to do. This was Peter's department. "That was a tough ending, but your team played great." Aaron snapped, "Yeah, we had it, and I blew it."

"That Reaper kid was doing dirty tricks the whole game," said Sarah. She cringed as she replayed the devious things Reaper had pulled on Aaron. She knew she couldn't protect her children from the unfairness of life, but watching Aaron experience this travesty was excruciating for her as well.

"Why didn't the refs call him on his cheating?"

Aaron kicked the ground making dirt fly. "He was too clever; they never saw him do it. I don't think the 'cheaters never prosper' thing is true. Ask Reaper." Sarah grimaced at Aaron's pain and tried to console him. "Life is long, Aaron. He'll have to deal with that at some point."

As the family drove home, Aaron stared out the window fuming in his thoughts alternating between anger and guilt. *Reaper stole our championship and cheated his way to victory. It's not fair. Reaper's the hero and I'm the goat. I lost the game. I didn't trust Jason. I messed up his route and caused the interception. How was I supposed to deal with Reaper's cheating? How did it go so wrong?*

Aaron's thoughts shifted to his dad. *Dad would have known what to do. How to deal with Reaper. Why can't he be here like the other dads?* Aaron pushed his tussled hair back to clear his mind of all the depressing thoughts. "Did you get any pictures for Dad?" Aaron asked his mom.

"Sure did. I got some great ones of you catching the screen pass for a touchdown. Your dad's going to love them."

Sarah sensed Aaron's pain and thought this was the perfect time to share the good news. "I talked to Papa today and he invited us to spend Christmas on the Ranch."

Aaron turned to his mom with the tiniest crease of a smile emerging. "I love the Ranch."

"Awesome! Can we leave tomorrow?" asked Benji. He loved life on the Ranch as well because it was simple and unstructured. He had the freedom to explore and do what he wanted. And it might help him forget about his absolutely atrocious last day of school. "First thing," replied Sarah trying to inject excitement into her children.

A ray of hope broke through the clouds of despair that surrounded Aaron. Christmas break had begun. Christmas was his favorite time of year, he simply loved everything about it. Even if his dad wouldn't be there, he loved spending time with Papa and Grandma on the Ranch.

***

Aaron was putting on clean clothes after his shower when Sarah called out, "Aaron, Benji, Hannah, we're making Christmas cookies."

Aaron loved making Christmas cookies and it had become one of their many Christmas traditions. When he arrived in the kitchen, he was happy to see that this year they were making sugar cookies shaped like angels, stars, and Christmas trees. Aaron loved to decorate the cookies with sprinkles, red hots, and white frosting, and he privately considered himself quite the artist. Benji was already at work using the star shaped cookie cutter. Hannah offered him first dibs on the other cookie cutters. Aaron knew Hannah loved making angels, so he took the Christmas tree shaped one and settled in to stamp out cookies.

As the three of them mastered their cookie artistry, Sarah brought out a large metal container to pack cookies to bring to Papa and Grandma's Ranch. After filling the container, they placed the rest of the cookies on decorative paper plates.

Sarah scanned the kitchen with dismay and sighed, "I think my bakers got a little carried away."

The kitchen looked like a bakery bomb had exploded. Flour and a sprinkling of the toppings covered the table, chairs, counters, and floor. Bailey licked the floor trying to get as much as he could before things got cleaned up. He was clever that way; always on the lookout for a snack when food was dropped. He seemed to have a sixth sense; he could be sleeping in another room, but when he heard a noise in the kitchen, he came running to look for an opportunity. Sarah brought out the cleaning supplies and they all pitched in to vacuum, scrub, and clean every last bit of the mess.

After dinner, the family put on their coats to deliver the cookies to neighbors and wish them a merry Christmas. They carefully loaded all the plates in the wagon, which Aaron was in charge of since he was the oldest. Bailey stood guard next to the wagon hoping for dropped cookies during the loading process. He was out of luck tonight. As they wheeled the wagon through the neighborhood, Benji and Hannah took turns ringing the doorbell for each house.

They spent the next hour visiting with each neighbor and handing out cookies. At each house Sarah caught up on news in the neighborhood, and friends shared Christmas plans. The evening air was brisk, so they were cold by the time they returned home. Aaron brought in three logs, placed them in the large stone fireplace, and started a fire. Sarah heated some milk and made hot chocolate for everyone. Aaron, Benji, and Hannah put on their pajamas and came out to the glow of a warm fire in the family room. It was a comfy room with pillows and blankets. Each night during the Christmas season, one of the children got to choose a Christmas story for Sarah to read aloud, and tonight it was Hannah's turn to choose.

As they snuggled with their blankets and hot chocolate, Sarah read Hannah's favorite, *Rudolph the Red-Nosed Reindeer.* Hannah liked this story because Rudolph showed that the littlest member of the family could end up being a star. Hannah also had a tender heart for anyone being picked-on or bullied. Seeing Rudolph overcome the teasing by the other reindeer appealed to her sense of justice — something she found missing in her world.

Sarah did her best to bring the story to life, but she was no Peter when it came to reading stories. He was a ham at heart and loved to use different voices and accents for each character in the story — Rudolph sounded like a German child by his telling. Sarah did her best to spruce up the story, but it was another reminder to the children of their dad's special place in the family, and his absence.

After the story, Sarah nudged the children to wake them and send them off to bed. Sarah tucked each of the children in and gave them a hug. As Aaron, Benji, and Hannah drifted off to sleep, all they could think about was Papa and Grandma and their snowy mountain lodge.

Sarah settled into the sofa downstairs and pulled out her phone to update Peter's parents. "The kids are over the moon excited to come tomorrow."

"We're getting everything ready," said Sam. "It'll be a wonderful Christmas, even if Peter won't be here."

"I hope so; the kids are pretty down about Peter. Life's hard, Sam, so much pain." Sarah paused, reflecting on the different ways her children were suffering.

"I know, Sarah, but the Ranch will be good for them. It's an incredibly special place. I know it will help the kids find their way."

"The kids? I hope it helps all of us find our way."

"It will," replied Sam in a reassuring tone. "The Ranch is an extraordinary place."

Chapter Two

The Ranch

Tomorrow started early. Bailey, with his tail wagging, jumped on Aaron's bed and licked his face. Bailey easily won the hospitality award in the Parsons family. Every time he greeted one of them, he acted like he was meeting a long-lost friend. Aaron pushed Bailey off the bed and reached up to the top bunk to wake Benji. Benji was a very sound sleeper; it seemed nothing could wake him from his slumber.

Aaron heard the heavy breathing, so he called out loudly, "Benji, wake up," and shook Benji's shoulder.

Slowly, Benji began to stir. He rubbed his eyes and grumbled, "I'm up, I'm up."

It was still dark outside, which was not a surprise since it was 5:00 in the morning. The drive to Papa and Grandma's Ranch was long, so Sarah liked to get an early start. She had prepared eggs and toast for breakfast. After they ate, Aaron and Benji packed all the bags in the car along with Bailey and his food and dog bed. Hannah helped Sarah straighten the kitchen, check the doors and windows, then load the basket of snacks for their long drive. With everyone packed and fed, they got on the road about 5:30.

Papa and Grandma lived on a gigantic ranch in the mountains called Parsons' Ranch, or just the Ranch for short. The Ranch had been in the Parsons family for as long as anyone could remember. The property had hundreds of acres of forests along with large meadows for grazing, a clear water lake, and a beautiful valley. It was hard to access, and the last miles were on winding, two-lane logging roads. The turn off to the Ranch was hard to see. The only clue was a small wooden sign that read: Parsons' Ranch. The private gravel road up to the Ranch was several miles long and the buildings on the property were invisible from the road.

The Ranch had a main lodge where Papa and Grandma lived. It was a rustic wooden home built long ago by previous members of the Parsons family. Papa had improved and updated it using his woodcraft skills. He used pine for all the siding and ceilings, and oak for the flooring. Aaron, Benji, and Hannah shared a room upstairs. It had a large window overlooking the mountains in the distance. Sarah had another room upstairs with its own bathroom. Papa and Grandma had a bedroom downstairs with its own private porch made of redwood where they would sit and read, or just talk, in the afternoons. There was a large family room with a stone fireplace where the family sat in the evenings to warm up by the fire.

A huge garage was next to the lodge. All the trucks, ATVs, and other vehicles used on the Ranch were parked there.

Papa and Grandma had a barn and a large pasture with lots of farm animals. They had horses, cows, goats, sheep, pigs as well as chickens, and a rooster named Romeo. A large meadow was behind the barn where Papa let the animals graze during the warm seasons. Snow covered the meadow this time of year, so the animals had to rely on the hay and grain Papa set out each day.

The Ranch also had a sawmill and a woodshop. Papa was a wood craftsman by trade. He started a furniture company when he was eighteen years old and grew it into a successful, unique luxury furniture enterprise. He kept the woodshop but sold the business about ten years ago so he and Grandma could enjoy retirement in peace and quiet on the Ranch. Papa still loved spending time in his workshop making handcrafted wood items as a hobby.

Grandma loved cooking and was always working on new recipes. She had a greenhouse where she grew lettuce, carrots, tomatoes, green beans, and every kind of herb. She had become quite an expert on all kinds of herbs and seasonings. She knew all about how to use them in cooking and also how the ancient Native Americans used them for healing and rituals.

"I can't wait to get to the Ranch and see Papa and Grandma," said Aaron.

"I bet there's snow all over the mountain!"

"Maybe Papa will let us pick out a Christmas tree this year," said Benji.

"I think this would be a good year for you boys to help Papa pick out a tree. You're old enough to join him. Your father started when he was about your age, so I'll talk to Papa when we get there," said Sarah.

The trip was long, but they were all so excited to see Papa and Grandma the time flew. Sarah started a game of "I Spy" and everybody got a turn. Benji picked a spec of white paint on the dashboard, which was nearly impossible to see. Once everyone gave up, Benji proudly called out the spec with a sense of victory.

Aaron groaned, "As usual, you pick a preposterously small thing." Benji gave a self-satisfied smile as he brushed his knuckles on his shirt sleeve.

"We have a way to go. Why don't you try to get some sleep," said Sarah. The children drifted off to sleep wondering what snowy adventures were ahead at the Ranch.

Dusk was starting to creep over the trees when they finally reached the mountain country. Sarah was cautious as she drove up narrow logging roads with snow and trees covering the mountain on either side of the road.

Aaron stirred from his sleep. "How close are we?"

"We're getting close. Only another thirty minutes to go," responded Sarah.

With Benji and Hannah still sleeping, Aaron gazed out the window at the snow-covered mountain. The natural beauty of the mountains near the Ranch was breathtaking. It was so majestic; it almost didn't look real. "Mom isn't it beautiful this time of year?" asked Aaron.

"Nature's beauty is pretty miraculous artwork." Sarah glanced across the white mountains and caught a deer nibbling on tree branches. "Points us to a pretty awesome artist, don't you think?"

Aaron had not considered nature as artwork, but he recognized the beauty of the country they were in. As he gazed across the majestic mountains, he wondered what this Christmas would bring. *Maybe Papa will take us to a new place on the Ranch. Maybe a place Dad explored when he was little.*

They were near the top of the mountain when they reached the long gravel road marked with the "Parsons' Ranch" sign. Aaron always liked seeing his last name on the sign to the Ranch. It made him feel important. Of course, this was Papa and Grandma's Ranch, but he felt like he was a part of it.

The bumpety bump of the gravel road woke Benji and Hannah. "We're here!" said Benji.

Papa and Grandma saw the headlights as they reached the lodge and came out to greet them. "We're so happy to see you. How was the trip?" asked Papa.

"Let me give you a big hug and kiss," said Grandma. After warmly embracing Sarah, she wrapped her arms around Hannah and gave her a kiss on the cheek.

Grandma was one of the few people in the world who could still give Aaron and Benji hugs and kisses. The boys had reached the age where such things were considered cringeworthy. But deep inside they relished hugs and kisses from Grandma.

"Benji, it's so nice to see you. You look like you've grown," said Grandma as she hugged him.

"Yeah, two inches, Grandma," exclaimed Benji as he stood on his tiptoes to make sure his impressive stature was noticed by Grandma and Papa.

"Aaron, you aren't too big for me to give you a hug and kiss, are you?" whispered Grandma as she wrapped her arms around him. Aaron smiled coyly. "No, Grandma."

They unloaded the car and brought all the bags into the lodge. Bailey jumped out of the car and sniffed the area, getting acquainted with his new surroundings. He did his "business" as Peter called it and then proceeded into the lodge to explore the interior. Aaron carried Bailey's bed and food into the lodge and placed it in the family room right next to the fire.

Grandma brought out a large platter of warm cookies. "Who wants homemade cookies and hot chocolate?"

"I'm kind of hungry," said Benji. "Me too," offered Hannah. "Me three," replied Aaron. The children rushed up to Grandma to take a cookie along with a mug of hot chocolate.

As the family enjoyed Grandma's mouthwatering snack, they caught up on the latest news, work, school, sports, and the coming Christmas season.

"Sam, I was talking to the boys today about how Peter used to love picking out the Christmas tree with you," said Sarah. She raised her eyebrows to signal her intentions to Papa.

"Ah yes, those were some fine adventures we had. These two strapping boys look ready, don't you think?" asked Papa.

Sarah winked at Papa with a smile. "Absolutely. Peter's been working with them on using a saw and handling a rope. They're both top-notch."

"Well, splendid. The three of us will go on an adventure to find a Christmas tree," said Papa as he broke out a wide grin and put his arms around Aaron and Benji. "But I need the boys' help on a project tomorrow, so maybe we can get a tree the day after." "Thanks, Papa. What kind of project?" asked Aaron.

"The woodshop has a leaky roof we need to patch. I'll show you an old trick, so we don't even have to go to the store."

Aaron shot his hand up to Papa and they exchanged a fist bump. "Fantastic, can't wait."

Hannah quietly withdrew as she listened to Papa discuss his big plans with Aaron and Benji. Grandma caught her by the arm and gave her a warm smile. "Hannah, will you help me in the greenhouse tomorrow? I'll show you some natural recipes using local herbs and plants. We grow all of them right here on the Ranch."

Hannah moved close to Sarah. "That sounds fun, Grandma."

Sarah glanced at Grandma with a grateful nod. "We'll make it a date, the three ladies out in the greenhouse."

***

Sarah's phone rang and she slipped into the study to get away from the noise. Her heart skipped a beat when she saw Jen's name on the caller ID.

Jen was a friend whose husband was on Peter's Navy Seal team.

"Sarah, can you talk?"

"Yeah, Jen. You hear anything?"

"I went to their Chief Warrant Officer, Briggs, and pleaded for any information they can give us."

"What did he say?" Sarah's heart was racing. She concentrated on every word Jen was telling her like it was pure gold.

"He couldn't give me much. He said it was a mission to Africa, real top secret, off the grid."

"Why haven't we heard anything?" asked Sarah. She was desperate for any information she could get. "It's been over three weeks." There was a silent pause on the other end of the phone triggering a rush of fear in Sarah. "Jen?"

"He had to be careful, but he said they're missing. The mission went sideways, and they're stuck in-country. That's all I know, Sarah."

"Oh, my goodness, Jen." Sarah's heart sank. She sat down on a leather sofa in the study stunned by the words she had just heard. She and Peter had been best friends since they were young children. Friendship grew to love and love to marriage. They were newlyweds during his Navy Seal BUDs training in Coronado, California. The dangers of his work were obvious, and she'd rehearsed a call like this in her mind a thousand times. But in this moment, the weight of the words "they're missing" was like a dagger to her heart.

"Sarah, are you OK?"

Sarah clenched her jaw in an effort to compose herself. "Yeah, I'm going to be OK. We're at the Ranch for Christmas. Thanks Jen, Merry Christmas."

Sarah stayed in the study and replayed the conversation with Jen. She held on to every word desperately trying to find hope in the news. Papa Sam and Grandma Chloe came into the study and sat next to her.

"We put the children to bed, Sarah. Stay here as long as you like," said Chloe as she stroked Sarah's back. Sarah softly replied, "Thanks, Chloe."

"What do they know?" asked Sam with an intense look on his face.

"Not much," replied Sarah as her mind continued to replay the word 'missing.' "His team is missing in Africa. Very dangerous mission."

The room fell silent except for the rhythmic tick-tock of the grandfather clock, cruelly marching time forward. They were each lost in their thoughts. Sarah was fighting her emotions trying to suppress all the worst-case scenarios bubbling up in her mind. Sam was grasping for something positive to encourage her, and Chloe faced a flood of memories of her little boy – lost, alone and afraid in Africa.

"From what they know, he's still alive, Sarah. That's something to hold onto." Sam placed his hand on Sarah's shoulder. "Peter's incredibly smart and skilled at his work. If anyone can find a way home, it's Peter."

Sam and Chloe sat silently with Sarah the rest of the evening, not saying a word. They simply held onto her as she quietly cried herself to sleep in their arms. Sam closed his eyes repeating his most urgent request in his head, *Father, bring Peter home to us.*

***

Hannah could see the excitement in Grandma's eyes while they ate breakfast. She was a masterful cook and had created hundreds of her own recipes over the years. It was one of her great passions. She also studied natural remedies and cultivated all kinds of plants and herbs on the Ranch. Sarah had only slightly embraced this passion, so Grandma was hoping to share her love of culinary arts and herbal uses and healing with Hannah.

"The greenhouse seems bigger," said Sarah as they walked in the large plastic covered nursery. "It looks like you've added some plants since last time we were here."

"We expanded it to add more herbs for natural teas and remedies."

"Hannah, remember that aloe plant from last time?" said Grandma as they walked by a group of large aloe plants. "We use them to treat infections."

"Yeah, Grandma. We use it at home for sunburn."

"Today, I'm going to show you how to make sleep tea. We've got some raccoons that keep getting into our trash."

"Will it hurt them?" asked Hannah.

"Oh no." Grandma plucked a small weed out of the raised nursery beds. "It just makes them woozy and fall asleep. After a couple of times, they stay away because they don't like being groggy."

"How do you make it?" asked Hannah. She pulled another weed out of the nursey bed imitating Grandma.

"It's an old recipe I learned from my mother." Grandma walked over to a group of flowers and herbs in the corner of the greenhouse and began cutting plants into a basket. "Let's see, we'll need some lavender, valerian, sage, chamomile, magnolia, passionflower, jasmine, rosemary, and lemongrass."

"How do we make it into sleep tea?" asked Hannah. She stared into the nursery bed reading the signs to remember all the plants.

Grandma finished cutting the last of the plants and placed them in her basket. "Grind these and let them steep in boiling water. Voila! Sleep tea."

"Can I grind the plants?" asked Hannah bounding out in front toward the lodge. Grandma was one of the few people Hannah felt absolutely safe with. Grandma's unconditional love and sweet disposition unlocked a side of Hannah that was hidden from most people.

"Absolutely, Hannah," said Grandma as she basked in Hannah's excitement. The time in the greenhouse filled Grandma's head with thoughts of hope. *Maybe my culinary love will live on.*

***

Grandma, Sarah, and Hannah passed Papa, Aaron, and Benji in the front yard as they returned to the lodge. Papa was taking the boys out to work on the roof patching project. They climbed into a Bronco and headed out into the forest. Papa had a funny habit of naming each of his vehicles. This one was named Billy.

"What's the stuff called again?" asked Aaron.

"Pitch glue," replied Papa. He maneuvered Billy through the snow and trees. "We're headed to the stand of pine trees in the upper part of the Ranch."

Aaron scribbled *pitch glue* in his small notepad as he quizzed Papa. "How'd you learn how to make it?"

"My dad showed me when I was about your age, and I showed your dad when he was little." Papa was smiling ear to ear as he passed on another bit of special family knowledge to Aaron and Benji. "Pitch glue's an ancient recipe. Native American tribes used it to seal their canoes and waterproof things. Ancient Egyptians used it to hunt birds. It's been around a long time."

"I don't know if we'll need it where we live," said Benji as he gazed out the window only half listening to Papa. Benji was practical and making pitch glue was not a skill he thought he would ever need. But still, they were out on the mountain traversing through the snow. Overall, a very good start to the day as far as Benji was concerned.

Papa saw the skepticism in Benji's face. "It's a great skill to learn, boys. If you're in the outdoors, it may come in handy someday." Papa pulled Billy off the trail next to a large hillside of large pine trees.

"Why pine trees?" asked Aaron as he grabbed a branch and examined the pine needles.

"Pine has the best resin which makes the strongest glue," said Papa. He pulled a hatchet from the back of Billy, and they walked up to one of the trees. "Aaron, can you grab that bucket from Billy?"

Aaron leaped into Billy and grabbed the bucket out of the back. He rushed back not wanting to miss anything important.

"This is how you tap a pine tree for sap," continued Papa. "First thing is to score the tree." Papa chipped away the top layer of bark. "Next, we score the cleared area to expose the sap." Using his hatchet, Papa carved rows of diagonal V-shaped notches in the cleared area.

"Where do you want the bucket?" asked Aaron.

"Right under the notches. That's all for today. It'll take a day or two for the sap to ooze out of the tree." Papa began loading their tools into Billy. "We'll come back later to pick up the sap."

Aaron loved discovering new outdoorsy things from Papa and asked as many questions as he could think of. He was an outdoorsman at heart and knew these little bits of survival knowledge might help him someday. But more importantly, his dad was a great outdoorsman and Aaron wanted to show him he was made in the same mold. This would be one more skill he could show his dad when he saw him next. Whenever that might be.

Chapter Three
The Redwood Grove

———— ✺ ————

"Cock-a-doodle-doo!" crowed Romeo, who reveled in his notorious role of waking up the rest of the animals and the entire Parsons household. He took immense joy in crowing as soon as the smallest sliver of sun appeared over the ridge. Aaron awoke disoriented by the crowing rooster in his disturbing mountain top dream. His head was jumbled. *Why would a rooster be at the top of a mountain when I'm clinging for my life?* He laid in bed for a moment to clear his head.

It was a wintry morning as the boys got out of bed to take in the view from their window. "I think it snowed last night," said Benji. "That looks like fresh snow covering the mountain."

"It covered up our footprints from last night," said Aaron, "and there's a ton of snow on the roof of our car."

Sarah poked her head in their room to make sure they were getting ready. "You better bundle up with lots of layers today, boys, because it's cold out there."

Aaron had three layers including a long sleeve shirt, a sweatshirt, and a thick leather jacket. "I think this will do the trick."

Benji was having trouble getting his layers on, so Sarah helped him pull on his sweatshirt and jacket. Hannah was still sleeping, so Sarah decided to let her rest peacefully. Aaron and Benji put their knit caps and gloves in their jacket pockets and went to find Papa. The tantalizing scent of bacon on the griddle drew them to the kitchen.

45

"Good morning, boys," said Grandma as she gave Benji and Aaron morning hugs. "I made a big breakfast for you to get ready for your day out on the mountain with Papa." Aaron's eyes lit up at the sight of pancakes, bacon, fruit, and hot chocolate calling out his name from the table. Grandma's breakfasts were better than any restaurant. She added crushed apples and cinnamon to the pancake batter and made her own syrup by mixing hot maple syrup and whipped butter.

Just as Aaron and Benji grabbed their forks to dig in, Grandma quietly called out, "Let's give thanks to God before we eat, shall we?"

They reached out to hold hands and Papa bowed his head and softly offered, "Thank you, God, for the safe arrival of our family yesterday. Help us recognize the many blessings You have graciously given to us. Please protect us and guide us through the day. Amen"

Benji buried his face in his plate, shoveling in his breakfast as fast as he could. He was not much of a conversationalist when food was involved, so Grandma would have to rely on Aaron this morning.

"The pancakes are even better than I remember, Grandma," said Aaron as he finished his plate and scooped up the last portion of syrup. The bacon is just how I like it, extra crispy." Grandma was like that, always remembering the little things about each of the children and surprising them with something special for no reason at all.

"Let's get our chores done so we can find ourselves a Christmas tree, shall we boys?" said Papa. As they got to the barn, Aaron volunteered, "I'll clean out the stalls with the rake, Papa."

"I'll fill the water bins for the animals," offered Benji. "Hey Papa, what do you get from a pampered cow?"

"I don't know, Benji. What?"

"Spoiled milk," shouted Benji. He got so excited about his joke he accidentally knocked over a shovel almost hitting one of the sheep in the barn. "Ooops."

"I'll have to remember that one. You know, these animals really do appreciate the care you're giving them, even if they can't tell you themselves," said Papa. Just as Papa was saying this, the sheep bleated out, "baaaah, baaaah." Papa laughed. "Well, maybe they can tell you how much they appreciate you."

After cleaning the stalls, they dropped fresh hay and grain in the food troughs. "We don't have to worry about the hens and Romeo today. Grandma and Hannah will tend to them when Hannah wakes up," said Papa.

"What do ya say we go find ourselves a Christmas tree," said Papa signaling that chores were done.

"Sounds good to us," said Aaron and Benji in unison grinning ear to ear with excitement.

"Let's take Rocky today. I think it will do just fine with the three of us," said Papa pointing to the red ATV parked in the garage. It had a closed cab that seated three, a small bed in the back to carry things, and four heavy-duty all-terrain tires. It also had a snowplow attachment Papa used to clear the roads on the Ranch. Papa named it Rocky because it was so good at getting up and down the hills on the Ranch.

Papa walked up to a large flatbed trailer. "Will you two help me hook the trailer to the back of Rocky? We'll use it to haul the Christmas tree back to the lodge."

Benji and Aaron stood at the tail end of the trailer and Papa stood at the end with the trailer hitch. "All ready," called out Aaron.

"On the count of three, push your end toward me," said Papa. The trailer was heavy and Benji and Aaron had trouble getting it to move.

Papa called out, "Plant your boots in the dirt and use your shoulder to push as hard as you can." Slowly the trailer began to roll, and Papa positioned the hitch onto the ball mount on the back of Rocky.

"This tree saw ought to be just right for the job," said Papa as he carefully examined the long saw with jagged teeth. "We'll need some rope as well," he added and grabbed a loop of rope from the shelf. Then he carefully tied them down in the bed of Rocky. "I think we're all ready. Let's go tell the ladies we're off."

"I have a basket of sandwiches and cookies for you to take," said Grandma. "Let me give you boys a proper goodbye." She embraced Aaron and Benji at the same time and quietly slipped a cookie in each of their jacket pockets. She winked and whispered to them, "In case you need a little energy out there."

Sarah was sitting on the floor sorting Christmas decorations. "I'm going to stick around here to help Grandma put up decorations around the lodge. Enjoy your adventure with Papa and pick us up a great Christmas tree!" She pulled Aaron aside, looked him straight in the eye, and whispered, "Aaron, look after your little brother."

"I will, Mom. I love you," replied Aaron in an earnest tone. Aaron wasn't bothered by her request. He was honored by her trust. Even if Benji got on his nerves, he would look after him for his mom.

Papa picked up the basket of food from Grandma. "Let's go, fellow explorers. Our Christmas tree awaits us."

***

Aaron and Benji grabbed their backpacks and climbed into Rocky. Aaron liked to be prepared, so he brought a bottle of water, first aid kit, and his notepad. Benji's backpack contained one of his prized possessions. His sketchpad and charcoal pencil set, just in case he happened upon a scene that spurred his artistic imagination. Papa noticed Benji's unzipped jacket. "It's a crisp day out on the mountain, boys. Bundle up."

Benji glanced down, oblivious to the chilly air rushing through his jacket. "Ah ha," he muttered as he zipped it up tight. Aaron rolled his eyes nodding at Papa as he positioned his gloves and scarf.

Papa made sure everybody was secure and started up Rocky. "Hold on tight, it's a bumpy ride." With all the fresh snow, Rocky had trouble maneuvering along the trail. As they travelled across the hills, Aaron gazed at the white spectacle blanketing the mountain. Snow covered the trees up to the low branches and a powdery layer sat gently on the upper portion of the trees. It was one of the most beautiful things Aaron had ever seen.

"The most important part of picking a Christmas tree is to look at the shape of the whole tree," said Papa as he navigated through the snow. "You don't want it to be lopsided or slanty. You also don't want it to have blank spots with no branches. Those sorts of trees are good for many other things, but not so good for a Christmas tree."

"Thanks, Papa. We'll keep our eyes peeled for the perfect Christmas tree," replied Aaron.

Benji stared out the window and scanned his brain for a joke. "What do Christmas trees wear at the pool?"

Papa so loved spending time with the children. It made him feel young to see the world through their eyes and to watch them explore the Ranch. He was prepared for Benji's steady flow of jokes. It had become a regular part of their time together. "What?"

"Trunks." Benji shot a wide grin and moved his eyebrows up and down as if they were cracking up.

Aaron rolled his eyes. He'd heard most of Benji's jokes and they were no better the second time. "Benji, knock it off. We're going after a Christmas tree."

They rode for a long time, until Papa pulled Rocky over to a small meadow. It seemed like they were a million miles away from everywhere. "Let's take a break to have a snack before we continue our search. I call this place Redwood Grove."

Aaron and Benji climbed out of Rocky and stretched their legs. Papa opened the basket and handed them each a sandwich. Everything Grandma made tasted like home. They sat in silence and admired the view. It was breathtaking. Large trees covered the hillside and snow blanketed the mountain. A "hoo...hoo" sound from above drew their attention. A white snowy owl perched high up in a tree watched them with wise eyes.

"Boys, I want to tell you about how special this Ranch is. The Parsons family has owned the Ranch a long, long time. It goes back many generations and I have lived on the Ranch my whole life. There's something extraordinary about this place."

"Papa, what do you mean – extraordinary?" asked Aaron.

"Something so special that you can't find it anywhere else in the entire world," replied Papa. "Anyway, as I was saying, when I was about your age, I explored every part of the Ranch. It's so big and so beautiful, you can spend a lifetime exploring and finding new things that will astound you."

"Papa, I love coming to visit you at the Ranch," said Aaron. "I think it's just about the most beautiful place in the whole world."

"Me too. I'd like to live here someday with you and Grandma," added Benji. "I could do amazing paintings."

Papa nodded in agreement with the boys' sentiments about the Ranch. "I had this same talk with your dad when he was about your age, so I think it's time for you to begin to discover the extraordinary story of the Ranch. It's a real wonder, boys. But the Ranch can also be dangerous, so you have to be very careful and make wise choices."

"We will, we promise, Papa," replied Aaron. Aaron was so excited he was about to burst. He was learning the secrets of the Ranch, secrets only his family knew, secrets he would share with his dad in a special bond forever.

"Me too," added Benji. The Ranch seemed safe and fun to Benji. He didn't understand why Papa was so cautious. But he knew Papa was wise about these sorts of things, so he figured it was best to go along for now. He could always make his own choices later.

***

Papa began hiking up a hill and pointed to the ridge. "OK then, let's take a little hike over that ridge." They climbed the snowy hill, surrounded by trees. They were deep in the forest and reached a small valley that seemed almost invisible, hidden from the rest of the world. It was strangely tranquil, and the sound of nothing was foreign to their ears. The only disturbance was the occasional gentle chirping of a small rosy finch that proudly displayed its pink feathers from a high branch.

Aaron's eyes widened as he trekked through the deep snow to get to the valley. The trees were different than others on the Ranch. They were giant redwoods, towering over everything else. And among them, there was one that stood out. It was the biggest and tallest of them all.

"These are ancient redwoods, boys. They're thousands of years old and they seem to reach all the way up to the sky." Papa pointed up the side of the tree craning his neck to look skyward. "This is the secret heart of the redwood grove, completely unknown to the outside world."

Aaron noticed the biggest tree had a wooden sign: *"The Way."*

"Why is this the only tree with a sign?"

Papa rubbed his gloves together. "Because of all the trees on the Ranch, this is the one tree that is truly extraordinary."

"Why is it so extraordinary, Papa?" asked Aaron as he walked closer to the gigantic tree.

"It's over three hundred feet tall, seems to reach all the way to the clouds." Papa paused for a moment and carefully considered his words. "Trees are funny things boys. I've been a wood craftsman all my life and have worked with every kind of tree."

"Like pines, oak, and spruce," said Aaron kicking a smooth spot in the snow with his boots.

"And many others. Some are good for building houses, others for furniture, still others for small, handcrafted things like the bowls I make for your grandma." Papa reached out and carefully touched the branches of the towering redwood.

"So what's this tree good for?" asked Benj.

Papa stepped back and lifted his arms to direct their attention to the soaring height of the tree. "Every tree has a connection to the world. Their roots go deep into the ground and their treetops reach high into the sky. Some trees were meant to stay trees and should never be cut down. That's what this tree is. A tree that should always remain a tree."

Aaron gazed up at the tree in awe of its dimensions and grandeur. "Wow, Papa, this is amazing."

"Papa, can I draw it?" asked Benji as he reached for his backpack.

Papa smiled as the boys' excitement filled the air. "We have a few minutes. Why not."

Benji removed a sketch pad and set of charcoal pencils from his backpack and began to reproduce the majestic picture in front of him. "The light shining through the trees is showing incredible colors."

Aaron craned his neck so he could peer straight up the tree. "This tree seems like it never ends. Can we climb it?"

"Absolutely. It's meant to be climbed," said Papa. "See how it's different than the other giant redwoods around it?"

Aaron spent the next ten minutes walking around the stand of redwoods closely examining them. They were truly a miracle. Their sheer size was stunning. But as impressive as all the trees were, he was strangely mesmerized by the one giant tree that stood above the others. Its branches were different than the other trees. "Its branches come all the way to the ground and are thicker than the other trees."

Papa smiled at Aaron. "Almost like it's inviting you to climb it." He patted Aaron on the back. "Wouldn't you say?"

"What do you think?" Benji held up his drawing waving it in front of Papa and Aaron. "It's a little rough, but I like the way I show the light streaming through the trees."

"I love it Benji," replied Papa. "You are becoming quite the artist."

"I can finish it up at the lodge." Benji carefully placed his sketchpad in his backpack. "I love this place, Papa."

"We better turn back to our mission." Papa brushed the snow around the tree with his boots to smooth out their footprints. "Our hunt for a Christmas tree. Aaron, do you want to drive Rocky?" asked Papa.

"Absolutely," exclaimed Aaron as Papa handed him the keys.

As they walked back to Rocky, Aaron and Benji stared up at the giant redwood tree with wonder.

Chapter Four

Christmas Tree in the Forest

———— ⌒o○⌒ ————

Papa helped Aaron get settled in the driver's seat. "Turn the key and press the accelerator gradually." He continued with a checklist of other details on steering, applying the brakes, and shifting gears. "Aaron, have you got this?" asked Papa.

Aaron had ridden in Rocky many times on visits to the Ranch over the years, so he was already familiar with the vehicle. "Yes, Papa. I think I'm ready."

Papa sat next to Aaron with his arm around Benji on his other side. "Go ahead Aaron, take it slow."

"Wow, this is awesome," said Aaron as Rocky began to move along the snow-covered trail.

They drove through the snow for about twenty minutes, and then Papa called out, "OK, you can pull over right here. This is a good spot to find our tree. Aaron, you did a fantastic job driving Rocky!" Papa untied the saw and rope, and they headed off to examine nearby trees. Benji grabbed the branches of a short fat tree. "This one looks pretty full."

"It sure does, Benji," replied Papa. "I think our lodge can fit a taller tree; let's see if we can find one a bit more grand."

They continued to search the area calling out prospects only to find flaws. The search continued for the next thirty minutes. Just as snow began to fall, Aaron yelled out, "I found it. Over here guys!"

Papa trudged through the deep snow and walked around the tree. "This one's a beauty, Aaron. What do you think, Benji?"

Benji held up his hands like an artist framing the tree. "I like it. This is the one."

Benji and Aaron knelt down and brushed away the snow from the base of the tree. Papa positioned them on each side of the tree and handed the saw to Aaron. "Boys, this is going to take teamwork." Papa held his hand together and made a push-pull motion to demonstrate. "Each of you hold on to one end of the saw and in unison saw the tree trunk as low to the ground as you can.

"Got it," called out Aaron. He ground his knees into the snow trying to get as much leverage as possible. "Ready."

"I'll stand here to make sure it doesn't fall on you." Papa grabbed a branch near the top of the tree. "On the count of three start sawing. 1-2-3, go."

Aaron and Benji had learned how to use a carpenter's saw from their dad, so they weren't afraid of the tool. But this was a new experience, cutting down a Christmas tree with a big, jagged, two-person saw. The sawing went slowly, but Benji and Aaron worked well together. They timed pushing and pulling in rhythm to keep the saw moving. Papa held the top of the tree straight so the saw wouldn't get pinched.

"Aaron, tell me when you're most of the way through the tree trunk," directed Papa. He craned his neck in a vain effort to see their progress.

As they continued to saw, Aaron kept his eye on the headway they were making. After another minute, Aaron thought it was time. "OK, Papa we're almost all the way through."

"Go ahead and back away from the tree," said Papa. "On the count of three, yell, timber!"

"1-2-3, timber!" yelled Aaron and Benji. They were rubbing their gloves together in excitement to see the fruit of their efforts fall to the ground.

Papa let go of the tree and it slowly toppled over onto the nearby snowbank. "Great job guys. You're real lumberjacks!"

"What's a lumberjack?" asked Benji. He stared at the tree stump marveling at their work.

"It's a job where they cut down very large trees from the forest. Those trees are taken on large trucks to the sawmills to make all kinds of things," replied Papa. "I guess we are. This tree's going to be a Christmas tree," cried Benji.

"Not just any Christmas tree," said Papa with a grin. "A Parsons' family Christmas tree."

Aaron slowly walked around the tree admiring its shape. "This may be the best we've had."

"I would say so. Your first Christmas tree should be the best one." Papa patted the boys on the back. "I'm real proud of you."

Papa grabbed the trunk of the tree and Benji and Aaron each grabbed a side. They dragged the tree to where Rocky was waiting and heaved it onto the trailer. Papa secured the tree to the trailer with the rope and put the saw in the back of Rocky. They sat in the snow to catch their breath and admire the picturesque countryside.

"It's days like this that remind me how magnificent the Ranch is," said Papa. He gazed across the mountain taking in the tree-covered hillside as gentle snowflakes fell around them.

Redwood Grove and *The Way* still gripped Aaron. "Did you climb the giant redwood tree when you were little?"

"Sure did." Papa paused for a moment, reflecting on those wonderful boyhood memories. "I had some remarkable times and gained a lot of wisdom up in that tree."

Aaron leaned closer to Papa. "What do you mean?" He had an unquenchable appetite to know more secrets of the Ranch, so he couldn't resist the urge to push further.

"There's a lot of goodness and beauty in the world." Papa pointed to the snowflakes gently falling to the ground. "But there's also evil and ugliness."

Aaron slid closer to Papa and asked, "How do you know the difference?"

"That's called wisdom, Aaron, the ability to see the difference." Papa drew a line in the snow with his finger. "That's one of the most important lessons to learn in life, boys."

"So how can I tell the difference?" asked Aaron. He used his finger to draw a circle in the snow around Papa's line.

"That's what I learned on that redwood tree. I could tell you my story, but this is something you'll have to discover for yourselves. It's something your dad discovered here."

Aaron jerked up with a twinkle in his eye. "My dad discovered it here too?"

"He sure did." Papa stood up and brushed the snow off his pants. "Wisdom is not only the ability to see the difference between good and evil — beauty and ugliness, it's the courage to act once you see. Recognizing the wise path and having the courage to take it."

Aaron felt a surge of curiosity about the mystery of Papa's words. They were talking about big things that mattered in life. Goodness, beauty, evil, ugliness. Especially after the ugly incident with Reaper, he wanted to learn more about them. He was also fascinated by the giant redwood tree. *What had Papa and his dad discovered?* He had to know.

"We better head back to the lodge. They'll be worrying about us." Papa opened the passenger door and motioned for Aaron and Benji to hop in. "Since we're carrying a big load, I think it's best if I drive Rocky back to the lodge."

"Sounds good to me," replied Aaron. He didn't want anything to do with driving Rocky with a large tree tied to the trailer.

As they made their way back to the lodge, Aaron and Benji were brimming with pride and confidence. They had gone on an adventure with Papa in the snow-covered mountains in search of the perfect Christmas tree, just as their father had before them. The large tree tied to the trailer was nature's treasure that would adorn the lodge with the scent of Christmas.

***

When they reached the lodge, Sarah and Hannah were in the front yard building a snowman. "We found a fabulous Christmas tree," called out Papa. "Aaron and Benji were like lumberjacks out there."

"You should have seen it! We sawed the tree down all by ourselves," shouted Aaron.

"Timber!" yelled Benji as the two boys fell into the snow laughing. Bailey bounded out of the lodge and jumped on the boys as he wagged his tail.

Aaron picked up a handful of snow, patted it into a ball, and hurled it at Benji. It hit him square in the chest.

"Hey, I wasn't looking," cried Benji. He faked a fall backward. Then he picked up a pile of snow and threw it at Aaron. It hit him in the side as he turned to avoid the snowball. Soon the whole family was making snowballs and heaving them at each other. Snowballs were hitting everyone, and they were laughing and falling into the soft snow.

Papa saw the chaos building and escaped the wintery battle to check on Grandma inside. She was cooking a mouthwatering meal. He gave her a gentle kiss on the cheek and whispered, "Chloe, I showed the boys the redwood grove."

"That's wonderful, Sam. They will so enjoy exploring." Grandma stopped stirring the pot and turned to Papa with a concerned look. "Did you warn them about the dangerous parts too?"

"I didn't give them too much detail. I want them to discover its wonders by themselves." Papa squeezed her shoulder to comfort her. "Aaron and Benji are smart boys. Just like Peter was."

The snowball fight was still raging outside, with nobody winning and everybody getting hit. Sarah decided it was time to wind things down before someone got hurt. "OK, let's call a truce so we can set up the Christmas tree."

"I'm the winner because I landed the most direct hits to the body," declared Aaron. He tickled Hannah causing her to fall backward in the snow roaring in laughter.

"No, I'm the winner because I had the best shot of the day. A snowball to your stomach that made you drop," said Benji. He feigned injury, closing his eyes and falling backward into the soft snow.

Hannah, still on the ground, grabbed another handful of snow and hurled it at Aaron. "No, I'm the winner because I threw the most snowballs for my age." In an effort to keep the peace, Sarah waved her arms and declared, "It's a tie!"

The children fell silent for a second and then grinned when Sarah continued, "Aaron, can you please get the Christmas tree stand from the garage? Benji, can you help me untie the rope? Hannah, please go ask Grandma to get the spot in the family room ready for the tree." "Yes, ma'am," they said in unison and took off in different directions.

Papa took charge of bringing the tree inside. He lifted the tree by the trunk while Aaron and Benji helped him by holding the top. They carried it into the lodge and placed it in the stand in the family room. It was a magnificent tree, about eight feet high with full branches all the way around. The fresh spruce scent drifted through the lodge, adding an extra dose of Christmas spirit.

Grandma slowly paced around the tree inspecting it top to bottom. "Aaron, Benji, this tree is beautiful. You boys did a superb job picking out a Christmas tree."

"Thanks, Grandma," replied Aaron as he admired the tree. "Papa told us what to look for. A tree with no blank spots."

"Dinner's ready, so let's take a break," said Grandma. "After dinner, we can decorate the tree."

They all sat at the big wooden table in the dining room. Papa had built the table and the chairs himself in his workshop. The table was solid and strong, and the chairs had a comfortable fit. Grandma adored the holidays because it involved two of her favorite things: Family and food. She had cooked homemade soup with warm buttered French bread; delicious smells wafted through the lodge. She knew they would need a bowl of hot soup after being in the cold all day.

After dinner, Papa brought out several large boxes filled with lights and decorations for the tree. Sarah set up the lights first while Aaron,

Benji, and Hannah separated all the Christmas decorations. Papa served as the quality assurance judge from the comfort of the sofa.

"I made eggnog and cookies for dessert," said Grandma. She teetered into the family room carrying a large pitcher of sloshing eggnog in one hand and a tray of cookies precariously balanced in the other. Bailey stalked behind her with his eyes locked on what he had good reason to believe would be his next meal. Sarah rushed over to grab the tray of cookies. "Let me help you with that."

Benji snatched a cookie off the tray and took a big bite. "Before Bailey gets a floor full of cookies."

"Nothing's too good for Bailey," joked Grandma as she set the eggnog down on the table.

The evening flew by as they hung ornaments on the tree while sipping eggnog and putting away more cookies than any of them cared to admit. Every so often, Papa chimed in with his artistic input, "A little more over here."

The stories were the best part of the evening for Aaron. He loved stories, all kinds of stories. The time Papa and his dad caught a huge fish that caused his dad to fall in the lake as he reeled it in. The night his mom helped a deer give birth to a baby fawn right in the front yard of the lodge. The stories gave Aaron a connection to the past. To his family.

Benji loved the stories about how much freedom kids used to have. Papa and Grandma described the way things were in the old days. Papa ended with, "We were free to do as we pleased. My mom told me to go out and play and not come back until dinner time."

Benji glanced at Sarah with a smirk, "See, that's how it should be. Papa's mom knew."

"That was a long time ago, mister," Sarah shot back with a coy smile.

Aaron and Benji shared their adventures with Papa – how they found the tree, sawed it down, hauled it to Rocky, and spotted the snowy owl and rosy finch in the trees. Aaron kept quiet about the redwood grove since it was still a big mystery to him – a mystery he intended to explore it as soon as possible.

Papa placed his hands under his chin as he listened intently to the boys recount their day in the snow. These times with his grandchildren were a treasure for him and reminded him of the times when Peter was young. "I remember the time your dad got stuck in a tree," said Papa with a chuckle. "He was about your age, Aaron."

Aaron sat up. "What happened to him?"

Papa paused as images of his little boy flashed in front of him. *Playing catch in the yard, projects in the woodshop, building snowmen*, so many wonderful memories. Suddenly, all the memories flushed from his mind as he remembered where Peter was now. The danger his boy was in. He clenched his jaw to regain his grip. "Ah... sorry, I was just reminiscing...I had to climb up to help him get down."

Sarah noticed Papa's eyes glistening with moisture. "Maybe that's why he decided to become a Navy Seal instead of an Army Ranger." They all chuckled, and Papa had the biggest laugh.

The end of the evening was marked by a finished Christmas tree. It was a masterpiece with colorful lights, glittering ornaments and tinsel, and topped with a sparkling angel. Papa and Grandma said their good nights and plodded off to bed. Sarah stayed to tidy up the boxes. Aaron, Benji, and Hannah made their way upstairs to their bedroom and changed into their pajamas.

"What a day, huh Benji?" said Aaron.

"The best! I still say I won the snowball fight," said Benji with a chuckle.

They climbed into bed and drifted off to sleep relishing their day and wondering what they might find in Redwood Grove.

***

Sarah was organizing the boxes when Jen's name appeared on her phone screen. She instinctively dropped the boxes in her hand and froze. The phone continued to ring as she hesitated, half afraid to hear any news. Finally, the urge to know won out. "Any news?"

"Briggs said they're still missing and no contact. All he could say is that the mission is Extreme Risk Profile."

"Extreme Risk Profile... that sounds bad." Sarah's mind was flooded with unimaginable horrors Peter might be facing. "Any word on if they can get them out? Or when?"

"That's all he could say."

Sarah took a deep, steadying breath and forced her brain to form words. "Thanks Jen. Have a nice Christmas if I don't talk to you before then."

Sarah retreated to the study, where she could be alone with her thoughts. Peter never shared much about his missions, and she assumed most were perilous. This one seemed especially so, judging by the few details she knew. He was the best at what he did, but the world was full of bad people and dangers. She realized she married a man who wanted to save the world. This torment was part of the price of that choice. She felt the tears rolling down her cheeks and quickly brushed them away. She had to be strong for him and for their children. She wanted to give them a memorable Christmas, even if he couldn't be there. She had to do her part to help Peter save the world.

Chapter Five

A Climb into the Fog

Aaron, Benji, and Hannah ran out to the garage, and Aaron pulled open the large door. They gathered around Rocky as Aaron explained the rules. "I promised Mom I would look after you two." "Yeah, yeah," said Benji in a mocking tone.

"Hannah, you sit in the middle," said Aaron as he helped Hannah onto the leather seat. "Hold on to the handles. Benji, you sit near the window and don't hang your head out. Grandma said to be back by 5:00 so I'm setting my alarm for 4:00."

Aaron climbed into the driver's seat and started Rocky. The engine kicked over with a loud rumble and Aaron slowly accelerated as he made his way towards the trail.

"I think that Redwood Grove is this way," said Aaron as he tried to remember the trail Papa had taken yesterday. "Yes, I recognize that hillside with the big rock. It's this way."

It was a beautiful day in the forest. The morning air was crisp, and the sun was just rising above the ridgeline. The white snow reflected the morning light creating a mysterious glow to the scenery.

Hannah was excited to be going on an adventure with her brothers, but at the same time, she was afraid to be venturing off like this. "What's so special about this Redwood Grove?" she asked.

"Papa said it's extraordinary," replied Benji. "You know, one of a kind."

"Look at the owl sitting on that tree," said Hannah as she craned her neck to get a better look.

"Yeah, we saw it yesterday," replied Benji. "It's a snowy-white owl." Aaron rolled his eyes, surprised that Benji had remembered.

After a while longer, they reached Redwood Grove. "I think we're here," said Aaron. "We hiked up that hill to get to the redwood grove."

"Wait for me," said Hannah in a nervous voice. The snow was above her knees, making it hard for her to keep up with her brothers.

"See, there are the redwood trees we told you about, Hannah," said Benji. He pointed to the stand of large redwood trees. The three of them stood frozen on the hill peering down into the clearing. The remains of their footprints from yesterday had disappeared under a fresh layer of snow, but this was definitely the place. The redwood trees were enormous and were blanketed with snow. It was an awesome sight. The large white owl landed high up in one of the trees.

They ran down into the clearing and Aaron pointed to the tree with *The Way* sign next to it. "Papa said we can climb this tree," he said.

Hannah stared up at the gigantic tree. "Whoa, it's a lot bigger close up."

"Papa said it's different than the other trees." Aaron pointed to the lowest row of branches. "Like it's inviting us to climb it."

"Then let's climb," cried Benji as he rubbed his hands together in the crisp morning air. "It's ginormous."

The children were experienced climbers since they had many large pine trees and oak trees in their backyard at home as well as years of tree climbing at the Ranch. But they had never climbed a tree like this one. This would take them to new heights. While most redwoods were difficult to climb, this was a particularly easy tree to climb. It had thick sturdy branches close enough together for the children to make their way up the tree, limb by limb. However, the branches were dusted with snow, forcing them to use extra care as they made their way up the wooden stairway into the sky.

Every few branches, Aaron paused to take in the view. "I can see all the way across the valley."

"Snow is falling on me, Aaron. Be careful," said Benji as he brushed snow off his face.

"Wait for me," said Hannah. She gripped each branch with all her might as she made her way up the tree behind Benji.

"Hey, I see something up a little higher," said Aaron. He moved to some branches above him to get a better look. "I think it's clouds or fog."

They were higher than they had ever climbed before. The tree was shrouded by a thick fog bank that made climbing difficult. They couldn't see anything, not even the branches right above them.

"Be careful," said Aaron. "Go really slow and make sure you have a good grip on the branch before you step up."

"I can't see a thing; I'm scared," said Hannah. She focused her attention upward, afraid to look down. "Should we turn around?"

"This is amazing! Let's keep going," shouted Benji as he climbed ahead.

"Hannah, I'll be right next to you," said Aaron. He stepped down a branch to creep close to Hannah. "We'll go as slow as you want."

Hannah held out her hand to grasp Aaron's. "OK, Aaron, make sure I'm safe."

They continued climbing through the fog for several minutes. Benji was climbing faster and was well above them.

"Hey, I think the fog is clearing," said Benji. "Climb up here; you're not going to believe this!"

Aaron and Hannah crept up branch by branch, and eventually caught up with Benji. They stepped off the tree branches and were standing on the ground. They had climbed into some kind of new place.

***

"Holy moly!" cried Aaron. His mouth fell open as he took in this new mysterious place.

As the three of them dusted the snow off their clothes, they looked around in bewilderment. They were standing in the middle of a meadow teeming with beautiful flowers of every color. The air was warm, the sky was blue, and all the snow was gone – it was like a summer day.

"Where did all the snow go?" asked Aaron spinning around to take in the scene.

"Where are we?" replied Benji. He peered down the giant redwood and saw nothing but thick fog.

"This's just about the most beautiful place I've ever seen," said Hannah. She bent over and picked a lovely yellow flower and put it in her hair.

As they looked around the meadow and tried to figure out where they were, they saw a family of deer staring at them nearby. There was a large buck with magnificent antlers, a smaller doe, and a fawn that had all been peacefully grazing on the flowers.

"Let's take a look around," said Aaron still trying to make sense of where they were. He took off his leather winter jacket and set it on the ground. "Leave our jackets right here near the opening, so we can find our way back."

"Yes, this is a wonderful place to explore," said the biggest deer with the antlers.

Aaron, Benji, and Hannah looked at each other in shock. Their eyes were as big as saucers. They took a step away from the deer family. "Dddd…. did that deer just talk to us?" asked Aaron.

"Of course I did," said the deer. "Why wouldn't I want to talk to you? Are you mean children? You look quite nice to me."

Benji scratched his head. "How can you talk to us?" he asked.

"We are nice children," added Hannah widening her grin to prove her point.

"Well, it's nice to meet you. I'm Jack Deer," said the big buck. "This is my wife, Ella Doe, and our son, Enzo Fawn."

"I'm Aaron, and this is my brother Benji and sister Hannah," replied Aaron not at all certain he was actually talking to a deer.

"Do you want some flowers? They're delightful and delicious," offered Enzo as he bent over to nibble on the colorful flowers.

"Ah... no thank you," replied Aaron. He cautiously stepped closer to the deer with his hands out in front of him as though he were feeling for reality in a dark room.

"We don't eat flowers," added Hannah turning her head to show off the yellow flower in her hair. "Do you like my flower?" Enzo pranced up to take a closer look at Hannah's unusual use of a flower.

"We'd be happy to show you around," offered Jack. "We're close to Lake Amari, and lots of animals live around the lake."

"That would be nice," replied Aaron. "We climbed up a tree and all of the sudden we were here. I'm not sure where 'here' is."

"Ah ha, so you're not from here," replied Jack. "Did you come up from the Parsons' Ranch?"

"Yeah, we climbed up the big redwood tree and found this place." Aaron reached out and touched Jack's antlers. "You know the Parsons? They're my Papa and Grandma."

"Yes, I know your Papa and Grandma from a long, long time ago." Jack ambled toward the lake with Ella and Enzo following behind him. "You'll love Lake Amari. You can meet our friends, and I'll tell you more about this place."

As they approached the lake, they saw all sorts of animals – squirrels, raccoons, skunks, bears, mountain lions, and birds of every color up in the trees. All the animals were talking, laughing, and frolicking around the lake. A squirrel was chasing a skunk around a tree as they chuckled. A mountain lion was gently playing with a baby bear. The birds were singing delightful tunes that filled the air with a lovely melody.

"We're very confused," said Aaron. His head swiveled back and forth as he beheld the mysterious beauty that surrounded them. "What kind of place is this?"

"This is the Kingdom of Himmel," replied Jack. He lowered his head and took a sip of water from the lake. "Technically, we're in the Highlands Province, but it's all part of Himmel."

A mountain lion sauntered up to them eyeing them carefully. Aaron, Benji, and Hannah maneuvered behind Jack. "We're about to play hide-and-seek. Do you want to play?" asked the mountain lion.

Jack shook his head as he stared at the mountain lion. "Jasper Lion, they just met us."

"Everybody likes hide-and-seek," replied an undeterred Jasper as he casually licked his whiskers.

Benji stepped in front of Jack to take a closer look at Jasper. "I'd like to play," said Benji. One of the laws of Benji was to never pass up a chance to play games. And playing with animals would be a first, so he was ecstatic at the prospect.

"Well then, it's settled," said Jasper. "We have three new players."

"Riley Raccoon, you go first," said Jasper. He looked at the racoon and directed her to walk over to the big rock they used as home base for the game.

"Everybody hide," said Riley. She placed her little paws over her eyes. "I'm going to find you all on the count of 10."

Riley began counting loudly and slowly, "1 – 2 – 3..." as all the animals scurried about looking for a place to hide.

Aaron, Benji, and Hannah looked at each other and shrugged their shoulders. "Well, we better hide," said Aaron.

"...4 – 5 – 6," could be heard from Riley in the distance.

"Follow me," whispered Aaron as he ran toward a large oak tree near the lake. They quickly climbed the tree and hid atop large thick branches so they could not be seen from the ground.

"Jasper, I saw you hiding by accident," called out Riley. "You can hide again. I'll add 5 more seconds."

"Thanks Riley," replied Jasper as he padded off to find a new spot.

"...9 – 10 – 11 – 12 – 13 – 14 – 15. Ready or not, here I come!" shouted Riley as she opened her eyes and began scanning the forest.

"I see you, Morris Squirrel," yelled Riley. She touched the squirrel with her paw and he kicked the dirt with his little claws.

"I thought I outsmarted you," cried Morris as he made his way back to the big rock.

"I see you too, Piper Bear," shouted Riley. She tagged the humongous bear who let out a thunderous roar that startled the children.

"I can't believe you found me," said Piper as she crawled out of the roomy cave towards the big rock. "I had the best hiding place."

"You hide there every time, Piper," replied Riley and chuckled at her friend. Piper was not very good at this game because she was too big for most of the hiding places.

Aaron, Benji, and Hannah crouched in the tree branches and tried their best not to be seen. Aaron saw Riley roam away from their tree. He heard a bird crowing next to them and lifted a branch to get a better look. A black raven with menacing eyes stared at them and crowed loudly. Nervous it would give them away, he quietly waved his arm, and it flew away.

"I see you, Jasper," said Riley. She touched the tail of the large mountain lion. "But that was a good hiding place."

"You're too clever for me, Riley," chuckled Jasper as he sauntered toward the big rock. "I thought I had you."

Riley tracked down and eventually called out the other animals' names as she found each one. They all laughed and joked about the hiding places and Riley's keen detective skills.

"I can't find Aaron, Benji, and Hannah," said Riley. "They're not in the cave, they're not in the meadow, and I can't think where else to look."

After a several more minutes, Riley called out, "Olly, olly oxen free," signaling that she was giving up and the game was over. Aaron, Benji, and Hannah climbed down the tree and ran over to the big rock. "Hurray for Aaron, Benji, and Hannah," all the animals cheered.

Benji thought something was strange about Riley's game strategy compared to what he was used to back home. "Hey, Riley, why did you tell Jasper to hide again?" asked Benji. "A better strategy would have been to keep quiet and then nab him."

"Telling him was the honest thing to do," replied Riley. She was surprised by his question. "I love Jasper and wouldn't want to cheat him. We don't do that here."

Benji cocked his head but was afraid to say anything to his new friends. He really wondered about this place, *No cheating, very strange.*

Ella Doe looked at the group with excitement. "Let's have a feast to celebrate our new friends."

"Splendid idea," said Piper as the big bear scooped some fresh honey with her giant paw.

The animals scurried off in every direction to gather food. Soon, the animals had laid out an assortment of delicious fruits, nuts, and vegetables including apples, strawberries, watermelon, boysenberries, almonds, walnuts, and carrots. Aaron, Benji, and Hannah cautiously tried the food, and it was the sweetest tasting food they had ever eaten. Somehow the taste was richer and more flavorful than back home.

Aaron bit into a crisp apple. "Wow, I've never had food so fresh and full of flavor."

"Yasha's water," replied Ella. "Makes everything taste better."

"This feast is terrific!" exclaimed Benji as he stuffed another plump strawberry in his mouth while simultaneously reaching for an apple soaked in honey. Benji was feeling a bit uncomfortable, this being his first feast with animals. His solution, as always, was a well-placed joke. It drove Aaron crazy. "Hey Jack, why did the deer get braces?"

Jack looked at Benji with a puzzled expression. "I don't know Benji, why?" "He had buck teeth." Benji grinned at Jack waiting for the laughter.

Enzo looked at Jack and Ella and saw them chuckle. He didn't know what braces were, but it sounded funny, so he laughed too.

"Very funny, Benji," replied Jack as he chomped his teeth up and down to imitate bucked teeth. "What do you call a cat that drinks lemonade?"

Benji was surprised that someone actually joined in his joke fest. He was really beginning to like this place. "What, Jack?" Jack began laughing before he even got the punchline out. Glancing toward

Jasper, he yelled, "A sour puss." Jasper pretended to laugh rolling over on his side. "Hilarious, Jackeroo."

Aaron's curiosity was bursting inside him, and he desperately wanted to stop the stream of dumb jokes that Benji had instigated. "Jack, you mentioned this is a kingdom. What do you mean?"

"Himmel is a land ruled by a king, King Yasha," replied Jack.

"Your king?" Aaron leaned closer to Jack with his ears perked. "You mean like the President?"

"Not at all like a president," replied Jack. He plucked a fresh strawberry with his mouth.

"King Yasha is everything," offered Ella. She lifted her head and pointed toward the tall mountains off in the distance.

"As I understand your president, he's your leader," replied Jack. "King Yasha is much more than that. He's a master artist who makes things that are good and beautiful. He's a king who knows us and cares for us much more than a president."

"We enjoy his beautiful artwork very much," said Jasper as he rolled over in the grass.

Benji was skeptical; it all sounded too good. In his experience, people in charge start making rules and take all the fun away. "Does your king tell you what to do?"

"Well, he guides us," replied Piper. She scratched her big furry back on the side of a tree with a big grin of delight. "Ah."

"Kings make rules, don't they?" Benji had a limited understanding of kings and queens, but enough to know they made all the rules in their kingdom, and nobody gets a vote. "What if you don't want to do what the king says?"

"Why would we not want to do what King Yasha says?" asked Jack with a befuddled look on his face. "He's the master artist of his kingdom."

"I don't know, maybe he doesn't know the right thing to do," replied Aaron. "Or maybe he isn't strong enough to take care of everyone in the kingdom."

"Or maybe I want to do what I want to do instead," added Benji as he grabbed another handful of strawberries and stuffed one in his mouth.

Hannah inched closer to Aaron holding onto his side. "Or maybe he doesn't like me," she said.

"That's Shadowlands talk," said Jack. He shook his head and gave a long look at the children. "Once you meet King Yasha, you'll understand."

"Where's Shadowlands?" asked Benji. Jack's response sparked his interest and got him thinking. *If the people in Shadowlands have these doubts too, maybe it's the place for me.*

Aaron could see Benji getting off track, so he interrupted. "I'd like to meet your king sometime. Does he meet with people?"
Ella perked up at the mention of King Yasha. "Yes," she said, "he loves to meet with people."

Piper pointed her enormous paw north to the mountains in the distance. "The City of Light is where you'll find him."

Aaron was curious why they'd only seen animals in Himmel and wanted to steer the conversation away from Benji's pointless questions. "Are there people like us in Himmel?"

"There are plenty of people in the kingdom," replied Jack. "Most live near the City of Light. Some unfortunate ones live in Shadowlands. Mr. Wigglebottom lives here with us animals."

"Who's Mr. Wigglebottom?" asked Aaron with raised eyebrows. "Can we meet him."

"He's a wonderful man. He lives in that cottage by the lake." Jack began sauntering down the trail. "It's this way."

Chapter Six

Mr. Wigglebottom

Mr. Wigglebottom's cottage was quite small, too small for a full-grown adult to live in. The cottage was made of large stone blocks with gorgeous lavender trumpet vines growing up the sides. The steep thatched roof was covered with a bright green moss. It had a neatly manicured yard, with colorful flowers growing all around the cottage and a gravel walkway out front.

An odd-looking little man stepped out of the cottage to greet them. "Greetings to all you beautiful animals. Who might these lads and the little lass be?"

"Good day, Mr. Wigglebottom," replied Jack Deer. "Aaron, Benji, and Hannah are our guests from afar."

"It's a great day indeed to make your acquaintance," Mr. Wigglebottom said, reaching out his hand to give a firm handshake to each of the children. "Fancy some tea? I just so happen to have a fresh pot brewing."

Aaron couldn't help but stare at Mr. Wigglebottom as they got closer to him. He was a good bit shorter than Aaron and only a little taller than Hannah. He was a stout little man with white wavy hair, chubby red cheeks, and piercing blue eyes. He wore a blue dinner jacket that went down to his knees, white slacks, and an English Bowler hat that gave him a distinguished look.

"Nice to meet you, Mr. Wigglebottom," replied Aaron. He tried to look Mr. Wigglebottom in the eyes without appearing to gawk. His mom and dad had taught him not to stare at people, especially if they had something different about them. Mr. Wigglebottom was certainly different.

"Come in, come in," replied Mr. Wigglebottom as he retreated into his cottage.

He moved with short quick little steps that were more like a waddle than a walk.

The door to the cottage was quite small and Aaron had to stoop down to fit through it. The inside of the cottage was clean and tidy with a wooden table in a tiny kitchen area and four petite stools. A small sitting area was next to the kitchen with a small sofa.

Mr. Wigglebottom waddled into the kitchen to pull a tray of chocolate chip cookies from the oven. The mouthwatering scent of fresh baked cookies filled the cottage. Ella Doe, Enzo Fawn, Jasper Lion, and Riley Raccoon had no problem fitting through the small front door, but Piper Bear and Jack Deer were a different matter. Piper tried to squeeze her enormous body through the door, but she was just too big. Riley tried to push her from behind without success. Jack twisted and turned his antlers attempting to slide through the door but all he got for his efforts was a sore neck.

Mr. Wigglebottom watched them straining to get through the door and chuckled at the strange sight of a full-grown bear and deer squeezing to get into his diminutive cottage. "Ms. Piper and Mr. Jack, may I suggest window seats for you." He opened two windows so Piper and Jack could enjoy the tea and cookies from outside the cottage.

Mr. Wigglebottom poured cups of tea and laid out a large plate of cookies for everyone as they gathered around his table, except for Piper and Jack who had their heads inside the window and their bodies outside. With a look of astonishment, Aaron surveyed the group of these new friends packed into this tiny cottage. He thought to himself, *this is the most peculiar thing I've ever seen.*

Mr. Wigglebottom stirred sugar into his tea as he looked over the children with a beaming smile on his face. "Sir Aaron, may I ask you. Are you from the Parsons line?"

Aaron was taken aback. Like Jack, Mr. Wigglebottom knew his family. "Yes, you know them?"

"I've had the great pleasure and privilege to meet them many, many years ago." Mr. Wigglebottom seemed pleased with the answer as he sipped his tea.

"Fine family, yes indeed."

Benji was curious about Mr. Wigglebottom. There were so many questions about this little man, but Benji had to think hard to find one that wouldn't be rude. "Why are you the only person who lives here with the animals?"

"I have the honor of being a caretaker for the animals, Sir Benji," Mr. Wigglebottom said, puffing out his chest in admiration of his unique calling in the kingdom.

Jack could see the children didn't understand, so he said, "Mr. Wigglebottom is what you might call a veterinarian."

Mr. Wigglebottom took a sip of tea. "If the animals get sick or injured, I have the privilege of tending to their needs."

"Ah, my mom's a veterinarian," said Benji. He chomped a big bite of his cookie dropping crumbs on the table. "A real good one."

Aaron hoped to get more information about Himmel and the King from Mr. Wigglebottom and was annoyed that Benji kept getting off on unimportant topics. "Jack says there is a King Yasha who is an artist. We want to meet him."

"It will be the highlight of your life to meet his majesty, King Yasha." Mr. Wigglebottom set his tea down and adjusted his hat as he reflected on King Yasha. "Sir Aaron, you're wise to seek an audience with King Yasha. He'll certainly delight in taking a meeting with you as well."

Aaron thought maybe Mr. Wigglebottom could give him more information about this artist king. "Jack says he's an artist who makes good and beautiful things. What kind of things?"

"He does indeed. Exquisitely good and beautiful paintings." Mr. Wigglebottom offered the plate of warm cookies around the table and encouraged everyone to take one. "You need to see his paintings. They're exceptional in every respect."

Aaron grabbed a cookie and placed it on the small plate in front of him. "With all his painting, does he have time to meet with people like us?" he asked.

"Every person should meet King Yasha," Mr. Wigglebottom said. He wiggled his nose and added, "He takes a special delight in meeting people; we're very special to him."

Aaron leaned in with furrowed brow and asked, "What do you mean special?"

"King Yasha loves all of the kingdom including all the animals, plants, and other parts of the kingdom." Mr. Wigglebottom swept his arm across the room slowly pointing at Jasper, Ella, Enzo, Riley, and then at Jack and Piper whose heads were poking in the open windows. "But people are like him and are very special to him."

The chime of Aaron's alarm interrupted Mr. Wigglebottom and startled the group into silence. Aaron looked down at his watch and realized it was 4:00. He was perturbed that he was just starting to get answers on this artist king. His questions would have to wait until another day. "I'm sorry but we have to go. Thank you for the delicious tea and cookies, Mr. Wigglebottom."

"I'm sorry to see you go." Mr. Wigglebottom escorted them out, waving from his front yard as they all departed. "Please come back soon."

Hannah was wistful as they made their way back to the redwood tree. The day had refreshed her spirit. For some reason, the fears that plagued her subsided in this place and she had enjoyed a day of sheer delight with these new friends. It was a feeling she had not known back home for a long time. Riley sensed Hannah's sadness and nuzzled up next to her and smiled. Hannah gently stroked Riley's head and said, "Thank you for the wonderful day."

Enzo trotted up next to Hannah and tickled behind her ear with his nose. "I hope you come back soon for more hide-and-seek."

"Yes, the hide-and-seek was a blast. Got to check the tree next time, Riley," added Benji. "Hey Piper, what kind of socks do bears wear?"

Piper raised her giant paw and pretended to scratch her head. "I don't know, Benji, what?"

"They don't wear anything! They go bear-foot." Benji raised his eyebrows with a big grin on his face. "Hey, is that good or what?"

"Quite true, Mr. Funny-boy," said Piper chuckling at Benji's corny joke.

"There're our jackets," said Aaron. He bent over and put on his jacket.

The animals gathered around the tree as the children prepared to leave. "You're welcome back anytime," said Jack. "Next time we can take you to meet King Yasha."

"That would be wonderful," replied Aaron.

***

The children climbed onto the redwood and soon were making their way down the snow-covered tree. They reached the bottom of the tree and hopped to the ground. As Aaron drove Rocky along the trail through the snow, they were all quiet, lost in their thoughts. This had been an extraordinary day for each of them. As they approached the lodge, they could see the lights on and smoke coming out of the chimney.

"I don't think Mom will believe us if we tell her," said Aaron. He tried to focus on his driving through the snow, but his mind kept returning to their day in Himmel.

"I don't believe it and I was there," said Benji chuckling.

"I liked Enzo Fawn," said Hannah as she twisted the yellow flower in her hair. "Can we see him again?" "We'll go back soon," said Aaron. "I want to meet King Yasha."

They walked into the lodge and were greeted by hugs from Papa and Grandma. Sarah was out walking before dinner. Papa looked at

Aaron with a wry smile. "Did you children have an interesting day out there?"

"Yeah Papa, we explored Redwood Grove." Aaron removed his jacket and hat and placed them on the coatrack near the door. "We had a fantastic day."

"I'm happy to hear that, Aaron," replied Papa. "Remember to be careful out there."

"I see Sarah coming up the walk; go wash your hands for dinner," said Grandma.

They enjoyed a wonderful meal together. Papa and Grandma told stories about when they were young and how the world used to be. Sarah listened mostly but added a few corrections when Papa and Grandma forgot things. Aaron thought life seemed simpler and kinder back then. He wondered what had changed, what was lost.

After dinner, Grandma brought out pumpkin pie. She topped each piece with whipped cream and served them on small plates. They settled by the fire as they ate pie and shared stories of past Christmases.

As Aaron ate his pie and listened to his family, his mind wandered to his day with the animals and Mr. Wigglebottom in Himmel. *We played hide-and-seek with animals! What is that place? How could we talk to animals? What is King Yasha like? Why did it feel so different?*

As the evening drew to a close, the fire began to flicker with the glow of orange embers. It was late, and the children fell asleep on pillows in front of the fire. Sarah gently woke Hannah and the boys and helped them upstairs to settle into bed. It didn't take long for the children to fall back to sleep, each drifting off to dream about their wonderful day in an extraordinary new world.

Chapter Seven

Shadowlands

———— ∽∞∾ ————

B enji woke up before sunrise and crept out of the lodge as quietly as he could. Himmel was amazing, but he was intrigued by Shadowlands. A place where there was no king. He put on a pair of snowshoes and headed out to Redwood Grove. It was a long hike, but he desperately wanted to explore this part of the kingdom they had just discovered. He knew Aaron wouldn't go to Shadowlands based on what Jack Deer had said about it. He was tired of being bossed around by Aaron. He was his own boy and he could do what he wanted. Right now, going to Shadowlands is what he wanted.

He climbed the big redwood named *The Way* and soon he was through the fog, standing in the meadow. Jack and the others were nowhere to be seen this morning. Jack had pointed west when he described Shadowlands yesterday, so Benji got his bearings as best he could and started out. As he got closer to Shadowlands, the sky darkened with black clouds as far as he could see. There was a chill in the air that reached all the way through his snow jacket. He walked toward a small hill in the distance where he thought he saw something moving. As he got closer, he recognized the thing moving was a pig splashing in a muddy swamp. The sight was quite odd; the pig was wearing a crown on its head.

"Well, that's bizarre," said Benji under his breath as he approached the pig.

"Oink, Oink," squealed the pig. It rolled in the mud while trying to steady the crown on its head with its front paw.

"A pig with a crown; twilight zone weird," muttered Benji. He kept his distance, not sure if this pig was safe.

"That's not a pig," said a boy with noticeably bloodshot eyes who appeared from the far end of the swamp. "It's an alligator."

"Ah, excuse me. I didn't see you," replied Benji, startled by the boy. "Alligator? That definitely looks like a pig."

"A pig?" The boy grimaced and pointed to a small circular screen on the leg of the pig. "Look at its SIM."

Benji glanced down in bewilderment at the picture of an alligator on the little screen. Benji considered whether he should call out this lunacy. *I need to get to Shadowlands, and I can't afford to be rude to this guy who might help me get there. What do I care if this pig wants to pretend it's an alligator?* "OK, so it's an alligator."

The boy smiled and propped up the crown sitting atop his own jet-black hair. "Very well, then."

Benji turned from the pig and noticed that crazy town had visited the boy too. "Hey, why are you wearing a crown?"

"Because I'm a king, and that's what kings wear," replied the boy. He adjusted his crown again and held his head up high.

"Is that why the pig…" Benji's eyes widened as he stared at the boy and the pig. "… I mean alligator is wearing a crown?"

"Yeah, it's a king too," replied the boy as he glared at Benji. "You got a problem with that?"

"No, not at all." Benji smiled in an attempt to ease the situation. "What are you the king of?"

"I'm a king in Shadowlands," said the boy as he straightened up and puffed his chest out, which gave him a regal look. "Ruler of my kingdom."

Benji fidgeted as the boy spoke. "You're the king of Shadowlands?" His thoughts intruded. *Jack said there are no kings in Shadowlands. This is concerning.*

"Well not all of Shadowlands," said the boy in a half mocking tone. "There're lots of other kings, but I'm king of my world in Shadowlands." He showed his SIM screen to Benji that displayed a picture of a deer. "I'm a deer, king of the forest."

Benji paused and looked at the boy. His thoughts distracted him. *Is he joking? This guy has a weird sense of humor. OK, I'll play along.* "Sure, you're a deer. I'm Benji, what's your name."

"Birsha, King Birsha," said the boy. He held his head even higher striking a regal pose. "Where's your crown?"

Benji replied, "I don't have one; I just got here from over there." He pointed to the area where he had climbed up the redwood tree.

"Oh, so you're not from here," replied Birsha as he looked Benji up and down. "Interesting..."

Benji shook his head and forced a smile thinking to himself, *definitely not.* "No, I'm new here."

Birsha relaxed his body and smiled at Benji. "Shadowlands is much different than Highlands. Everyone's a king here." He reached out to shake Benji's hand. "Do you want to meet some other kings?"

"Yeah, that would be great," replied Benji as he offered a firm shake. "Let's meet some kings."

"See those lights in the distance? Birsha pointed off to the west. "That's Dustmore."

"Can people from Highlands be a king here too?" asked Benji. "I want to be a king."

"Certainly," replied Birsha. He gave an inviting smile at Benji as he strode westward toward Dustmore. "Dustmore is the District Office for the southern region of Shadowlands. It's the closest place to get your crown to rule your own kingdom."

***

The atmosphere grew danker as they trekked toward Dustmore. Benji noticed that the countryside was very different than where he played with the animals yesterday. The sky was coal black, and the meadow lacked the vibrant colors of Aspen Meadows. Benji was surprised that the kingdom of Himmel could have such drastically different regions. Aspen Meadows was so beautiful and Shadowlands was so...so dreary. Inhospitable in every way, but still it offered Benji a kingship. They encountered many other animals along the way, all wearing crowns. The animals were quarreling and shouting back and forth. One squirrel seemed to be arguing with a fox.

"Why are they fighting?" asked Benji with a puzzled expression. "They've all got their crowns."

Birsha narrowed his eyes. "It's a very serious thing in Shadowlands to be called the wrong name."

"What do you mean 'wrong name'?" Benji scratched his head. "I see a squirrel and fox."

"Yes, but in their kingdom, they're both lions," replied Birsha. "Their SIM is the final word on what's true."

"So can I be anything I want in Shadowlands?" asked Benji. Shadowlands seemed absolutely whacky to Benji, but he saw an angle. *If a person can be anything they want, I just might like this land of the loons.*

"Well, almost anything." Birsha paused and grimaced at Benji. "You can't be an enemy."

"An enemy?" Benji gasped and turned toward Birsha. "Of whom?"

"His Eminence," shot back Birsha. A slight smile appeared on his face. "Don't worry, you'll learn all that when you get your crown."

As they entered Dustmore, Benji noticed a bevy of activity, with animals and people scurrying about. Most of the people were staring into their SIMs; their green glow drawing them into their own world. In the center of town, there was an enormous white building made of stone with large pillars. The words *"Shadowlands Administration – Dustmore District"* were etched on the front of the building.

"That's where you register to become a king," said Birsha pointing up the stairs to the large building. "I've got some things to do. I'll catch up with you later."

Benji thanked Birsha and said goodbye to his new pretend "deer" friend. He walked up the stairs and entered the building. A series of windows filled the room, and a line of people waited in front of each window. Above each window was a sign, and a clerk waiting on customers. He saw the window with *"Kingdom Applications"* on its sign and decided to start there.

Luckily, only one young girl stood in front of him in line. "My name's Benji, and I'm trying to become a king. Is this the line for that?"

"Sure is," replied the girl as she twirled her hair with her finger. "Nice to meet you. I'm Julia, and I'm becoming a queen today!"

"Why aren't you a queen already?" asked Benji. He stared as she twisted more and more of her hair into what looked like a painful knot around her fingers. "I thought everyone in Shadowlands is a king or queen."

"I just turned ten, and we get to become kings and queens when we turn ten." Julia gave a cross-eyed look upward as she released the tightly wound hair. "With my crown, I can get a job at the water treatment plant."

"What are you before you get your crown?" asked Benji. He was curious how this place worked with kids. *Probably like back home, where they get bossed around by the adults.*

"We're princes and princesses," replied Julia. "Our parents get to be the king and queen of us before we turn ten." She reached the front of the line and turned toward the clerk.

"Good morning, what can I do for you?" asked the clerk. He busily shuffled the papers on his counter into a pile without looking up. "Speak up please. We don't have all day."

"I just turned ten and want to become a queen," replied Julia. She began twisting her hair into a knot again. "This is where I do that, isn't it?"

"Here's the application," said the clerk. He handed Julia a long application form. Julia quickly completed the form and returned it to the clerk. He put on his glasses and carefully examined all her answers on the application.

"Everything seems in order, Julia," said the clerk. He finally looked up with the tiniest of smiles. "Here's your crown and SIM." He handed her a golden crown and small circular SIM device.

Julia grabbed the crown and placed it on her head. "Fantastic." She began fidgeting with the SIM. "In my kingdom, I'm a fierce mountain lion. The most fearless in all of Shadowlands. Can you help me?" Julia handed the SIM back to the clerk.

"Scroll through the list of animals until you get to mountain lion, right here," said the clerk as he helped her adjust the settings on her SIM. "There you go. All set, Queen Julia."

"Congratulations, Julia," said Benji. He wondered, *maybe with that crown, she won't tie her hair in knots anymore.* "You look very queen-like."

"Thanks, Benji," replied Julia. She adjusted her crown and stepped aside to make room for Benji. "I've been waiting for this day a long time."

"Hey, Julia. When is a piece of wood like a queen?" Benji tilted his head with a toothy grin.

"Ah… I don't know," replied Julia. The crease in her brow telegraphed her confusion. *How could he joke at a time like this? My royal coronation!*

"When it's a ruler." Benji let out a loud chuckle inviting her to reply. Her silence was her reply. She simply shook her head and strolled away with her eyes fixed on the green glow of her SIM.

"Next," called out the clerk. His head was down again organizing Julia's papers. "What can I do for you?"

"I want to become a king," replied Benji. He tapped his foot uncontrollably as he awaited his glorious ascension to royalty. "King Benji."

***

Aaron woke up to Romeo's crowing. The crazed rooster had joined his horrifying mountain top dream once again. He shook the cobwebs from his head and looked in on Benji's bed only to find it empty. Benji had already gone, which was very unusual for his sleepyhead brother. He woke Hannah, and they ate a quick breakfast followed by daily chores taking care of the animals in the barn.

After chores, Aaron went to the garage and saw that Rocky was still there. He thought for a moment, then examined the winter supply closet and noticed a pair of snowshoes was missing. Aaron was seething. His brother had gone back to Redwood Grove without him. He packed supplies and the lunch Grandma had made.

"We have to find Benji," said Aaron as he helped her get settled in Rocky. "He left without us."

Hannah tilted her head. "So, we're going to search for him?" She wanted to go back to Himmel to see her new friends, but was unsure how or where they'd find Benji.

"That's right, we're a search party for Benji." Aaron climbed into Rocky and started the engine. "It'll be an adventure."

Aaron saw snowshoe tracks and they seemed to follow the trail leading to Redwood Grove. As they continued along the trail, Aaron was surprised Benji had made it so far on his own. He parked Rocky near the redwood grove and scanned the area. As he suspected, Benji's snowshoes were laying in the snow by the redwoods and there was no sign of him anywhere. Aaron placed the snowshoes in the back of Rocky and he and Hannah climbed the redwood tree into the fog.

Jack Deer and his family were in the meadow enjoying breakfast when Aaron and Hannah climbed through the fog.

"Good morning, it's nice to see you back so soon," said Jack. He looked over the two of them with a quizzical expression. "Where's Benji?"

"That's what we're trying to figure out." Aaron dusted off the snow and placed his leather jacket by the tree as a marker. "I think he climbed up early this morning. You haven't seen him?"

"Not today," replied Jack. "We were down at Lake Amari earlier, so we would have missed him."

"Why don't you ask Mr. Wigglebottom," said Ella Doe. "He's got a very good eye for people coming and going."

"That's an excellent idea," replied Aaron. Aaron wanted to continue his conversation with Mr. Wigglebottom anyway, so he had more than one reason to visit him.

Enzo Fawn jumped up to greet Hannah still chewing on a mouthful of flowers. "Do you want to play games?"

Aaron smiled inside and patted Enzo on his furry head. "Why don't you come down to the lake with us." He clapped his hands in anticipation of more time with Mr. Wigglebottom. "You and Hannah can play a game down there."

So, Jack and his family, along with Aaron and Hannah, headed for Lake Amari to find Mr. Wigglebottom. As they approached, they found him talking to a squirrel. He was pouring water on the squirrel's paw.

"That rock must have been sharp, Morris Squirrel." Mr. Wigglebottom's face was creased with concern as he wrapped a bandage on the little squirrel's paw.

"This is a nasty cut."

"It sure was," moaned Morris. "I was running so fast I didn't even see it."

Mr. Wigglebottom wagged his finger. "Well stay off it the rest of the day and come back tomorrow. We'll take a look to see how it's healing."

Morris thanked Mr. Wigglebottom and hobbled off. Riley Raccoon was down at the lake drinking when she saw Hannah and Enzo. She quickly ran up to them and gave them a sort of hug, as best as she could with her short little arms.

Enzo sprung into the air with excitement. "We're going to play a game; do you want to join us?"

"Yeah, what can we play?" replied Riley. She scratched her head with her little paw as she racked her brain. "What's a good game for a raccoon, deer and little girl?"

Mr. Wigglebottom saw the delight in their eyes. "How about marbles? I've got a set inside." He waddled into his cottage and returned with a bag of marbles. He used his finger to draw a big circle about three feet in diameter in the dirt and emptied the marbles onto the ground in the middle of the circle.

Riley looked at Mr. Wigglebottom with a puzzled expression. "How do you play marbles?"

"The object is to knock the smaller marbles out of the circle with your shooter marble." Mr. Wigglebottom held up the large marble. "Each of you gets a shooter marble. The winner is the player who knocks the most marbles out of the circle."

Hannah had never played marbles before and loved having another day in Himmel with her new friends. After they got their game of marbles underway, Mr. Wigglebottom invited Aaron for tea in his cottage.

Aaron sat down on the sofa and stirred some sugar into his tea. "Mr. Wigglebottom, have you seen Benji this morning?"

"No, I haven't seen him today, Sir Aaron." Mr. Wigglebottom brought out some of the cookies from yesterday. "No doubt he'll show up."

Aaron was annoyed that Benji had taken off on his own, but he thought he could use this time to learn more about Himmel and this artist king. "While we wait, I have a couple of questions for you if you have time."

Chapter Eight

King for a Day

———— ∽∞∾ ————

B enji was deep in thought when the clerk handed the application to him. He imagined what it would be like to be a king. *I can be anything I want to be, and I can make all the rules. No more being bossed around. No more homework. I can eat anything I want when I want.*

The clerk's voice stirred Benji out of his daydream. "Son, do you want the application?" The clerk bristled as he tapped his pencil on the counter.

"Yes, I'm sorry, thank you," replied Benji. He sensed the man was in no mood for a joke, so he resisted the urge. "I'll fill it out right now."

The application had an extensive list of questions. Some were easy like his name, age, and so on. About halfway through the form, the questions took on a more disquieting tone. They seemed to be testing his loyalty to something. Or someone.

- Do you trust the Shadowlands authorities?
- If the Shadowlands authorities says something is true, does that make it true?
- Will you rule your kingdom as directed by the Shadowlands authorities?
- Do you pledge your loyalty to His Eminence?

"Excuse me sir, but do I have to fill out all of the questions in the application?" Benji hoped to skip the questions at the end. After all, he had just arrived in Shadowlands and didn't know if he could trust the people here. His mind raced as he considered his options. *Who was it he was supposed to trust anyway? This whole thing seems shady, but maybe that's what it takes to be a king.* His instincts told him to run, but the allure of becoming a king was deafening. It overwhelmed the faint voice of his better judgment.

"Every question has to be completed before we can make you a king," replied the clerk. "Don't be troubled by those questions. We have to be careful that we don't make crazy people kings." The clerk leaned forward with a frown and whispered in a low voice, "You're not crazy, are you?"

"No, I'm not crazy," replied Benji. He wondered what crazy meant in this world, since most of the people he had met in Shadowlands seemed to be fulltime residents of crazy town. "I'm quite normal."

"Then I can help you." The clerk reached across the counter and pointed to the section with the troubling questions. "Just answer "Yes" to all those questions, and you'll be a king this afternoon."

Benji felt uneasy, but he so much wanted to be a king. He suppressed the inner battle in his mind and quickly finished up the questions. He bolstered up his courage, *seize the moment, Benji,* and handed the application back to the clerk. "Here you go, sir."

"Very well, let's take a look," said the clerk. His head swiveled between the application and Benji's face as he scrutinized Benji's answers.

Benji felt a lump in his throat as he awaited the results. His mind wandered to his math test debacle with Mr. Jacobson. *Will this be another fiasco? How could it? I'm going to be a king and kings don't have fiascos...or math tests.*

"Congratulations, King Benji," said the clerk in a loud voice. He handed Benji a crown and SIM. "You are now officially a king in Shadowlands."

"In my kingdom, there's no bedtime, no homework, and I can eat dessert any time I want." Benji lifted his head high attempting to strike a regal pose. "Can you help me adjust my SIM?"

"That shouldn't be a problem. Adjust these settings right here," replied the clerk as he fiddled with the SIM. "Enjoy your kingdom, Benji!"

"Sir, one final question." Benji stared down at his SIM unable to turn away. "What does SIM stand for?"

"Self-Image Mirror," The clerk said, offering a coy smile at Benji. "You should know that ... certainly you will come to learn."

Benji didn't give it another thought - he was a king. He adorned his head with the crown and strutted out of the building imagining what he'd do with his royal status. *I'm a king, and kings make the rules!*

Birsha had been waiting outside the Shadowlands administration offices and jumped to his feet when he saw Benji. "King Benji, congratulations." He patted Benji on the back. "What do you want to do as your first act as king?"

"I want to get something to eat," answered Benji. He pointed to a restaurant across the street and headed that way. "We would like a table for two outside on the patio please," said Benji to the waitress.

"Why certainly, right this way," answered the waitress as she led them to a table with a view of the courtyard. Benji and Birsha took their seats and looked over the menu.

"I'll have a piece of chocolate cake" commanded Benji. He looked up at the waitress with an air of regal authority. "And an ice cream sundae."

The waitress scribbled his order on her notepad. "Certainly, King Benji. I see from your SIM that you can eat dessert any time of day."

"I would like a big plate of grass and leaves," said Birsha. "That's what deer eat, right?"

"Why yes, I see that you're a deer today," replied the waitress without giving Birsha a second look. "That sounds perfect for you."

Benji looked around the restaurant while they waited for their food and noticed all the customers were glued to their SIMs. Their eyes were transfixed to the green glow staring back at them. Benji glanced at his SIM every so often. He had to admit, the more he looked at it, the more drawn to it he was.

The waitress returned a brief time later with two large trays. One had a large piece of chocolate cake on a plate and an enormous ice cream sundae. The second tray had a plate of grass and leaves for Birsha.

Benji picked up a spoon and scooped heaps of ice cream into his mouth. The sundae had three scoops of ice cream, hot fudge, caramel sauce, and whipped cream. "Holy cow … this is amazing" He funneled the ice cream into his mouth like a conveyer belt until his head began to throb. "Ugh… brain freeze."

Birsha grimaced as he picked at his leaves and grass. "Nothing like a genuine deer meal." He eyed Benji's sundae with envy, but stoically worked on his plate of leaves.

Having devoured his sundae, Benji grabbed a fork and began shoveling cake into his mouth. The cake was decadent. It had melted chocolate chips in it with rich creamy chocolate frosting. "Scrumptious," cried Benji as crumbs of cake flew out of his mouth.

Birsha chomped the last portion of his grass and leaves. "I'm still getting used to eating deer food," he said in a fawning manner.

As they were relaxing after their meal, they heard a commotion in the courtyard. There was a short man with a furry shirt yelling at another older bald man about something. Soon a large policeman strolled up.

"What seems to be the problem?" said the officer. His steely eyes were fixed on the men as he slapped a baton into his palm.

The man with the furry shirt yelled, "This guy called me a man when I'm clearly a dog." His cheeks were quickly blossoming into a bright red as he awaited the officer's response.

The officer's eyebrows lowered, creating a menacing crease in his forehead. "Let me see your SIM."

"But he's clearly a man," said the bald man throwing his arms in the air. "Look at him. This is insane."

"Look at his SIM." The officer stepped closer to the bald man. "He's a dog in his kingdom."

"But it's not real," yelled the bald man." He began jumping up and down hysterically. "He can't become a dog by just saying so."

"I am a dog... I am a dog..., rough, rough," shouted the man with the furry shirt. Now his face was the color of a fire engine. "Call me a dog right now."

The officer strolled behind the bald man. "I'm sorry sir, but I'm going to have to arrest you." He yanked on the bald man's arms and slapped handcuffs on him. "You can't go around breaking the rules of other people's kingdoms."

As the police officer escorted the man away, the man with the furry shirt howled with delight, "Woof, woof!"

Benji's face was frozen in disbelief as he glanced at Birsha. "What was that?"

"Some people don't believe in the Shadowlands kingdom," said Birsha as he shook his head. "It's a real problem. I mean what kind of kingdom would it be if no one followed the rules of the kings?"

"I guess that's right," replied Benji still puzzled by the whole event. He was so excited about his new place in royalty that he had little interest in understanding the craziness of the people around him. He was a king and that was all that mattered.

"How was your dessert, King Benji?" asked the waitress. She surveyed their empty dishes and nodded, impressed that they knocked back their entire meals.

"It was the best," replied Benji straining to smile. His stomach was screaming that he had eaten way too much, way too fast. "But I think I maybe ate too much; my stomach doesn't feel very good."

"Well, that's to be expected, but it's your kingdom, Benji," said the waitress. "Here's your bill."

"Bill? I thought I was king, so I didn't have to pay for my food." Benji's already queasy stomach didn't take the news well - at all. "I don't have any money."

"That's a problem." The waitress scowled at Benji. "Your SIM says you can eat desserts any time. It doesn't say anything about free food."

Benji's face turned pale. "Are you sure?" He considered his go-to strategy, but her dower expression told him to stay away from the jokes.

She examined Benji's SIM and looked at the fine print of his rules. "Sorry, King Benji, but you have to scrub dishes in the back to pay off your bill."

"That's right, Benji, and since I'm a deer, this is your problem." Birsha snickered as he set down his napkin. "Deer don't pay bills and don't do dishes. I've got to go, but thanks for the meal."

Benji's stomach was in full revolt. The waitress escorted him to the back of the restaurant and a burly man named Nick threw an apron at him and pointed to a big stack of dishes. Benji spent the next two hours cleaning dishes, emptying trash bags, and mopping the floor under Nick's brooding glare. Nick was a taskmaster without a sense of humor. Benji tried a couple of jokes, but Nick's funny bone was impenetrable.

Benji was beginning to think the freedom and power of becoming a king felt more like a prison sentence. He was exhausted and dirty by the time he finished. He didn't feel much like a king.

As he left the restaurant, he saw Julia across the courtyard. "Hey Julia, it's me King Benji." He jogged toward her, happy to see a familiar face. And happy to be done with Nick and that horrid restaurant.

Julia looked up from her SIM when she heard Benji's voice. "Hi, Benji. You look great as a king."

Benji adjusted his crown to make sure it was still on straight after his "quality time" with Nick. "Well, I'm still getting used to being a king; it's harder than it looks."

"Roar!" belted out Julia as she lifted her head in the air and shook it as though she was shaking her fur. "I'm practicing my mountain lion roar for my job at the water treatment plant. What do you think?"

"Very impressive." Benji was consumed by curiosity as he watched her. "Julia, I have a question. What's the joke here about pretending to be something you're not?"

Julia looked at him, puzzled by the question. "What do you mean pretending?"

"I just had lunch with a guy who says he's a deer, and he's clearly a boy." Benji fiddled with his SIM as he played out how to word his next question. "You say you're a mountain lion and your SIM has a picture of a mountain lion on it. But when I look at you, I see a girl."

"I am a mountain lion, Benji," replied Julia sternly. "I'm the queen of the mountains and if I say I'm a mountain lion, I'm a mountain lion."

"But that's what I don't understand." Benji needed to know more, but he knew to tread lightly after watching the bald man get arrested. "When I became king, I made new rules about eating dessert, bedtime, and homework. I made rules about real stuff; that's what kings do. They make rules about real stuff. But…"

"Yes?" said Julia. She began twisting her hair in a knot. "What is it?"

Oh no, not the hair knots again, thought Benji as he played out the most delicate way to probe a little deeper. "But you made up something that's not real. You're a girl and saying you're a mountain lion doesn't make you a mountain lion."

"In my kingdom it does, Benji. I get to say what's real in my kingdom and you have to agree with me about my kingdom." Julia looked like a bomb, about to explode into tiny bits. "That's how it works in Shadowlands."

"OK, OK, I agree," replied Benji. He wanted to avoid the trouble he had seen in the courtyard. "You're a mountain lion."

Julia pushed herself right up into Benji's face spraying spit as she spoke. "That's not enough, Benji. Say I'm the most fearless mountain lion in all of Shadowlands. Say it right now!"

Benji wiped his face, took a step back and tried to calm the situation. "But I haven't met all the mountain lions in Shadowlands. I've met a couple of other mountain lions and they seem pretty fearless too." Julia's beet red face made it clear Benji was not making any headway. "Do you know Jasper Lion? What if I say you're *a* fearless mountain lion in Shadowlands."

Julia stepped closer giving him another saliva shower. "Benji, you're not getting it. In my kingdom, I'm the queen, and what I say goes." Her knotted hair was standing on end like an angry cat's fur. "If you don't honor me as the most fearless mountain lion in all of Shadowlands, I'll report you to the Shadowlands authorities."

Benji knew better, but his instincts took over in the desperation of the moment. "You mean, I have to lionize you... get it lion-ize." He offered a weak chuckle hoping upon hope this one landed.

"You're joking about something like this," screamed Julia. She began stomping on the ground like an angry bull.

Benji could see she was holding back tears and quickly tried to recover from his ill-timed joke. "I'm sorry. Just kidding. Your roar was fantastic, Julia."

Two boys sitting nearby overheard the conversation and approached Benji and Julia with a menacing stride. One was tall and built like a brickhouse, with muscles bulging out of his too small t-shirt. The other had spiky red hair to match what looked like a blazing hot temper from the expression on his face.

"Is there a problem here?" said the human brickhouse. He looked at Julia's SIM. "I see Queen Julia is the most fearless mountain lion in all of Shadowlands." "Are you questioning Queen Julia's kingdom?" asked the raging inferno.

"No ... Not at all," stammered Benji trying to calm everyone down. He sized up the two boys in his head as he tried to buy time. *One's a musclebound bone crusher and the other's a psychopath with the temper of a raging inferno. I like my bones just the way they are and I have an affinity for not burning up. I'm not getting into a fight over Julia's whacko kingdom.*

"Why won't you say Queen Julia is the most fearless mountain lion in all of Shadowlands," shouted the human brickhouse as he poked his finger in Benji's chest.

"I think I've made a mistake," said Benji. He backed away from the boys and Julia. "I'm very sorry."

"I think you've made a big mistake. You can't just disobey another person's kingdom," said the raging inferno.

At this point, Julia was on her SIM calling the Shadowlands authorities to report Benji. The two boys began to stalk Benji, and he continued to back away. Remembering what had happened earlier to the bald man in the courtyard, Benji turned and ran as fast as he could toward the redwood tree. He just wanted to reach the tree, climb down, and leave Shadowlands. Benji was a fast runner and stayed ahead of the boys even though his stomach was still in a state of revolt from the cake and sundae.

When he got outside of Dustmore, he hid among a big stack of logs. The boys searched the area for over thirty minutes but finally gave up. Benji took off his crown and placed it in his jacket along with his SIM. He walked as quickly as he could back toward the redwood tree. He never wanted to see Shadowlands again.

***

Aaron smiled at the sound of Hannah's laughter with her new friends in the front yard of Mr. Wigglebottom's cottage. "Mr. Wigglebottom, you said the king makes good and beautiful paintings. How do you know?"

"I've seen many of his paintings over the years and each and every one of them is both perfectly good and perfectly beautiful." Mr. Wigglebottom glanced out the window to watch Hannah, Enzo Fawn, and Riley Raccoon playing and giggling. "That's all he makes."

Aaron set his tea down and picked up a cookie. "What do you mean?" he asked.

"King Yasha's very nature is good and beautiful, so everything he makes must be both good and beautiful." Mr. Wigglebottom scrutinized Aaron's face to see if he was tracking. "The artwork is a reflection of the artist."

Aaron pondered Mr. Wigglebottom's words, but something didn't make sense to him. "Does that mean everything in Himmel is perfectly good and beautiful?"

"Not at all." Mr. Wigglebottom motioned out the window to the splendor of the youngsters playing and the animals relaxing by the lake. He said, "Everything the artist makes is good and beautiful, but there's no guarantee it stays that way. There are also bad and ugly things in Himmel, but they don't come from King Yasha."

Aaron had not spent much time thinking about such lofty things as goodness and beauty. He found it exhilarating to consider these ideas to help him understand the world around him. His desire to meet King Yasha only grew as he learned more about him.

"Sir Aaron, you should speak to King Yasha about these matters when you meet him. Go straight to the horse's mouth as they say." Mr. Wigglebottom heard screaming and squinted out his window. "I think Sir Benji has found some trouble."

Aaron stood up and ran to the window. He saw Benji running toward them with several people chasing him and screaming at him to stop. The situation looked dire, and his mind immediately went to Hannah's safety. He bolted out of the cottage. "Hannah, I'm sorry but we have to go right now. Say goodbye to your friends."

"What's wrong, Aaron?" asked Hannah. She was frozen by Benji's yelling and Aaron's stern voice. "What about Benji?"

"I'll explain later; we've got to go." Aaron grabbed her hand and ran as fast as he could to the redwood tree. They jumped on and started climbing down the branches. "Climb all the way down and wait for us. I'm going to get Benji."

"Aaron, I'm scared." Hannah clung to the branch paralyzed to climb down. "Are we going to be all right?"

"Yes, Hannah, but climb down now and wait for us." He gave her a reassuring smile. "You can do this. Be brave."

***

Benji was exhausted when he finally saw the redwood in the distance. His stomach was still in a disagreeable mood, and his legs were rubbery from the ordeal. Suddenly, he heard a commotion behind him and turned to see the police gaining ground on him. The human brickhouse and raging inferno were also running hard toward him.

Benji mustered his last bit of strength to sprint toward the redwood screaming for anyone to rescue him from yet another fiasco he had gotten himself into. He could see it ahead, but the brickhouse and raging inferno along with a squad of police were catching up fast. His heart was racing, and one thought played over and over again in his head, *make it to the redwood, get to the redwood.*

A police loudspeaker screeched, "King Benji, this is the Shadowlands Kingdom Enforcement Squad. We have a warrant for your arrest. You have violated the kingship law of Shadowlands. Lay on the ground and put your hands behind your back."

Benji was only a few steps from the redwood and the danger pushed him to keep going and get to the tree. The brickhouse and raging inferno were almost on top of him, and they were shouting horrible things. Benji leaped onto the redwood. He was half in Himmel with his head and arms still above the fog and half back in his world with his feet resting on a tree branch.

The brickhouse grabbed one arm while the raging inferno grabbed the other arm and tried to pull him back up into Himmel. Benji knew he couldn't fight off these ruffians for long. They had a good grip on his arms and were pulling him back up to Himmel. Suddenly, Benji felt a tug on his leg —someone was pulling him down.

"Benji, it's me, Aaron. What's going on?" shouted Aaron.

"I'm in trouble, Aaron. They're trying to get me. Pull me down. Pull me down!"

"I got you, Benji," shouted Aaron.

Aaron grabbed Benji's legs and pulled with all his might, but it was no use. The brickhouse and raging inferno tandem had a tight grip on Benji and were pulling him up into Himmel. Suddenly, Benji heard Jack and Piper shout, "Let go of that boy!"

Jack and Piper had seen the commotion and were running full speed toward the attacking brickhouse and raging inferno. They lowered their heads and slammed into the two boys causing them to lose their grip on Benji and fly into the air waving their arms like rag dolls. Benji fell into Aaron's arms where they rested for several minutes to catch their breath and settle their nerves.

Hannah yelled from the ground, "What's going on?"

"We're fine, Hannah. We'll be down in a minute," replied Aaron. He was breathing hard as he stared at Benji. Benji was panting like a dog and shaking uncontrollably. Seeing Benji was in no condition to talk, Aaron urged him to begin climbing down the tree. Together, they crept down the tree one branch at a time.

When they finally made it to the ground, Hannah rushed up and clenched Aaron with all her might. "I didn't know if you were going to ever come down."

"We're all right. Just a little shaken up." Aaron stroked Hannah's hair.

"Benji, what happened up there?"

Benji's breathing had slowed, but his hands were shaking like leaves. "I don't want to talk about it. That place is horrible." "What place?" asked Aaron.

"Shadowlands," Benji replied. "And I said, I don't want to talk about it."

Papa's words came rushing into Aaron's mind. "Remember what Papa said? 'The world has goodness and beauty, but also evil and ugliness.'"

Benji was still trembling as he replayed in his mind his ghastly day in Shadowlands. "Yeah, I think so."

Aaron rubbed Benji's shoulders in an effort to rub the shock out of him. "Maybe that's what Papa meant when he said wisdom is the vision to see the difference."

"Mmm…Maybe," stuttered Benji as he blankly stared at the white canvass of snow in front of him.

Aaron was furious with Benji for going back to Himmel without him, especially to Shadowlands, a place they had been warned about. Benji had ruined his plan to meet the artist king. He was paying the price for Benji's selfishness, like so many times before. It was exhausting. He so missed his dad at times like this. His dad understood him and had a way of calming him when his perfectionist idiosyncrasies overwhelmed him. But today, he was consumed by anger and frustration.

Aaron sat in the snow looking at Benji balled up next to him and Hannah clinging to his arm. He could see the terror in Benji's face. It was clear that something perilous had happened to Benji in the Shadowlands part of Himmel. He decided the best course was to let his anger subside during the ride back to the lodge. Time would give him perspective that he didn't have right now.

They climbed into Rocky and drove back to the lodge in utter silence, each person far away in their own thoughts. Aaron filled with anger, Benji with terror, and Hannah with fear. One thing they all knew for sure. All was not right in Himmel.

Chapter Nine

An Adventure Awaits

It was dark when they pulled up to the lodge. Lights were shining through the windows and smoke rose from the chimney. They could see Grandma's face in the window keeping watch for them. She looked relieved to see the headlights of Rocky pull into the driveway. The children were spent from their terrifying encounter. As they climbed out of Rocky, Papa, Grandma, and Sarah ran out the front door to greet them.

"We were worried sick," said Grandma as she embraced Hannah. "Where were you?"

"You stayed out a bit late." Papa playfully wrapped an arm around the neck of each of the boys. "Did you boys run into trouble out there?"

Sarah examined each of the children only as a mother could. After confirming they were all right, she let out a sigh of relief. "Let's go inside to get warm."

"I've made beef stew for dinner," said Grandma as she headed into the kitchen to serve large bowls for everyone. "This will warm you up."

The lodge was filled with the smell of Grandma's cooking and a warm fire blazed in the family room. Aaron could almost taste the stew as he took off his jacket. Grandma brought out the bowls of stew and fresh biscuits with homemade honey-butter. Papa had bee colonies on the Ranch, and he harvested the honey for Grandma. Biscuits and honey-butter was a favorite of the children, so it was a welcome sight after their frightening day. Aaron, Benji, and Hannah were curiously silent as they ate their stew and biscuits.

"Tell us about your adventure today," said Papa as he spread honey-butter on a biscuit.

"Rocky worked really well today, Papa," said Aaron. He kept his eyes on his biscuits hoping to say as little as possible.

"Did you go back to the redwood grove?" asked Papa. His eyes creeped up from his biscuit to meet Aaron. "The place we went the other day?"

"Yeah, we did," replied Aaron. He felt Papa's stare and raised his head briefly, trading eye contact.

"Grandma, you outdid yourself on this honey-butter," said Papa with a soft chuckle. He scooped another spoonful of honey-butter in the hopes of easing Aaron's nerves. "Did you see anything new today?"

"Well, we climbed the redwood tree," said Aaron hoping that was enough. "Yeah, Grandma, it's awesome." He reached over and grabbed a scoop of honey-butter and lathered it on his biscuit.

"Oh, tell me. What did you find?" asked Papa.

Aaron fidgeted with his spoon as he crafted a response. "We found a passage of some kind, high up in the redwood tree above the fog," he said.

Benji kept his eyes on his stew and seemed barely interested in the conversation. He was hoping Aaron would do all the talking as he was better at this kind of thing. Hannah enjoyed the family conversations but didn't usually have a lot to say; she just liked hearing the others share stories and the like. Aaron recognized the look of fear in Hannah's eyes, so tonight, it was up to him to do the talking for his brother and sister.

"A passage; very interesting, Aaron." Papa set his biscuit down and dusted the crumbs off his hands as he focused on Aaron. "Where did it go?"

Aaron squirmed as he chewed over Papa's question. *I can't say anything about Benji's harrowing trip to Shadowlands. He's in no position to tell his own story. How can I protect him and tell the truth? Maybe part of the truth is the best I can do for now.*

"We found a place called Himmel," said Aaron. "It was amazing, Papa. We met animals that talked, and we played hide-and-seek with them. They made a big feast for us." Aaron sized up Papa who seemed to have a laid-back response to this mind-blowing news. He kept going. "They told us about their king. We met a funny little man named Mr. Wigglebottom who said he knows you. It was the most awesome day ever, Papa."

Papa sat back in his chair and took a deep, long breath. "Well, that sounds incredible, Aaron." He broke into a broad smile at Aaron and the other children. "I hope Mr. Wigglebottom is well."

Grandma placed her hand on Papa's arm and turned to Aaron. "You know, Aaron, we have known about Himmel for ages." She leaned in with a warm smile and whispered, "That's why we say the Ranch is so extraordinary."

Papa smiled coyly. "Your dad spent plenty of time in Himmel when he was about your age, Aaron."

Aaron felt a great weight slide off his shoulders as he shared their trip to Himmel with Papa, Grandma, and Sarah. He suspected they may have known about Himmel, but their casual response to his news was surprising. He thought his family must be a bit odd if exploring another world was everyday news. But his real interest at the moment was to learn more about King Yasha. "Papa, did you meet King Yasha?"

"I've met King Yasha many times, Aaron. I visited Himmel often when I was young." Papa smiled and gazed up at the ceiling with a distant stare. "Now that you've found the passage, you should visit Himmel as often as you like. When you meet King Yasha, please say hello for me."

"Will you come with us tomorrow?" asked Aaron. His mind was already planning all that he would do in Himmel. "Jack Deer said he'd take us to the king."

"The redwood tree is a special passage for children, so it's just for you, Benji, and Hannah." Papa's smile was replaced by a forlorn look. "I visited when I was younger. This is your time."

Aaron nodded. "I understand." Aaron rubbed his hands together. "We have a lot of planning to do. Will you help us?"

Papa leaned close to Aaron. "Sure, love to."

"Awesome." Aaron reached out to give Papa a fist-bump.

"One thing is particularly important, Aaron," said Papa as he fist-bumped Aaron. "This secret was given to our family long ago when our ancestors bought the Ranch. Don't share this secret with anyone."

Aaron sat back in his chair and his face grew serious. "Why, Papa?"

"There are people who want to harm Himmel and King Yasha, so we need to help them stay safe." Papa's eyes fixed on Aaron with an intensity that he rarely showed. "Do you understand?"

"Yes, Papa. We won't tell anyone," replied Aaron. Benji and Hannah nodded their heads in agreement.

Aaron was anxious to end the evening. Looking after his brother and sister had consumed all of his energy, and he just wanted to get to sleep and plan his trip back to Himmel. "The dinner was fantastic, Grandma. I'm a little tired after our big day, so I think I'll go to bed early tonight."

The children hugged their mom and Papa and Grandma and headed up to their bedroom.

Benji's clothes were spread across the floor, so he rummaged through the pile to find his pajamas. He felt guilty for putting Aaron and Hannah through the worry of his solo journey to Shadowlands and then making Aaron do all the talking. "Thanks for telling them about Himmel."

Aaron glared at him. His anger had retreated during their ride back to the lodge but being forced to cover for Benji during dinner had only renewed it. It was time for Benji to spill the beans, even though he seemed petrified by the day's events. "Benji, what happened to you up there? Who was trying to pull you back up into Himmel?"

"It's a long story," replied Benji. "It started as the best day of my life, but then it turned into the worst day of my life."

Benji pulled out his crown and the SIM from his jacket pocket and showed them to Aaron and Hannah. He told them all about his visit to Shadowlands, meeting Birsha, going to the Shadowlands Administration Office to become a king, the cake and sundae, cleaning the dishes with big Nick, and the terrible trouble he got in with Julia, the brickhouse and raging inferno boys, and the cops.

Aaron leaned back on the bed in disbelief. "That's horrible, Benji."

"I never want to see that horrible place again," said Benji. He looked down at his crown, and then he placed it along with the SIM in the drawer next to his bed and firmly closed it.

Benji wanted to change the subject. "Did you go to visit the king?" he asked.

"Not yet. We stayed at Mr. Wigglebottom's looking for you. We're all going back tomorrow to meet King Yasha. I still have lots of questions for him," said Aaron.

"But I'm not going anywhere near Shadowlands," said Benji as he clicked the light switch off and climbed into bed. "King Yasha it is."

"Those kids are so mean," said Hannah. Even though she hadn't seen anything, she was terrified by Benji's story. She grabbed Aaron's hand for comfort. "Is that OK?"

"Sure, Hannah." Aaron's shoulder was twisted in an awkward position, but he knew Hannah needed him tonight. As he lay in bed reassuring Hannah, his mind was busy planning all the details of their trip to Himmel. As far as he was concerned, it was his responsibility to make the perfect plan.

***

Aaron woke early to the sound of Romeo, who somehow had escaped his familiar mountain top dream last night. His mind was still fixed on their return to Himmel, and he couldn't wait to explore some more. Benji and Hannah were crashed out, so he quietly dressed and went downstairs. Grandma was preparing breakfast and Papa was at the table sipping his coffee while reading a book.

"Good morning, Grandma. What's for breakfast," said Aaron.

"Oatmeal with fresh fruit, Aaron. Take a seat and I'll make you a bowl," replied Grandma as she scooped oatmeal into a bowl.

"Papa, can I do the chores right after breakfast?" asked Aaron. He rubbed his hands together anxious to get the day going.

"Sure, the animals always welcome an early meal," joked Papa. "Are you three going back to Himmel today?"

"Yeah, we're going to meet King Yasha," replied Aaron. "If they get up in time."

"Aah, I see. Well then, you best get your chores done and pack a lunch," said Papa.

"I made turkey sandwiches," said Grandma. She handed Aaron a bag and wrapped her arms around him whispering, "Be careful."

"We will, Grandma," said Aaron as he packed the lunches in his backpack.

Aaron had spent the night racking his brain for supplies that might come in handy during their return trip to Himmel. His dad had taught him to always be prepared with the supplies and equipment suited to the environment of the mission. His dad used Navy Seal language when he discussed this type of thing, and Aaron was an attentive student of these lessons. It was part of what made his dad so awesome, and why he missed him so much right now. He was embarking on the biggest adventure of his life and his dad wasn't there to share it or give him the final tips he would need.

Fortunately, he had Papa, who was just about as good as his dad. Papa had what his dad called "old school" survival skills. "Will you help me find supplies for our trip today?" asked Aaron.

"Sure, Aaron." Papa jumped out of his chair and gave a big smile at Aaron.

"We can go to the garage right after chores. I've got some fantastic equipment for you."

Aaron raced out to the barn singing to the animals. "We're going on an adventure today... meeting the King." Energy was bursting out of him like a shooting star. In no time at all, he had raked the stables, laid out fresh hay and grain for the animals, and filled their water bins.

Papa approached the barn just as he was walking out. "Whoa, you're already done with your chores?" Papa let out a loud laugh watching Aaron bounce up and down with excitement. They marched over to the garage and Papa pulled open the creaky wooden doors.

Papa surveyed his gigantic collection of wilderness supplies. "I taught your dad about camping outdoors. The key is navigation, water, communication, and warmth." Papa rubbed his hands together and started picking up camping gear. "Here's a compass; that'll come in handy. Canteens for each of you. Radios." "Sure," said Aaron as he slipped the supplies into his backpack.

"Every explorer needs binoculars," said Papa. He had caught Aaron's rush of excitement and hauled more items down from the shelf. "I have three pairs you can take. Oh, this rope is great to have. Let's see: Swiss army knife, first aid kit, bug repellent, and hand shovel." Papa handed supplies to Aaron to fill his pack.

Aaron juggled all the supplies in his arms as Papa kept loading more and more things. "Thanks Papa!" He set all the supplies down on the bench and meticulously stowed them in his backpack.

"Before you head off on your adventure, I can use your help with the pitch glue."

Aaron had forgotten all about that project and was dying to get back to Himmel. "Papa, do we have to do it today?"

"It'll just take half an hour or so." Papa patted him on the back with a reassuring smile. "I already picked up the bucket of sap this morning."

"OK, what's next?" asked Aaron as they walked into the woodshop.

"We need to melt the sap resin." Papa placed the metal bucket on a burner and began to heat the resin until it was gooey and runny. "Now add one part hardwood charcoal to reduce the stickiness." He began stirring in a black charcoal.

"Why do we want to make it less sticky?" Aaron absolutely loved this outdoorsman lesson and temporarily distracted him from his great adventure.

"Can I stir it?"

"Sure, here you go." Papa handed the stir stick to Aaron and showed him how to turn it to avoid splashing the scalding hot sap. "If it's too sticky, it's hard to work with. The charcoal makes it easier to apply."

Aaron kept stirring until all the charcoal was invisible. "What next?"

"Next, we add one part sawdust for filler." Papa picked up a bucket from the corner near the table saw. "It strengthens the glue."

Aaron dumped a scoop of sawdust into the sap bucket and mixed it for several minutes. "It looks pretty mixed." Aaron slowly turned the stick and lifted it in the air to show Papa.

"I think it's done," said Papa. "We have pitch glue." Papa handed Aaron a small bag of charcoal and sawdust to add to his backpack. "Take this with you. You never know when it may come in handy."

"Thanks Papa," said Aaron stowing the additional supplies.

Papa climbed up the ladder along the side of the woodshop and began applying the pitch glue. "You spread it with a stick and make sure you cover the whole area." Aaron craned his neck to see Papa's work on the roof. "OK, gotcha."

"It dries pretty quick, so you have to work fast." Papa finished his work and stepped back to admire the finished product. "Pretty good for a couple of amateurs."

Aaron let out a loud laugh as he tried to brush off the sap from his hands. "Thanks for letting me help, Papa."

"Thank you, Aaron. You're always a big help to me." Papa had a big grin as he climbed down the ladder. He brushed Aaron's hair with his hand.

"You're quite a boy. A lot like your dad."

Benji and Hannah strolled out of the lodge with Bailey in tow. Until his attention was diverted to a squirrel. "Bailey, stop that," shouted Hannah. After seeing Morris Squirrel in Himmel, she felt sorry for the little squirrel.

"Did we miss chores?" asked Benji with a wry smile. "We were busy with Grandma's oatmeal."

Aaron shook his head. "Yeah, I bet you were really sweating it, wrestling with that oatmeal."

"It's OK, we've got chores every day. We'll let you make it up." Papa chuckled and tussled Benji's hair as he walked past. "I'm going to check on Grandma."

Aaron began loading supplies into Rocky. "Are you two ready?"

"I was thinking." Benji kicked the ground with his boots causing snow to fly. "We're going to steer clear of Shadowlands, right?"

"What do you think?" replied Aaron. "After your little fiasco, I wouldn't get near that place if you paid me."

Hannah crept up to Aaron. "I want to see my new friends, but I'm scared." She looked up at Aaron with her big eyes searching for security.

Aaron knelt down so his face was right in front of her. "I won't let anything happen to you. You can stay right by my side the whole time."

"Promise?" said Hannah softly. She held up her hand crossing her two fingers.

"Parsons Cord," replied Aaron. He held up his hand crossing two fingers and gave her a hug.

Aaron finished loading the provisions in Rocky and they pushed it out of the garage. Papa, Grandma and Sarah appeared out of the lodge to see them off. "So, you're going to see King Yasha?" called out Papa.

"That's our goal," replied Aaron. He reached into the bed of Rocky to make sure all the provisions were secured.

"That may take days," said Papa. "It's a considerable distance and you may run into distractions along the way."

"Listen to Mr. Wigglebottom if you have any questions," said Grandma. "He's a wise man." She gave each of the children a hug and stashed a cookie in each of their jackets.

"Benji, listen to your brother." Sarah chewed on her lip as she watched the children prepare for their adventure. "Hannah, stay close to Aaron the whole time." She got down on her knees and gave them a group embrace. "I'll look after them," replied Aaron, smiling at his mom.

Papa slung his arm around Aaron, and they retreated away from the others. "Remember: The vision to tell the difference, and the courage to act."

Aaron squeezed Papa with all his might and buried his face in his chest to hold back tears. The pain of not having his dad with him was like a punch in the gut, but his Papa softened the blow. "Yes, sir. I love you, Papa."

"I love you, Aaron. Take care of yourself and your brother and sister." Papa held up his hand with two fingers crossed. "Parsons Cord."

Chapter Ten

Aspen Meadows

Aaron started up Rocky and they headed down the trail toward Redwood Grove. By this time, Aaron remembered the trail and they traveled swiftly through the snow. As they drove, they saw a family of deer eating small twigs off the trees and an owl up in a tree watching them speed by. It was a spectacular day; the sun was shining, and the sky was a deep blue. When they got to the redwood grove, Aaron pulled over and parked Rocky.

They ran to the big redwood tree and began climbing. It seemed shorter today and they rapidly made their way through the fog and stepped out onto the familiar beautiful meadow. Jack Deer, Ella Doe, and Enzo Fawn were there grazing on flowers.

Jack lifted his head. "It's good to see you, Aaron."

"Benji and Hannah, it's so nice to see you again," said Ella.

"Hi, Hannah," exclaimed Enzo as he pranced over to Hannah.

Jack strode up to Benji and looked him up and down. "That was quite a commotion you had yesterday, Benji."

"Yeah, I got into some trouble in Shadowlands." Benji looked down, kicking the flowers. "Thanks for the help."

"I'd say you did get yourself into a pickle." Jack smirked at Benji. "Best for you to keep your head down from now on."

Aaron was still peeved by Benji's selfish excursion to Shadowlands and was determined to keep the focus on meeting King Yasha. "I couldn't wait to come back. Will you take us to King Yasha?"

"We'd love to," replied Ella. "It's always delightful to visit the king."

"Let's tell the others. They'll want to visit the king too," said Enzo. "But first, I want to show you my secret Razzle-Dazzle Den."

"Sounds cool, Enzo," replied Benji. He and Hannah followed Enzo to explore his lavender vine cave. "We'll meet you at the lake after we see Enzo's cave."

Aaron shook his head in frustration. "Don't be long. You're not going to keep me from the king today."

***

Enzo Fawn led Benji and Hannah to the edge of the meadow along a winding path into the trees. Soon they reached a clearing and it was the most breathtaking scene they had ever come across. Lush flowers of every color carpeted the ground and spectacular lavender trumpet vines adorned the entrance of the cave. The varying shades of blue, purple, magenta, yellow, and orange rushed into their eyes, exhilarating their sense of sight like never before. They were standing in nature's rainbow of beauty. Benji and Hannah tiptoed through the flowers, not wanting to damage even one, as they made their way to the cave.

"See, it's pretty spectacular, isn't it," said Enzo. He pranced to the entrance of the cave and motioned them to come closer. "The cave is even more beautiful."

The lavender bouquet welcoming them into the cave had the sweet aroma of honey. The interior of the cave was dark, and it took a few seconds for their eyes to adjust. Hannah blinked her eyes several times, and she was astounded by what she saw as she opened her eyes. The darkness of the cave had been transformed into a light prism of fluorescent color. "What is this?" whispered Hannah.

"I call it my Razzle-Dazzle Den," replied Enzo. "These mosses give off fluorescent light in shades and colors found nowhere else. Isn't it dazzling?"

"I've never seen these colors before," said Benji. He swiveled his head around the cave taking in all the gorgeous color. He began to reach for his sketchpad and pencils, but then abandoned the idea. "I wish I had time to sketch this, but Aaron would blow up."

"I knew you'd like it," said Enzo proudly. "It's pretty extraordinary."

The Razzle-Dazzle Den had a serene ambiance. It was so quiet that Benji could hear his heartbeat. Benji and Hannah settled next to Enzo and let their minds meander through the beauty of the cave. Hannah was in awe of this florescent paradise Enzo had introduced to them. Benji marveled at the artistry of the scenery he was beholding. *What kind of artist could create such beauty?*

***

While Benji and Hannah explored Enzo Fawn's Razzle-Dazzle Den, Aaron rushed down the trail to investigate strange noises coming from Lake Amari. It sounded like huffing and puffing combined with hooting and hollering. He found Mr. Wigglebottom in the middle of the lake darting back and forth like a madman. He was laughing hysterically while huffing like he'd just finished a climb up a mountain. As Aaron got closer, he saw that Mr. Wigglebottom was standing on top of the water. Aaron rubbed his eyes in an effort to shake reality back into his head. But it didn't work. Mr. Wigglebottom was definitely standing on top of the water. Mr. Wigglebottom noticed Aaron and paused from his erratic convolutions on the lake.

"Sir Aaron, good to see you again," called out Mr. Wigglebottom between gasps. "Do you want to join me in a game of Ziggety-Zag?"

"You're standing on the water." Aaron's eyes widened as he stood frozen on the lakeshore. "How?"

"Step out and you'll see." Mr. Wigglebottom waved at Aaron with a big smile. "King Yasha added a little fun to this part of the lake."

Aaron placed one foot out on the lake and tapped the top of the water. Sure enough, his shoe stopped at the surface of the water. He planted both feet on the lake and stared down as his body stood over the water. He was standing on top of the lake. The surface of the lake felt like ice, but it wasn't frozen. Aaron shuffled his way to meet Mr. Wigglebottom in the middle of the lake staring down the whole time.

"You probably haven't played Ziggety-Zag before." Mr. Wigglebottom pointed to the school of fish below the surface of the lake. "It's zany tomfoolery and the best morning workout you can get."

"How do you play?" Aaron peered into the water and saw a school of small fish darting every which way. "Who do you play with?"

Mr. Wigglebottom chuckled. "We play with the fish." Mr. Wigglebottom began darting back and forth following the quick movements of the school of fish below. "Try to keep up with them."

Aaron zigged and zagged on the water imitating the school of fish and quickly found himself exhausted. Now he was huffing and puffing while laughing uncontrollably. "This is zany!" He was determined to master this new game, as crazy as it was, so he studied the fish to see if there was a pattern to their evasive movements. As he learned how the school moved, he gradually improved, almost keeping up with them.

Benji and Hannah strolled down the trail and saw Aaron doing some kind of weird dance on top of the middle of the lake. "What are you doing?" screamed Benji.

"Playing Ziggety-Zag," replied Aaron. He was too tired to explain. "Come on out. It's gonzo fun!"

"Hannah let's play Ziggety-Zag," said Benji as he stepped out onto the lake. "I don't know what it is, but it looks major league off the hook."

Hannah and Benji crept their way to the middle of the lake and Mr. Wigglebottom explained how to play Ziggety-Zag. Soon all three of the children were darting and cavorting on the lake trying in vain to keep up with the speedy little fish below the surface.

"I'm going to head in for a shower," said Mr. Wigglebottom. "Keep playing. The fish love it."

Aaron, Benji, and Hannah spent the next twenty minutes playing ZiggetyZag with the fish. The game revealed a beauty in the school of fish that was otherwise hidden. Their movements were rhythmic and orchestrated in intricate patterns timed in perfect unison. What had seemed like meaningless darting by fish became a beautiful dance performed by a community of the king's creatures.

***

Mr. Wigglebottom stepped out of his cottage as he rubbed his thick silver hair with a towel. "Isn't that the zaniest most invigorating way to start your day?" He stared at Benji, and his face grew serious. "I trust you made it home safely yesterday?"

"Yeah, Benji was in a tight spot in Shadowlands yesterday," said Aaron as he placed his hand on Benji's shoulder. "Lucky to get away."

"You don't want to be in a predicament in Shadowlands," replied Mr. Wigglebottom. He placed his derby hat on his head and carefully positioned it just so. "Very perilous. I suggest you stay away."

Benji shot a smug look at Mr. Wigglebottom. "That's exactly what we plan to do."

Aaron redirected the conversation again. "Jack Deer and our friends are taking us to meet King Yasha. Can you go with us?"

Mr. Wigglebottom removed his hat and patted his forehead with a handkerchief. "I don't want to slow you down. It's a long journey to the City of Light. Besides, the other animals may need me here."

"Before we start, there are things I need to tell you about Himmel," said Jack in a serious voice. "We live in the Highlands Province. As you see, it's beautiful and very safe. Not all of Himmel is like the Highlands." Jack raised his head and pointed his large antlers toward Shadowlands. "As Benji learned yesterday, there's another province that's unsafe... in fact, it's downright dangerous. We'll need to avoid Shadowlands Province at all costs."

As Jack described Shadowlands, Hannah scooted next to Aaron and hid behind him. "We'll stay away. Right, Aaron?" she asked.

Aaron put his arm around his sister and gently squeezed her. "What do you mean by dangerous?" he asked.

Mr. Wigglebottom stepped closer to Aaron speaking softly and slowly for emphasis. "There's a sickness some people get and it's extremely serious."

Benji listened intently and replayed the events of yesterday in his mind. "I know what you mean. I saw it in their eyes – all red."

"Sickness?" Aaron stroked his chin with a frown on his face. "What kind? How do you get it?"

"There's a flower called Midnight Clover. It's dark purple, almost black," said Mr. Wigglebottom. He pointed to his eyes. "It makes you blind if you eat it or spend too much time around it. It's a sickness called Midnight Madness."

Aaron made meticulous mental notes to adjust his plan to account for this new hazard. "Does it grow here in Highlands?" asked Aaron.

"We've started to see it here," said Jack. "It was first spotted in Shadowlands and must have spread to the western edge of Highlands."

"It's important to travel along the stream," said Mr. Wigglebottom. He pointed up the clear blue stream. "As long as you stay near the stream and avoid the Midnight Clover, you should be fine."

"We don't have to go near Shadowlands, do we?" asked Hannah. She had one arm tightly wrapped around Aaron and the other around Enzo.

Jack tilted his large antlers toward the stream. "No, we're going to steer clear of Shadowlands."

Mr. Wigglebottom clasped Aaron's hands with both of his hands. "Sir Aaron, as you journey through Himmel, I offer this advice to you: A successful journey is had through clarity of mission and purpose, in your case, meeting his majesty, King Yasha."

Aaron nodded his head. "Yes, meeting King Yasha."

Mr. Wigglebottom peered into Aaron's eyes. "Clarity comes from focusing on the good and beautiful, what's real. Confusion comes from entertaining the bad and ugly."

Aaron thanked Mr. Wigglebottom and then filled the three canteens in the stream. The group traveling to meet King Yasha had grown with the animals' excitement to go on an adventure to see the king. Jack and his family had agreed to serve as guides. Piper Bear, Jasper Lion, and Riley Raccoon volunteered to provide security.

Jack took the lead and directed them to walk along the side of the stream away from Lake Amari. The first leg of their journey would take them through Aspen Meadows. It was a glorious day with the blue sky above and meadows painted with gorgeous flowers as far as the eye could see.

"This is such a beautiful place," said Aaron. "Is it like this every day?"

"Yes, every day," replied Jasper. "The king makes sure of that."

Hannah gazed up to the sky and scanned the horizon. "It's so bright and beautiful, but I don't see the sun in the sky," said Hannah.

Ella gave a soft snort. "King Yasha provides the light and warmth for us to enjoy each and every day."

"Today is a particularly fine day," added Enzo. "The king has made a marvelous day."

"Huh?" Hannah stared at Enzo with a scrunched face. "The king makes your days?"

"He's a master artist," replied Jack. "He makes every day for us."

"That's a peculiar idea," said Aaron. He made a mental note to ask King Yasha about this. *An artist making the days?*

Jack stopped in his tracks and sniffed the air around them. He pointed to his left with his left hoof. "See that? It's Midnight Clover."

About twenty yards west of the stream, the bright multi-colored meadow suddenly turned dark purplish black. Aaron walked closer and saw hundreds of tiny dark clovers growing in the field and a boy lying in the middle of them. He was about thirteen and had a disheveled look. His hair was unruly. His fingernails were too long and had dirt under them. They looked more like claws than fingernails. His tee shirt was about two sizes too small, and his rather expansive stomach bulged out for all to see. Aaron also noticed that his eyes were bloodshot, like he had been swimming in a pool too long, which obviously this boy had not.

"Hey, where are you going?" asked the boy. He stood up and rubbed his generous belly. His eyes were stuck on his SIM, so he barely looked at them.

Jack stepped up in front of the others. "We're going to the City of Light to visit the king," replied Jack sternly.

The boy casually picked something out of his teeth. "That's a waste of time. He can't do anything for you."

Ella strode up next to Jack in the front. "These three have never met him so we're taking them up the mountain," said Ella. "I'm Ian," said the boy as he stepped closer to them. "What're your names?"

"I'm Aaron, and this is my brother and sister, Benji and Hannah." Aaron stayed behind Jack wanting nothing to do with this loathsome boy. "Why is it a waste of time to visit the king?"

"Why?" Ian roared with laughter. "Because he's not really the king."

Jasper stalked up front. "He is the king," he snarled. Jasper rose to his full height, and the fir on his neck stood straight up. "The one and only artist, King Yasha."

"Even if he is a king, he's not a good king," replied Ian. He let out a long yawn with a strange growl. "Not good at all."

"He's an exceptionally good king," said Jack. "Just look at the day he made for us."

"I don't think his paintings are beautiful. They're downright ugly if you ask me," uttered Ian. He contorted his face with a look of disgust. "Even if he's a king, I'm a bear and this meadow is my kingdom."

Jack motioned for the children to step further away from Ian. "I think he's got Midnight Madness," he whispered. "Be careful not to touch him."

"My eyesight is just fine. I'm a bear, and this is my meadow." Ian began pawing at the ground and growling to himself. "I'm the boss of me, and I don't have to listen to any stupid rules by anyone else."

Jack, Jasper, and Piper formed a wall protecting the children. "Keep your distance, Ian," yelled Jack.

"I do what I want, say what I want, and eat what I want. I'm free and no fake king can tell me otherwise," declared Ian as he grabbed a handful of Midnight Clover and stuffed it in his mouth. "I'm about to make a pot of tea with Midnight Clover. Would you like to join me?"

"You seem like you're insanely … I mean exceedingly, attached to Midnight Clover, Ian," said Aaron as he backed further away from Ian. "Are you sure you're free?" he asked in a concerned voice.

"Yes, I'm free." Ian broke out a crazed look as he chomped on his Midnight Clover. "King Ian, the bear who rules this meadow!"

Piper Bear stood up on her back legs and heaved a thunderous growl.

"We're going to the City of Light to visit King Yasha and we're not staying with you or having your tea."

"Suit yourself," said Ian as he turned to walk deeper into the Midnight Clover field. He laid in the Midnight Clover drawn to the green glow of his SIM.

"We best be going," said Jack and he led the group back to the trail near the stream. "I'd say that boy is lost." "You see how perilous the Midnight Madness illness is," said Ella. "Poor lad."

"Yeah, he seemed to be blind to the world around him," replied Aaron.

"Why was he so against King Yasha?"

"I'm not exactly sure," replied Jack. "You'll have to ask the king. But I can tell you people with Midnight Madness dislike the king and they hate his paintings."

"I've done silly things," joked Benji, "but that guy is as nutty as a walnut orchard."

Jack turned the group back on the trail along the stream. "They scream about being free, but as you saw with Ian, I don't think they know what it means to be free," he said.

"He seemed to be obsessed with Midnight Clover," said Aaron. "Like whacko crazy about it."

"Yeah, he was stuffing it in his mouth like he was a cow," said Benji with a laugh.

"It's quite sad," said Ella. "The more Midnight Clover you eat, the more you want, and it just makes you sicker and sicker."

"Is there a cure for it?" asked Hannah. "Maybe Mr. Wigglebottom can help."

Jack turned toward Hannah and paused for a moment. "I'm not entirely sure. I've seen people get better, something to do with the water. I'm not sure how it works. You should ask the king when you meet him."

Chapter Eleven

City of Light

The beautiful meadows gave way to rolling foothills of Asha Grasslands, home to hundreds of animals peacefully grazing – horses, cows, sheep, goats, and buffalo aplenty. But there were also more exotic animals like antelopes, gazelles, zebras, giraffes, elephants, wildebeests, impalas, and others. The array of animals all living peacefully together was an incredible display of the artist's beautiful creativity. In some places the animals congregated in gatherings of their own kind, while in other places the animals mixed together like one big happy family. Aaron, Benji, and Hannah turned their heads side to side, taking in the majestic sight of so many different kinds of animals.

The open range of Asha Grasslands seemed vast, and it took them over half the day to get to the upper terrace, which had large parcels of farmland. As they hiked through the upper terrace, they saw families busily tending to their crops – carrots, lettuce, beans, tomatoes, broccoli, artichokes, peppers, strawberries, blueberries, boysenberries, and many others. The farmers were busy but not rushed. They were focused on their work, but at the same time they paused to spend time with neighbors and lend a helping hand. Aaron noticed that the farmers were unusually friendly to travelers as they passed by. They waved with enthusiasm at Aaron's group without a second thought of the strange combination of children and animals strolling by the stream.

"Wow, feels like we're in a parade," said Aaron under his breath. "What a welcome party." Hannah stepped away from Aaron for the first time, her hand in perpetual motion waving to the farmers. Aaron's face lit up at the sight of his sister's smile radiating her joy out to the farmers.

"You're a fine-looking group of travelers," said an elderly man wearing overalls and a big straw hat. He set down his pick and wiped the sweat from his brow. "Where are you heading?"

"We're going to meet King Yasha in the City of Light," replied Aaron. He stepped over to shake the man's hand. "I'm Aaron, and this is my brother Benji, and sister Hannah."

"Mighty fine to meet you all," replied the man. "I'm Hank. Meeting the king, that's no small thing."

"We've never met him," replied Hannah. She approached Hank, staring at him with sincere eyes. "Have you met him?"

"Sure have." Hank removed his hat and carefully shaped the ends with his fingers. "King Yasha's the finest king you could ever imagine."

Benji hung back standing next to Jasper. "Why is he so special?" asked Benji.

"See all this," replied Hank pointing to the massive expanse overflowing with hearty fruits and vegetables. "All this is from him. He makes every day. The water comes from his stream, the nutrients from his soil, the sun from his light, the whole thing."

Benji stepped closer to Hank. "Why are you helping each other?" Benji's eyes narrowed as though he were a scientist dissecting an alien creature.

"What's the angle?"

Hank broke into a wide smile. "Angle? We're all one big family here in Himmel." He dusted dirt off his hands. "We all have challenges that come our way."

"But why help?" Benji leaned in even closer. "Why not finish your work and sit back munching down a few strawberries on your porch?"

"I care for them… I love them." Hank's eyes glistened as he shifted his gaze from Benji to Aaron and then Hannah. "Just like King Yasha cares for me and loves me."

Benji's brow furrowed as he tried to figure Hank out. "King Yasha… seems to be all over Himmel."

Aaron stepped in to seize the conversation from Benji's pointless questions. "Hank, I've got a question for you." Something had been bothering Aaron since they started their journey in Himmel. It felt like they had traveled hundreds of miles, maybe thousands of miles. They had seen so much, yet they had only travelled a day. "How can we see so much of the kingdom in one day?"

"Pretty amazing, isn't it," replied Hank with a friendly laugh. "That tells you something about King Yasha. I'll tell you what, Aaron … you ask the king when you see him."

Aaron gave Hank a warm smile. "Thanks for your time." He reached out and clasped Hank's calloused hand. "We'll let you get back to your work."

"We better be on our way," said Jack Deer. "We've got to make the City of Light."

"I understand. It's a bit more of a trek to the City of Light." Hank put his hat back on and picked some carrots and strawberries. "Here's a little something for the road. Please give my regards to King Yasha when you see him."

Jack pointed to a trail head as the road to the City of Light. This portion of the journey was more challenging; the trail was steep and narrow. Hannah was exhausted. Her cheeks were red, and beads of sweat were running down her face as she staggered along.

Piper Bear noticed Hannah's distress and whispered to Riley Raccoon, "Poor little girl. Giving everything she's got to keep up with her older brothers."

Riley leaped up on Piper's back and whispered back, "Yeah, and us animals too. We're used to these long travels over the countryside. We should do something."

Piper strode up next to Hannah. "Hannah, why don't you hop on my back. You'll enjoy the view up there."

Riley jumped off Piper's back. "It's great up there. You'll love it." She nuzzled Hannah's side nudging her toward Piper.

"Thanks Piper, I am kind of tired." Hannah hopped on the bear's back and held on to her shaggy fur, relieved to get some rest. "Just for a little while, then I can walk again."

"Sure thing, Hannah, just for a while." Piper smiled coyly and added, "But it's kind of nice having you up there. Stay as long as you like."

They gradually made their way up the trail, and finally they reached a small meadow with grasses, flowers, and the stream running through it. They were all ready for a rest.

"This is a good spot for a break," said Jack. The animals began grazing on the grass while Aaron, Benji, and Hannah took out their sandwiches and sat back on the bank of the stream.

Aaron stepped over to Jack who was quietly grazing next to Enzo Fawn and Ella Doe. "Hank seemed to break up back there when he was talking about King Yasha." Aaron took one of Hank's carrots and held it out for Enzo. "What was that about?"

"Benji's question made Hank reflect on how much King Yasha loves him." Jack lifted his head and gazed at Aaron. "That's enough to make a grown man cry, Aaron."

Jack's response reminded Aaron of something Mr. Wigglebottom had said. "The other day Mr. Wigglebottom told me that we're very special to the king." Aaron held out one of Hank's strawberries and Enzo quickly gobbled it up. "What is so special about us?"

Jack gently prodded Enzo with his nose. "This whole world is special to the king; we animals are also special to him." Jack lifted his head peering into Aaron's eyes. "But you're different. You were made like the king, so you have always been very special to him."

Hannah had been listening from the bank of the stream. "I hope he likes me." She took a big bite out of a fresh strawberry. "Wow, this is wonderlicious."

"I assure you, Hannah, he likes you very much," said Riley, "In fact, he loves you more than you can even imagine."

"What do you mean by, 'made like the king?'" asked Aaron. He strolled down to the stream to grab another handful of strawberries, plopping one into his mouth. "You're right Hannah. These are wonderlicious." They all laughed at Hannah's funny expression.

"You can ask him when you see him, Aaron. We better get a move on," said Jack.

When they reached the end of Asha Grasslands, the foothills turned to mountains that were steeper. The trail narrowed and they had to walk single file at the edge of the stream. The grasslands gave way to forests of large pine trees.

"We're entering Sane Forest, but it's getting late. We better sleep here tonight. We can finish the journey in the morning."

***

"Hey, let's play a game tonight," said Enzo Fawn. He jumped up and down with excitement so contagious, it was impossible to refuse him. "What should we play?"

"We shouldn't play hide-and-seek since the children aren't familiar with Sane Forest," replied Ella Doe. She smiled and shook her head at the sight of Enzo's unbridled enthusiasm. "Pick something else."

"Uhm…" Enzo stopped jumping and furrowed his brow as he considered his options. "How about Simon Says?"

"Excellent choice, Enzo," replied Jack Deer. "Since you thought of the game, you go first."

Everyone lined up facing Enzo, and he thought about his first command. "OK, Simon says put your left front hoof on your nose." Enzo thought for a second. "Or hand or paw, whatever you have." Everyone giggled as Enzo looked down the line at each player.

Enzo continued, "Simon says, put your right front hoof, or hand or paw, on your tail."

"Hey, we don't have a tail," shouted Hannah. They all began howling with laughter.

"I know, I wanted to get you." Enzo snickered as he placed his hoof on his tail. "Your right hand on your backside, how's that."

The game continued this way well into the night. Each player took a turn and had similar problems directing the game with players having such different bodies. It was the most unusual game of Simon Says the children had ever played, but it was also the most fun.

Jack directed the children into the center of the campground and each of the animals laid in a circle around them. Piper Bear, Riley Raccoon, and Jasper Lion took turns keeping watch through the night. It was a warm night, and the stars provided a magnificent glimmer to the sky above. Aaron, Benji, and Hannah were in a strange new place, but they felt safe under the care of their new friends. They finally fell asleep imagining what it would be like to meet King Yasha. They would learn very soon.

During Jasper's shift as lookout, he noticed a man in the distance staring at their campground. The man had dark hair and a pale white complexion. It was difficult to make out details in the darkness, but Jasper's superior night vision helped him spot identifying details. The man had severely bloodshot eyes of a flaming red color. Jasper took several paces toward the man and rumbled a growl from deep down in his throat. This seemed to startle the man and caused him to rush away westward toward Shadowlands. There was something sinister about the man. He seemed out of place in the Highlands, and Jasper made a note to keep an eye out for him.

***

"Good morning," said Jack Deer as he stood near Ella Doe and Enzo Fawn looking over the children.

Aaron got to his feet and rubbed the sleep out of his eyes. He felt refreshed. His dreaded mountain top dream had not visited him last night.

"Good morning, Jack. Can we see King Yasha today?" asked Aaron.

"That's the plan," replied Jack as he chomped on one of Hank's carrots.

"Let me wake up the others," said Ella. She strolled over to Piper Bear and nudged the bear's gigantic head with her nose. "Time to get up sleepy bear."

Piper let out a long loud yawn as she took in the new morning. "Look at the beautiful day the king's made for us." She rose to her feet and padded over to Jasper Lion. "How's our night watchman?"

Jasper was curled up twitching in some sort of dream, but suddenly leaped to his feet when Piper approached him. "I was just resting my eyes."

Piper snorted and laid a big paw on Jasper's back. "Sure, that's what we thought."

"I was," replied Jasper. "And don't sneak up on me." He didn't want to scare the group, so he kept his late evening encounter to himself. At least for now.

After breakfast, they continued their trek toward the City of Light. It was another gorgeous day in Himmel. Forest animals scurried about taking on their daily tasks. Birds of interesting colors fluttered from tree to tree as they sang their morning tunes. The Sane Forest also had many animals the children had never seen outside the zoo. Monkeys, orangutangs, and gorillas rested up in the trees, flying squirrels flew from tree to tree, and leopards, tigers, cheetahs, and pumas lounged in the shade calmly watching the group of adventurers go by.

Aaron was astonished by so many wild animals almost close enough to touch, and surprised none of them were tearing into each other with the ferocious killer instinct he had seen in books and TV shows. "Why are all the animals so peaceful?"

"They live in the beautiful harmony of King Yasha's masterpiece," replied Jack. "In Himmel, there's no need to hunt each other because King Yasha provides all our needs. You see, King Yasha's beauty comes in many forms."

"Wow, amazing," replied Aaron. "This artist king is really someone special."

"Another masterpiece," said Jack. "King Yasha never fails to impress."

Enzo began humming a tune. "Do you want to sing a song while we walk?" He stepped next to Hannah and tickled the back of her neck with his nose.

"Hey that's wet," cried Hannah as she giggled and wiped the back of her neck. "Sure, I'm not a very good singer, but I like to sing."

"Fantastic, this is how it goes."

> *You've made the day for my delight.*
> *You bring us warmth and light.*
> *And keep us safe at night.*
> *You guard our lives with your love and might.*
> *Oh, what a good and beautiful King.*

"What a lovely song, Enzo," said Hannah. She began humming the tune. "What's it called?"

"*My King,*" replied Enzo as he trotted ahead of the group to lead the chorus.

The melody and words of the song filled the air as they travelled through the forest. The time flew by as they sang and joked along the way. It was almost midday when they finally reached the City of Light.

The City of Light was situated on a large mesa near the top of the mountain with open meadows and fields, and fruit trees along the banks of a stream running through the center of the city. The streets were immaculate, and the homes were modest but meticulously maintained. All the buildings had an architectural splendor to them. They were simple yet exquisite in their beauty.

The entire city offered an array of magnificence, but it was the people who provided the unique character to the city. The spirit of community and shared joy permeated the city. The community was bursting with purpose and activity, but not in a harried way. People were milling about, devoted to various activities, but eager to pause to chat with or help a neighbor. The people oozed a sense of joy and contentment as they went about their day.

"Welcome to the City of Light," said Jack breathing heavily after the long climb.

"This is an amazing place," said Aaron as he surveyed his surroundings. "Jack, can we meet some of the people here?"

"Sure." Jack led the way toward a small group working in a grove of fruit trees near the stream. "Hi, this is Aaron and his family. They've come to meet the king."

"Why hello, Aaron. It's wonderful to meet you," said a man on a ladder picking apples. He glanced toward Benji and Hannah. "Might these be your brother and sister?"

"I'm Hannah, Aaron's sister." Hannah sensed the people in the City of Light were like Hank and others she had met along the way. Except Ian. The nagging fear she had about her classmates at school was a million miles away for her here in the City of Light.

"I'm Benji," he said, eyeing the man's apples. "Tasty looking apples you've got there."

"Would you like one?" asked the man. He picked a crisp red apple and tossed it to Benji. "Here you go. My name's Thomas."

"So, you're here to meet King Yasha, are you?" said a woman working on an orange tree nearby. "You'll love him, absolutely love him."

"We're just about done with our work," replied Thomas as he climbed down his ladder. "Sophia, why don't we take these nice children to King Yasha." "Splendid idea," replied Sophia. She climbed down her ladder and brushed her hands off. She picked an orange off the tree and tossed it to Aaron. "Try this. Sweetest juice you've ever had."

"Thank you for the help," said Jack. "We'd appreciate your escort to the king's residence."

"King Yasha is very busy, but he always has time for us," said Thomas as they walked. He lives in that building up on the hill. It's called the Mishken Chateau. Of course, he's all around Himmel, but the chateau is where he makes his home." It was a beautiful building with ornate stained-glass windows and a tall spiral roof reaching up to the sky.

"He particularly loves children. You three are in for a real treat," added Sophia.

***

Their pace quickened as they approached Mishken Chateau where two men stood next to large wooden doors. The men were taller and bigger than other people they had met in Himmel. Certainly taller than Mr. Wigglebottom. Even bigger than the human brickhouse Benji met in Shadowlands. Something about them incited fear. But there was also a warmth to them and a kindness in their faces. Without a word, they beckoned the group to come through the enormous doors and into the chateau.

The inside walls and ceiling were decorated with gorgeous landscape murals. Aaron recognized some of them. One wall had a painting of Aspen Meadows with animals lounging by Lake Amari. Another wall had a huge mural of Asha Grasslands showing the animals grazing and farmers gathered at some sort of celebration. A landscape depiction of Sane Forest adorned another wall. The ceiling was transformed by a 3D rendition of the sky with deep blue shades speckled with fluffy cumulus clouds, and birds gliding through the air. The birds almost looked alive. As they walked, Aaron, Benji, and Hannah craned their necks and took in all the exquisite artwork.

At the far end of the room Aaron could see open doors leading to a large patio. The view from the patio overlooked the entire countryside below, all the way down the mountain and across the meadows as far as the eye could see. Aaron, Benji, and Hannah glanced at each other in amazement. They had never seen anything so magnificent. A man was sitting on a stool at the edge of the patio in front of a canvas resting on an easel.

"Aaron, Benji, Hannah, I've been expecting you," said the man without turning around to face them.

"A…Are you King Yasha?" asked Aaron. He stared at King Yasha, frozen without blinking. This was all he could think about the past few days. Now, here he was, standing in front of him.

"Why yes," replied Yasha as he stepped away from his canvas. "Let me take a look at you; it's so nice to have you visit."

King Yasha approached Aaron, Benji, and Hannah and extended his arms. The children felt his deep affection for them, and a sense of peace, as he wrapped his arms around them. He was not especially tall or strong or good looking, so at first glance, he didn't appear to have the royal qualities Aaron pictured in a king. Still, there was something quite unique about him, something otherworldly and majestic. He had kind eyes, but at the same time, his stare was penetrating. His smile was warm and comforting. His voice exuded supreme confidence, but with no hint of arrogance. The children felt a sense of calm in his presence allaying every fear they had ever known.

"You've had a long journey; let's sit down together. I want you to tell me everything that's on your mind and in your heart," said King Yasha. He led them back into the chateau and motioned for them to settle onto a large sofa.

"I've been so excited to meet you. I've been keeping my eye on you for a very long time. You know you are very special to me, real treasures."

"I have so many questions, I don't know where to start," said Aaron. He couldn't take his eyes off King Yasha and his mind was whirling. *What do I ask a king?*

King Yasha smiled warmly at Aaron. "I suppose the beginning would be a good place." He had an inviting twinkle in his eye as he leaned back on the sofa.

Chapter Twelve

An Audience with the King

"King Yasha, I heard you're an artist and that you make each day," said Aaron. He sat up and cleared his throat. "What kind of artist are you?"

"That's a very good question to start with, Aaron. Let's go out to the patio and I'll show you," said King Yasha as he stepped outside. "I love to make things. I specialize in making beautiful things, good things. Everything I make is designed to bring delight to the people of Himmel."

"Can we see?" asked Aaron as he followed close behind King Yasha.

"Of course. You actually see my artwork every day." King Yasha pointed at the breathtaking landscape beyond the patio. "What I paint, I give freely for all to see and enjoy."

King Yasha beckoned the children to move closer to his canvas. "You see this painting? It's a picture of tomorrow. I'm not done yet, but it's coming along."

Aaron, Benji, and Hannah fixed their eyes on the canvas and were astonished. It was the most exquisite painting they had ever seen. It showed Lake Amari, the stream running all the way up to the City of Light, Aspen Meadows, Asha Grasslands, Sane Forrest, all the animals they had met, the rolling foothills, the orchards with Thomas and

Sophia and Mishken Chateau. The detail of the painting was so fine, every tiny feature of Himmel was present. The entire world they had seen exploring in Himmel was in the painting in every color imaginable.

King Yasha stepped away from the painting. "Do you like my painting?"

Aaron was starstruck by the image in front of him. "Yes, it's the most wonderful thing I've ever seen," he replied.

"It's lovely," added Hannah still wide-eyed peering at the painting. "I see our new friends."

"Do you want to see something extraordinary?" asked King Yasha. He placed his hands over their eyes. "Open your eyes and look at the painting."

"Holy moly, the things in the painting are moving," exclaimed Aaron as he blinked his eyes several times. "I see Mr. Wigglebottom playing Ziggety-Zag. This is crazy, I can't believe this."

Benji cocked his head as he scrutinized the painting. "This can't be. Is this real?" he asked.

"Yes, exactly. That's a good word for it." Yasha waved his arm and the painting stopped moving. "Every day I make a painting of Himmel that's real. That's true."

Hannah's face crinkled. "Your paintings are alive?"

"Not alive like that," replied King Yasha. He placed his hands together under his chin as he formed the words the children would understand. "I imagine a day in Himmel and then paint that day in the finest detail, even beyond what you can see. When I finish, it becomes real to all in my kingdom.

Today, you're enjoying the day in Himmel I painted yesterday."

Aaron scratched his head and muttered, "Confusing."

"I know, don't worry." King Yasha placed his hand on Aaron's shoulder. "Just know that I make every painting with you in mind. Down to the tiniest detail."

"Do you have Jack Deer, Ella Doe, Enzo Fawn, Jasper Lion, Piper Bear, Riley Raccoon and the rest of our friends in mind too?" asked Hannah.

"I sure do," replied King Yasha. He chuckled and gestured outward to the expansive kingdom below. "I have all the people and animals in Himmel in mind when I make a painting."

"You really are a marvelous artist," said Aaron. He was fixated on the painting, grasping new intricate details the longer he gazed upon it.

"From one artist to another, I'd say you're pretty good," joked Benji. "Actually, you're awesome."

King Yasha let out a jovial laugh as he urged Benji to move closer. "Well, I like to think so. I've had a lot of practice over the years."

The children couldn't take their eyes off the painting, so King Yasha quietly sat on his stool and enjoyed their delight in his creation. They were pointing out all the places, people and animals they had met along their journey to the City of Light. Hannah kept giggling as she remembered the fun times they'd had with the animals and Mr. Wigglebottom.

After what seemed like five minutes to the children, but was actually more than an hour, King Yasha invited them back inside. "Let's go inside again and relax on the sofa. Would you like some lunch?"

As they left the patio, Aaron saw a second easel at the other end of the patio with a tarp over the canvas. It seemed peculiar to him that King Yasha would have a second easel, but he decided he'd asked enough questions about the painting for now.

"That would be nice," said Aaron. "We finished the sandwiches our grandma packed for us."

"Oh my, how I love your grandma. She's a treasure and such a good cook." King Yasha gazed upward as he cherished his memories of Grandma. "Her apple pancakes are the best. I've never had better biscuits and honey-butter."

"You know our grandma?" asked Benji. He knew that Papa and his dad had met King Yasha, but this was news to him.

"Yes, I know the whole Parsons family going all the way back," replied King Yasha. "That's why I've been so eager to meet you three." Yasha lifted his hand and a servant appeared with a tray of enormous sandwiches, homemade potato chips, and fresh strawberries and apples.

"Jack told us we're very special because we're made like you," said Aaron as he took a bite of his sandwich. "Even more than Jack and the other animals."

"Jack's right, Aaron." King Yasha moved his hand as though he was painting. "When I make a painting, I care for all the things I put in the painting, but I add parts of myself to the people I put into my paintings, so they'll be kind of like me – not exactly like me, but in certain ways like me."

"How are we like you?" asked Benji as he chewed on a strawberry. His eyes narrowed as he stared intently at King Yasha. "You're a king."

"In lots of ways, Benji." King Yasha pointed to the beautiful murals covering the walls. "When I paint people, I paint them with colors that are deeper than just the outside. These colors add so much more to the people."

"You paint inside colors?" asked Aaron. He scrunched his mouth as he wrestled with King Yasha's explanation. "I've never seen an inside color."

"It's more than just color, it's part of my image that I put into you." King Yasha smiled and waved his arm at the children. "Look at you three for example. You're smart and can think about complicated ideas."

"So you give us our smarts," said Aaron. He placed his sandwich on the table and ran his fingers through his hair. "So we can make brilliant plans?"

"Yes, your intelligence. Your ability to reason out complicated things," replied King Yasha. He turned to Benji and said, "You paint like me and can make beautiful things too."

Benji sat up with excitement. "Yeah, I love painting things." Benji thought for a moment and picked up an apple spinning it in his hand. "That's part of you?"

"Exactly. You all have the ability to create good and beautiful things." King Yasha continued, "You know there's a difference between right and wrong and you want things to be fair, to be just."

Aaron perked up. "Yes, but that's not my experience." He crunched down on a potato chip with anger.

"I know, Aaron, and that saddens me to no end," replied King Yasha. "I call it morals. I add an understanding of my morals and a desire for justice into people. Deep inside. Some don't feel it, but it's there."

"I know some kids who don't feel it." Aaron grimaced as he recalled Reaper and the horrendous ending to his football game. "That's for sure."

"Another way I make people like me is friendships...relationships." King Yasha laughed as the children sat up and moved closer to him wanting to hear more. "You love friendships with each other and care for each other. You were made to have loving relationships with others. And with me. Your capacity to love comes from me. These are just some of the ways I paint you to be like me."

Aaron sat back in silence and pondered everything King Yasha had said. It was beginning to make sense, but he had a nagging question. "Why do you make us like you?"

Benji nodded his head as he turned from Aaron to King Yasha. "Yeah, we're not kings or queens." He took a big bite out of his apple with a loud crunch.

"You're like my ambassadors in my kingdom. I make you like me to represent me." King Yasha stood and pointed out the patio toward the expansive kingdom below. "Himmel is a very big place and I want people to help me care for the entire kingdom."

"How can we help you care for your kingdom?" asked Aaron. He finished his sandwich and stood up to take in the view of the city below. "We're not kings. We're just kids."

"By making you like me, you'll know how to care for Himmel and all who live in it just as I would." King Yasha rose and draped his arm around Aaron's shoulder. "I've given you the things you'll need to do that well."

Benji set his apple on the table and approached King Yasha. "But we're not from Himmel." His eyes narrowed as he tried to read the king. "You mean you need our help?"

"I wouldn't say I *need* your help," replied King Yasha. He chuckled and patted Benji on the back. "I can certainly do all that needs to be done myself. I want your help because I know it will bring you delight. And the funny thing is, the more you serve like this, the more you are transformed to be more like me."

"So, we work for you?" asked Benji. He sensed an angle. *Maybe this king just wants some free labor. He makes the rules. We do the work.*

"Not really, Benji," said King Yasha. He cracked a smile that telegraphed something Benji couldn't decipher. "It's more like a family."

Benji's ears perked up when he heard "family" as he recalled Hank's comment. "We met a guy named Hank. He said to say hello."

"Hank is a treasure to me," replied King Yasha. "Anyway, you know your Papa's furniture business. When your dad was young, he worked with your Papa and helped him make furniture. I think of you as part of my family business. Every time I make a painting, I want members of my family to help me."

"So, are you in our family?" asked Hannah. She was up on her knees keenly listening to everything King Yasha said.

"You're very close Hannah, but not exactly," replied King Yasha. "You're in *my* family. The entire Parsons family is in my family."

"So, are you our father?" asked Hannah. Images of her dad ran through her head bringing a somber note to their conversation. "I already have a dad."

"No, I'm not. And you have a wonderful dad," replied King Yasha. He placed his hand on her shoulder. "You know how you have a father? Well, I have a father too."

"What's your father like?" asked Hannah as she leaned forward soaking in every word.

"He's very much like me," replied King Yasha. He strolled over to the sofa and sat next to Hannah. Aaron and Benji paced behind him and joined him on the sofa. "In fact, if you know me, then you know my father."

"What's his name?" asked Benji. He scratched out his theory in his head. *Maybe this father guy is the one with the angle. Somebody has to have an angle.*

"Most call him Dio or just plain Father." Yasha leaned closer to the children and whispered, "but you can call him Abba."

Hannah stepped close to Yasha, excited to learn she was part of his family. "Can we meet Abba?"

Yasha stroked Hannah's hair and said, "Not today, but I'm sure you'll meet Abba very soon."

"Sorry, I have a few more questions," said Aaron. He couldn't resist. He had a million questions, but maybe just three more — for now. "Who made you king?"

"No one made me king. I've always been king, even before Himmel existed. I'm the king because I'm the artist who made Himmel and who maintains it." Yasha scrutinized Aaron. "Doesn't that make sense?"

"Yeah, I guess it does," replied Aaron as he studied the beautiful landscape murals on the wall. "Since you made the kingdom, it figures you would know best how to live here. Second question, if you're a king, why don't you wear a crown?"

Yasha chuckled, "I don't wear a crown now, but I suppose I could if I wanted." He ran his fingers through his long brown hair. "My paintings and my work in Himmel show my royalty, not some crown. It would probably just get in the way of my painting."

"Makes sense." Aaron continued to press. "Do you paint everybody like you, even crazy Ian, the boy we met on the way here?"

Yasha paused before answering the third question. "Aaron, that question is a bit more complicated, so I'll answer it later when we have more time. The short answer is, yes, I do make everyone like me, but that's not where it ends."

Aaron wasn't sure what to make of King Yasha's answer, but he trusted that he'd have a chance to follow up later.

They spent the afternoon on a tour of the chateau. It was a humongous building with every sort of space: big rooms, little rooms, banquet halls, libraries, atria, vestibules, chambers, and chapels. A series of hallways, concourses, and corridors created a gigantic maze, leading every which way. The children were starry-eyed as they took in the spectacle. "It's far too big to see in one day," said Yasha.

As they turned a corner on the tour, Benji peered down a distant corridor. "What's down there?"

"That's the Eternal Hallway," replied Yasha. His face telegraphed a seriousness to that part of the chateau.

Yasha's response triggered a voracious curiosity in Aaron. "What's there?"

"There are many places, many mansions down that hallway. The Reminiscent Room, the Aviary... many more enchanting places." Yasha waved his arm pointing toward the patio. "But that's for another day. Today, we'll take in the beauty of the kingdom of Himmel."

Aaron yearned to explore the Eternal Hallway, but Yasha was insistent and directed the children to the patio again. The children were not disappointed as Yasha pointed out many of the wonderful places in Himmel. With each new sight, the children discovered a spectacular new part of the kingdom of Himmel.

"We have so much to discuss, but it's getting late." Yasha waved his arm from the patio seemingly signaling something. "You can stay here tonight; we'll have a banquet to celebrate your visit. Grace will get you settled."

***

A beautiful woman strolled onto the patio and introduced herself as Grace. She wore a flowing white gown and had long brown braided hair. Her skin was like porcelain and her chestnut brown eyes and soft smile conveyed a caring warmth. She escorted them to the guest wing of the chateau and led them into an enormous suite with three big, soft beds. At the far end of the room, large French doors opened onto a balcony that overlooked a huge fountain below.

Aaron felt bad that he'd left their new friends all day to meet with King Yasha. "Grace, what about our friends?"

Grace smiled at Aaron as she opened the French doors. "I've made arrangements for them to stay at the chateau too. They're all invited to the banquet. Mike and Gabe will see to it."

Aaron, Benji, and Hannah walked to the massive wooden front doors and the same two large men greeted them.

"Are you Mike and Gabe?" asked Aaron. He kept his distance; still not sure how safe they were. "Grace said to see you about our friends."

"Sure are." Mike and Gabe stepped closer and gave Aaron and Benji hearty pats on the back. "Why don't you get your friends? They're down in the plaza."

The children walked to the plaza below the chateau and found Thomas, Sophia, Jack Deer, Ella Doe, Enzo Fawn, Piper Bear, Jasper Lion, and Riley Raccoon standing near the large fountain. They were with a group of townspeople and Jasper was telling a story about the time Riley got her head stuck in a knothole of a tree and Piper had to save her by clawing her way through the bark. They all had a good laugh, including Riley as she rubbed her head recalling the frightful event.

Thomas' face lit up when he saw the children approaching. "How was your visit with King Yasha?"

Aaron rummaged through his head trying to put words to his day with King Yasha. *How can I describe a day with a king? Not just any king, but the king who perfectly makes everything. Including me!* "Amazing, and confusing."

As a fellow artist, it was King Yasha's painting that stuck-out to Benji. "We saw his painting and it moved around like it was real." Benji waved his hands imitating King Yasha. "He does one every day."

"We're part of his family," said Hannah. Her joy in King Yasha glowed all around her. "He has a dad named Abba."

Sophia gave two loud claps with her strong hands. "As it should be. A wonderful visit with King Yasha." She dipped her hands in the fountain and took a drink of water. "Gali Fountain, best water you'll find."

Aaron gathered up the group and directed them toward the chateau. "Yasha said you can stay here too. Mike and Gabe will get you settled. He's having a banquet tonight and you're all invited!"

After everyone got settled, they went out to explore the City of Light for the rest of the afternoon. It was mind-boggling. All the people were so gracious and kind, some even invited them into their homes to talk and share tea and cookies. As they left one of the homes, Thomas and Aaron sat on the steps of the Gali Fountain to take in the splendor of the countryside.

"They're good people," said Thomas. He dipped his hand in the fountain and drew out a drink of water.

"Some of the kindest people I've met," replied Aaron. Thomas' comment reminded him of something Mr. Wigglebottom had said. "A man named Mr. Wigglebottom told me that King Yasha's very nature is good, so everything he makes is good."

Thomas' eyes lit up at the mention of Mr. Wigglebottom. "Ah, a prince of a man. How is he?"

"He's doing fine." Aaron wanted to get back to his question. "How about what Mr. Wigglebottom said. How do we tell if something is good?"

Thomas dried his hand on his pants as he considered Aaron's question. "Think of goodness as a measuring stick. It measures how closely something matches its nature and purpose. You know, what it's made for."

"What do you mean?" asked Aaron with a crinkled face.

"Everything is made for something. That something is its nature and purpose." Thomas pulled a pencil from his bag and showed it to Aaron. "Take this pencil. What's its nature and purpose?"

"I suppose to draw or write something," answered Aaron.

Thomas began to draw on a piece of paper. "So, we can say this is a good pencil because I can use it to write and draw." He then snapped the tip of the pencil. "Now, it's not so good."

"How do we know the nature and purpose of something? What it's made for?" asked Aaron. He dipped his hand into the fountain and drew out a small taste. "Wow, that's good water."

Thomas gave a small chuckle. "We have to look to the artist who created it." Thomas glanced up to the chateau. "It all comes back to King Yasha, the master artist. He's the artist who creates everything including the nature and purpose of all things. Even us."

Aaron's brow furrowed as he contemplated the implications. "So how do we know our nature and purpose?"

Thomas placed the pencil back in his pocket. "We're made like Yasha, so our nature and purpose are to be like him. To live like him."

Aaron cringed as he thought about Reaper. "I know a boy who cheats to win, and he thinks that's a good thing to do."

"His cheating is certainly not good because cheating is not part of Yasha's nature." Thomas pointed up to the chateau toward the balcony where King Yasha's painting rested on its easel. "King Yasha is the final standard for what's good. If something is worthy of his approval, it's good. Let that be your guide."

"But I don't know Yasha." Aaron scooped some more water out of the fountain and drank it. "At least not well."

"You can know his nature by what he's made," replied Thomas as he waved his arm around the beautiful scenery of the City of Light. "And by his words..." Thomas paused in silence for several seconds. "And by his actions."

Aaron's mind replayed the images of Himmel and King Yasha's words to him. "So, can you help me know Yasha better?" he asked.

"That, my boy, is the most valuable ambition a person can have." Thomas leaned closer to Aaron with a smile. "King Yasha is the truth. His very nature is true and honest. So, he doesn't approve of cheating, lying, stealing and those sorts of things. Since those behaviors are against his nature, they're not good. They're bad."

"Interesting." Aaron peered into the fountain, letting the words sink it. "Through him, I know what is true, what is good."

"Exactly," replied Thomas. "If you keep your focus on King Yasha, you'll see what is really good and true in the world."

Just as they finished their conversation, Sophia strolled up to check on them. "What are you boys talking about?"

Thomas stood to greet Sophia, clasping her hand. "Aaron wants to know King Yasha better – his goodness." Thomas smiled at Aaron, impressed by his curiosity.

"Ah, such important matters. Beauty is another grand idea of our kingdom, Aaron." Sophia gazed out at the hillside painted with a rainbow of flowers. "Isn't it beautiful?"

"Sure is." Aaron slid over making room for Sophia. "Mr. Wigglebottom told me Yasha's nature is perfectly beautiful."

"That's true." Sophia sat down and scooped up some water. "Beauty invites wonder and delight. Don't King Yasha's paintings give you wonder and delight?"

"They do," replied Aaron. He scooped some water from the fountain. "Do we all get to decide what's beautiful? I think Yasha's paintings are very beautiful, but a boy I met, crazy Ian, doesn't think so."

"To a point, King Yasha's given us a desire to seek out beauty. In music, artwork, a lovely spring day, a mother deer caring for her little fawn, a school of fish darting about. All these things offer the gift of beauty." Sophia shook her head and grimaced as she thought about Ian. "But something that's against King Yasha's nature can't be beautiful. I think Ian was deceived. Ultimately, the way to know what's beautiful is through King Yasha."

Benji and Hannah approached the fountain eating fresh strawberries from a bowl. "Timothy gave us a tour of the strawberry field and shared these with us."

"Hey Aaron, do you want some?" asked Hannah as she chewed on a strawberry. "They're wonderlicious!"

"Thanks, Hannah." Aaron plucked a plump strawberry and plopped it in his mouth. "This is a beautiful strawberry, and it tastes very good."

Thomas laughed and patted Aaron on the back. "Now you're seeing things clearly, Aaron."

The daylight was giving way to darkness, so Aaron steered the group back to the chateau to get ready for the banquet. As the children walked through the city, they sang the *My King* song Enzo had taught them,

> *You've made the day for my delight.*
> *You bring us warmth and light.*
> *You keep us safe at night.*
> *You guard our lives with your love and might.*
> *Oh, what a good and beautiful King you are.*

For Aaron, Benji, and Hannah, there was a newfound passion for the song.

They were family to the King.

Chapter Thirteen
A Royal Banquet

G race entered the guest suite to escort Aaron, Benji, and Hannah to the banquet room. As they walked down a long corridor, Aaron heard a sound out on the patio. He stepped away from the others, crept out to the patio, and found King Yasha, weeping. Aaron stood in silence, not knowing what to say or do. Yasha was gazing across Himmel as tears rolled down his face.

Aaron's thoughts drifted, searching for what to say. *Kings are strong, fearless. I just met him, but I certainly didn't expect to see him crying. What would bring a king to tears?* "Sir, what's wrong?"

"I was thinking of Ian and all the sick people in Shadowlands," replied Yasha in a soft, almost imperceptible voice. "My paintings are beautiful and good, and I make them to bring delight to everyone in Himmel. It breaks my heart when people become sick... utterly blind."

Aaron felt bad for even mentioning Ian to Yasha. He had no idea it would cause such distress. After his conversation with Thomas, he was at a loss as to how Ian could be part of Yasha's good and beautiful artwork. "So, Ian is made like you?"

"Yes, everyone is made like me." Yasha turned to Aaron with a penetrating gaze. "But as they get sicker, they become less and less like me. It's like the image of me becomes blurry to the point they can't recognize they're made like me."

Aaron's mind automatically turned to planning a solution. "Can you make them better? There must be a way."

"There is a way. At great cost." Yasha smiled at Aaron and wiped the tears from his face. "This is a matter for the future. Tonight, you're the guests of honor. We have a banquet to attend."

Aaron and Yasha strolled into the banquet room and were greeted by all their friends. The stately room had an elegant ambiance. The walls were adorned with gorgeous paintings of natural landscapes and sites in Himmel. A large sturdy wooden table marked the center of the room with a white linen tablecloth and ornate place settings in front of each seat. A large crystal chandelier radiated light through the room. Thomas, Sophia, and all the animals were chatting as they ate hors d'oeuvres.

Grace approached King Yasha and he whispered to her, "The guests of honor have arrived."

"King Yasha would like to welcome you all," called out Grace. She gestured for the guests to find their place. "Please take your seat and dinner will be served shortly."

Grace had arranged special seating for each guest so each of the animals had a place made specially for them to eat at the table. Servers in white suits brought out dishes of fresh grilled fish and vegetables, including carrots, broccoli, and potatoes. Freshly baked French bread with butter was laid out for each guest. Benji could hardly wait and grabbed a piece of bread when he heard Yasha's voice.

King Yasha stood with a glass in his hand. "A toast to our guests," he said. "May your visit to Himmel bring you an adventure into our good and beautiful kingdom." Everyone stood, toasted glasses, and cheered the children as guests of honor.

"If it's OK, I would like to propose a toast to our host, the King," said Thomas as he lifted his glass. "To our King, we give thanks and praise for your paintings and everything you do for the citizens of Himmel."

There was a whole lot of oohing and aahing among the guests. The chef at the chateau had a special skill in bringing resplendent flavors out of every kind and type of food. Each of the animals was served food to their liking, so even they were in a food festival like never before.

Hannah was eager to show off the etiquette skills her mom had taught her, this being dinner with a king and all. She held her fork in two fingers and lifted a tiny bit of grilled fish to her mouth. She closed her eyes and meticulously chewed the bite with her mouth closed. The taste was so extraordinary, she completely lost sight of her ladylike plan. "Wonderlicous," she yelled at the top of her lungs.

The room fell silent as everyone's eyes turned on Hannah. Her face blushed bright red and her eyes were as big as stars. After an uncomfortable moment, a boisterous howl came from Yasha as he stood and applauded Hannah, saying, "A girl with good taste. Wonderlicous, indeed."

"Sorry, but it is," said Hannah sheepishly. She scooped up some carrots with a big grin.

"Remember, we're family," replied King Yasha gazing at her, and then at Aaron and Benji. "You must have questions for me."

Aaron put down his fork and wiped his mouth with his napkin. "How big is your kingdom?"

"It's everything you see and even the things you can't see," replied Yasha. He directed his arm across the room taking in all of the beautiful paintings covering the walls.

"It felt like we saw thousands of miles of the kingdom when we traveled through Aspen Meadows, Asha Grasslands, and Sane Forest." Aaron recalled the vastness of the kingdom they had seen in just one and a half days. "How can we see so much... so quickly?"

"Ah, time and space," replied King Yasha as he took a bite of potatoes. "Time and space, or distance as you put it, work differently here in Himmel than in your world."

"How do you mean 'different'?" asked Aaron as he leaned in with bewildered curiosity. "Aren't time and distance kind of the same everywhere?"

"Himmel is far too vast to see everything, even in a lifetime." Yasha swiveled his head taking in the beautiful landscape paintings on the walls. "As part of my paintings, I compress time and distance, so people can enjoy the fullness of the kingdom. It's a gift to the people I love to bring delight."

Aaron shrugged his shoulders and shook his head in confusion. *Compress, that doesn't answer anything. He seems more interested in the why than he does with the how. Maybe I'll never fully understand the mysteries of Yasha and his kingdom. Maybe his ways are just simply higher than my ways.* Aaron's mind shifted to Shadowlands and his face crinkled as he thought about that dreary place Benji visited. "Jack Deer told us about the two provinces of Himmel, Highlands and Shadowlands. You mean you're king of all that?"

Yasha nodded his head at Aaron and filled his fork with grilled fish. "Yes, and even more."

"Are people free to go anywhere they want in Himmel?" asked Aaron. He savored his grilled fish as he stared at Yasha. "Their choice?"

"Yes, I've given people freedom to choose." Yasha glanced over at Thomas and Sophia. "When they choose wisely, it brings me immense happiness."

"Even Shadowlands?" Aaron's face grew serious as he recalled crazy Ian. "You let them choose Shadowlands?"

"Yes," Yasha said as he set his fork down and stared at Aaron like a laser beam. "That's an unwise choice, and it's very dangerous."

"What does Midnight Clover do to them?" asked Aaron. He grabbed a biscuit and took a big bite. "I saw Ian eating it."

"It's a very serious thing," replied Yasha. He looked down at his plate and wiped his eyes with his napkin. "Midnight Clover makes people sick. It causes a type of blindness and insanity. It's called Midnight Madness."

Benji had been listening closely trying to make sense of what he'd seen in Shadowlands "Your paintings are so good and beautiful." He pointed to the beautiful painting of deer grazing in a meadow of colorful flowers. "But Shadowlands is so ugly."

Yasha turned to Benji with a smile and said, "My paintings depict the goodness and beauty of Himmel, including Shadowlands, ... what is real and true. The image of Shadowlands I paint is far different than the Shadowlands you have seen or heard about."

Aaron interrupted, "What do you mean real and true?"

King Yasha took a sip of water and wiped his mouth with his napkin. "I'm the artist who made Himmel and I work to maintain it every day," he said. "That means I'm the ultimate source of what is real and true." Yasha's stare grew more penetrating as he added, "Anything else is counterfeit, a lie. This is a very important thing to know. Your safety depends on it."

Aaron sat up startled by the sternness of Yasha's warning. "That sounds serious. I'm glad we have Thomas, Sophia, and the animals to help us with that."

"They will be of great value, Aaron," replied Yasha with a gentle smile as he glanced at Aaron's new friends, "but you must know the difference as well."

Aaron lathered butter on a biscuit and said to Yasha, "You were telling us about Midnight Madness. You said it makes them insane?"

Yasha shook his head and turned back to Aaron. "Yes, thank you Aaron, back to that ghastly illness. People with Midnight Madness can't see the goodness and beauty in my paintings, so they begin to doubt." Aaron craned his neck forward with curiosity. "Doubt what?"

Yasha pointed to his chest with a pained look on his face and said, "Doubt me, doubt my goodness, my beauty. My paintings become blurred to people with Midnight Madness. They can't see them clearly."

"That's horrible," replied Aaron. He sensed the torment Midnight Madness caused Yasha. "It's like your paintings have been smudged."

"The worst part is that if left untreated, the doubt becomes so great the person begins to doubt what is real." Yasha swept his arm around the room pointing to the artwork. "They distrust me and my paintings and eventually depart from me."

Aaron leaned back replaying Ian's odd behavior in his mind. "I think crazy Ian was at that point."

"Shadowlands is full of people who suffer from Midnight Madness. That's why it's so dangerous there." King Yasha shook his head with a dower expression. "My paintings are not even recognizable in Shadowlands."

"Is there medicine to cure Midnight Madness?" asked Hannah. She slid a carrot to Riley, who was sitting next to her. "Can't you cure them?"

"There is, Hannah, but they have to want it." Yasha straightened up in his chair and handed another carrot to Riley as he smiled at Hannah. "Enough of this sad talk for now. I'll take you on a tour of Himmel tomorrow and we can talk more about this."

"My turn to ask a question," said Benji. "If you're the king, do you make all the rules in Himmel?"

"I do." Yasha took a bite of grilled fish and looked over at Benji with a reassuring smile. "There are a number of rules that govern how to live in peace together in Himmel. To make it simple, you can boil them down to two basic rules. First, love me and my paintings, and second love others."

Benji's face grew serious. Talk of rules was always a grave matter for Benji. "Why do we have to love your paintings?"

"My paintings are what is real in Himmel, and they include the best way to live in Himmel." King Yasha sat upright in his chair which gave him a commanding appearance. "You can call them rules. It's my direction on the best way to live in the kingdom I created. Doesn't that make sense?"

Benji saw how happy all the people and animals were in the City of Light and Highlands, so King Yasha made sense to him. But it still seemed like someone bossing him around. "I guess so. What if a person doesn't want to follow your rules?"

"People are free to choose," replied King Yasha as he glanced over to Thomas and Sophia. "But my rules help people, so that's the wise choice."

Benji ran everything through his mind straining to find an angle... a chink in the armor. "Do you ever make mistakes?"

"I see across the entire kingdom – both what has happened in the past and what will happen in the future. That allows me to carefully make each painting include perfect rules for the good of everyone in Himmel." Yasha leaned forward peering deep into Benji's eyes. "You can trust me; I care deeply for each person in my kingdom."

Benji began to lower his skepticism with Yasha, but he couldn't get over Shadowlands and crazy Ian. "Ian seemed to hate your paintings and your rules."

"Midnight Madness is a horrible thing." Yasha nodded at Benji with a look of concern and said, "They can't see and get confused about what is good and beautiful. As their sickness worsens, their rebellion against me grows."

Benji's anger towards crazy Ian, Birsha, and Julia started to turn to compassion. They could be as happy as Thomas, Sophia, and the others he had met in the City of Light, if only they could see properly. "That's very sad that the blindness twists their minds so badly."

The conversation made Aaron think about what Papa had said to him: *Wisdom is the vision to see the difference between the good and beautiful and the evil and ugly.* He now saw what Papa meant and it pushed him to explore these ideas even more.

"I'll tell you more about this tomorrow on our tour." Yasha could see this topic required more time than the evening provided, so he turned his attention to Hannah.

"My turn," said Hannah. "There's a big fountain below our balcony. It's very beautiful. What's it called?"

"It's called Gali Fountain. It feeds the streams, lakes, and ponds." Yasha was pleased to hear a question that was lighter and more cheerful. "It supplies all the water throughout Himmel. I replenish it daily so it will refresh and sustain all the living creatures and plants."

Hannah took a big drink of water and grinned at Yasha. "We drank some on our trip here. It's very cold and fresh."

"It certainly is," said Yasha lifting up a glass filled with fresh water. "It's a source of flourishing for the whole kingdom. You might even call it living water."

"Speaking of water…" Hannah stood to make sure her voice carried to Yasha. "We played a zany game of Ziggety-Zag with Mr. Wigglebottom on Lake Amari."

"I'm so pleased you had fun," Yasha said, giving them a self-satisfied smile. "I particularly like that little bit of amusement I added to the lake. The fish find it rousing fun as well."

"But how do you do that?" asked Hannah. "We walked on water."

"The artist can create anything in his imagination, Hannah." Yasha smiled and picked up his water glass. "I added a little exhilarating play to my painting of the lake. Beauty comes in many forms. Tomfoolery can be beautiful too."

***

After dinner, servers brought platters of pastries for dessert. The guests moved to small tables around the room to enjoy their dessert and tea in more intimate settings. Benji grabbed a cherry tart and apple turnover and sat at a small glass table by himself in the corner.

"May I join you?" asked Yasha taking a seat next to Benji. "I see you're a fan of desserts."

"Sure," said Benji. He really wanted to sit in peace and gobble up his pastries, but he couldn't bring himself to turn down King Yasha, him being the king and all.

"Thank you for asking about rules in Himmel, Benji," said Yasha. His eyes widened as he watched Benji hoover up the cherry tart. "I know you don't like rules. You have to live with a lot of them at home, don't you?"

Benji finished chewing his tart, swallowed, and wiped the crumbs off his face. "Yeah, they're always telling me what to do."

"Having a big brother can be tough." Yasha glanced toward Aaron who was enjoying a pastry nearby with Hannah. "Your dad and mom tell you what to do, and then your big brother does on top of that."

Benji's face grew serious. "I don't have a dad right now, he's missing. Aaron acts like my dad."

"I'm sorry your dad's missing, Benji." Yasha placed his hand on Benji's shoulder. "That must be a very scary thing for you."

"I try not to think about it. I hope he comes back, but I never know." Benji put down his fork and wiped away some cherry that was stuck on his face. His appetite was fading with the thought of his dad. "He's a Navy Seal and his job is super dangerous."

"He's a very brave man." Yasha shifted in his seat as he thought of Peter. "It saddens me to hear your father is missing."

"It doesn't seem fair." Benji sat defiantly staring at Yasha. "My dad is missing, and all my friends' dads aren't missing."

"The world can seem unfair, Benji." Yasha leaned in closer to Benji. "But I can assure you, all things will work out for good in the end to those who love me."

"What's my dad have to do with rules?" asked Benji. He thought that all the talk of his dad was ruining this absolutely scrumptious dessert-fest.

Yasha raised his eyebrow and peered at Benji. "I think maybe you're angry about your dad being missing, so you don't want to follow any rules."

"I tried following rules like a good little boy, and my dad still went missing."

Benji's face became blazing red. "What's the point of following rules?"

Yasha leaned back in his chair. "Do you know why I have the two rules I mentioned earlier?"

Benji took a deep breath as he tried to collect himself. "I guess because that's the way you want it and you're the king."

"That's true." Yasha laughed at Benji's bluntness. "I want it that way because it's what's best for you and everyone in Himmel."

Benji returned to his thoughts. *He's back to his rules. Always rules with these adults. Can't I have even a little freedom?* "OK, but it would be nice to be able to decide what I eat and when I do homework."

"You tried that didn't you?" King Yasha laughed as he took a bite of apple turnover. "How was your visit to Shadowlands?"

Benji's eyes widened at Yasha's question. "Aah, how'd you know I went there?"

"I know everything that goes on in Himmel," Yasha smirked as he chewed his turnover. "Did you like being your own king?"

"It was fun at first. The ice cream and chocolate cake were out of this world." Benji set down his fork and looked up to Yasha. "Then it got worse when Julia went crazy about being a lion. And big Nick, don't get me started on him."

"That's what the world would be like if everyone got to be king," said King Yasha.

Benji's mind was whirling, *He's got a point. It was horrendous in Shadowlands.* "So maybe some rules are OK."

Yasha sat up and clasped his hands together. He said, "Let me try to explain the two rules. On the first rule, if you love me, you'll love the things I love. You're giving me honor as the painter who made Himmel and maintains it every day."

"That makes sense," Benji nodded and said, even letting a crease of a smile emerge. "But loving others seems too hard. People can be mean, or bossy, or lie, or cheat, or do all kinds of terrible things."

"That's true, Benji," replied Yasha. "But loving them is still the right thing to do. Loving others means treating them as I would treat them. That's why I have the second rule."

Benji's mind still fluttered with skepticism, *what's the angle.* "Even if they don't deserve it?"

"If it were about deserving it, a lot of people would not be loved. It has nothing to do with deserving it." Yasha looked into Benji's eyes with a deep penetrating gaze. "Under your rules, what should we do about a boy who cheats on a test at school to get a prize? Should that boy still be loved? Think about the other students who didn't cheat and who didn't get a prize. Was it loving of that boy to cheat?"

Benji felt the blood rush to his head and he got dizzy as he reflected on what King Yasha said. He was mystified that Yasha knew about his shenanigans at school. "Aah, I guess not."

"You see, my two rules bring about a world where everyone treats each other with kindness and respect. A world that is good and beautiful." King Yasha drew close to Benji and placed his hand on his head. In a soft, almost imperceptible voice, he whispered, "The things we love tell us who we are."

Benji began to whimper and leaned over to embrace Yasha with every bit of strength he could muster. Yasha had reached a place inside him that was broken and, he thought, beyond repair. His heart felt different, softer, more tender. He was beginning to understand what the two rules meant in his own life, and he wanted desperately to start living this way.

***

Aaron and Hannah walked up to Benji's table as he and King Yasha were embracing. "Are we interrupting anything?" asked Aaron.

"No, we were just finishing our conversation." Yasha said. Benji sat back in his chair, and Yasha moved a couple more chairs up to the table. "Please join us. I want to hear about your family. I have not seen them in a very long time, but so enjoyed their company when they were young. How are your mom and dad, and your Papa and Grandma?"

They spent the rest of the evening telling Yasha all about their parents, Papa and Grandma, the Ranch and all that was going on with their family. After candles had burned down to nubs, they retired to the guest suite and drifted off to sleep with a peace they had never felt before.

Chapter Fourteen

Kingdom Tour

⸻ ❧ ⸻

They woke up to the gentle trickle of the Gali Fountain outside their balcony window. Grace showed them to King Yasha who was busy on the patio putting the finishing touches on his painting.

"I thought we'd visit Lake Enid and then Mt. Superior today." Yasha laid down his brush to greet his guests. "I think you've seen most of Aspen Meadows, Asha Grasslands, and Sane Forest, but the western part of Highlands has some beautiful sights too."

"Can our friends go too?" asked Aaron. He subtly strained to get a peek at tomorrow's painting, but King Yasha was blocking it with his body. "They wouldn't want to miss this."

"Certainly, Grace is seeing to it." Yasha stepped away from his painting. "I'll finish this later. We'll meet them at Gali Fountain."

Aaron filled their canteens at Gali Fountain as they waited for the others to join them. The fountain was made of white marble with a large statue of a tree in the middle of it. Extending from the tree's highest branches were white doves flying into the air. The water was cold and pure and was the best tasting water he had ever had. The fountain flowed into a channel that fed into the City of Light stream leading to the water system for the entire kingdom of Himmel.

"I think everyone's here," said King Yasha as he surveyed the large group. "Shall we go?"

"Where are we going first?" asked Aaron. He was uneasy about the mystery of the day's agenda. Not only did he have no say in the itinerary, but he also had no idea how to plan for what lay ahead. He was several zip codes away from his comfort zone.

Yasha sensed Aaron's inner turmoil, so he pulled out a map and handed it to Aaron. "We'll follow the stream down to Lake Enid and have lunch there." Aaron quickly grabbed the map and began analyzing the itinerary in his head.

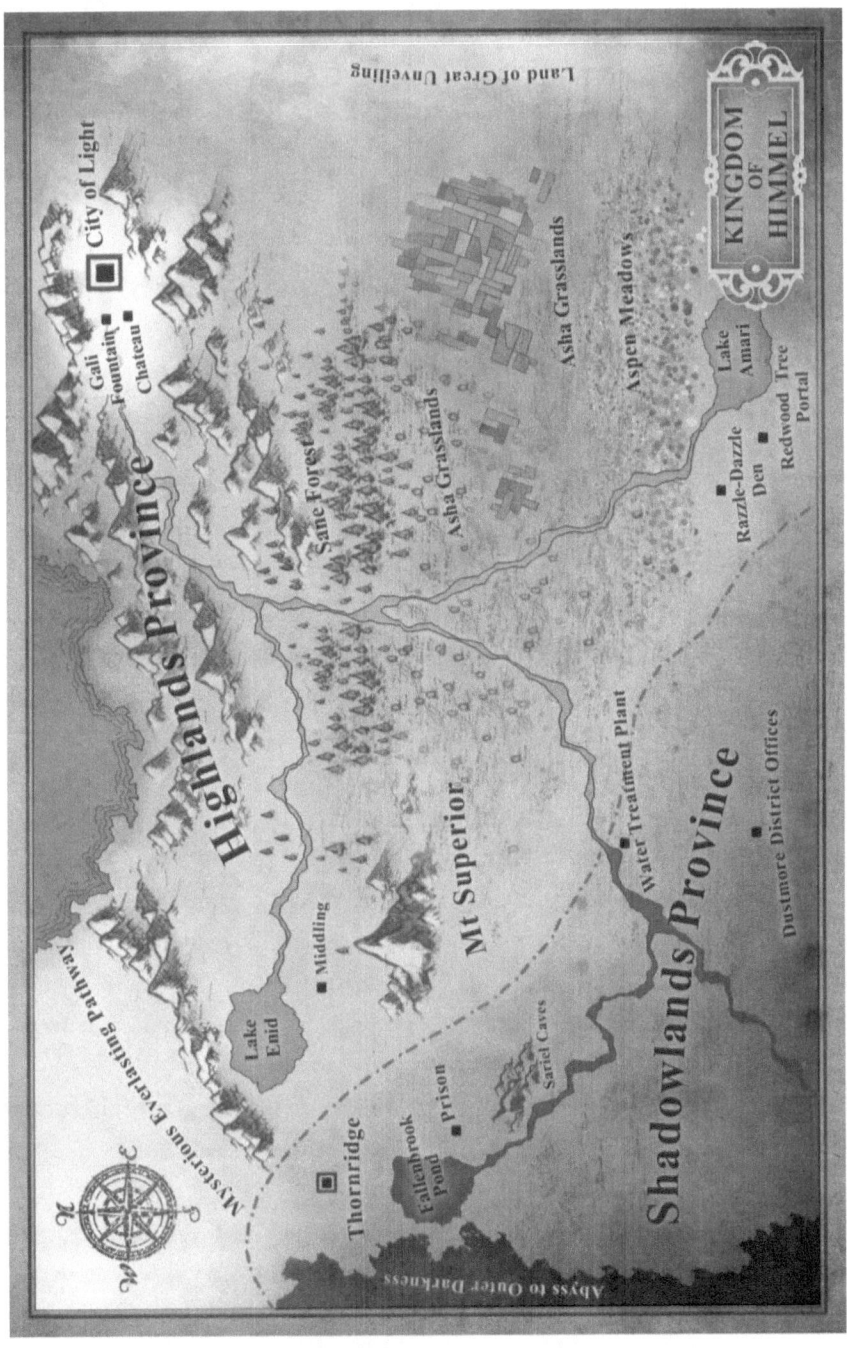

"We learned a new song from Enzo Fawn," said Hannah. She ran alongside Yasha. "Can we sing it?"

"I love Enzo's songs," replied Yasha. He laughed and stroked Enzo's back as they hiked along the trail. "Please share it with me."

Hannah started the song, but soon they were all singing it as they hiked toward Lake Enid. Except Aaron, who was buried in his map.

You've made the day for my delight.
You bring us warmth and light.
And keep us safe at night.
You guard our lives with your love and might.
Oh, what a good and beautiful King.

"Aah, one of my favorites. Lovely, Hannah," said King Yasha.

The hike to Lake Enid was beautiful and not too difficult. They traveled through the western side of Sane Forrest and listened to a chorus of birds chirping their unique melodies in the trees. Aaron, Benji, and Hannah were amazed by the splendor of their surroundings and enjoyed watching their friends. Jack Deer saw deer families and stopped to chat along the way. Piper Bear met a friend, and they went into the stream to catch fish. Riley Raccoon chased squirrels and stopped to share a snack with a fellow raccoon. When they reached Lake Enid, Yasha directed them to a large rock perched along the lake.

"This is a nice spot with a wonderful view." Yasha pulled three swimsuits and towels from his backpack. "Would you like to take a swim before lunch? Grace packed your swimsuits."

"Is this lake like Lake Amari with the Ziggety-Zag?" asked Aaron. "It'll be hard to swim if we can walk on the water."

"No, it's very swimmable," replied Yasha. "In fact, I made something special just for you. Take a look at that rock."

Aaron walked toward the giant rock and saw a gigantic water slide carved into the rock. Fresh water rushed down the slide making it smooth and shiny. "It must be a hundred yards long," yelled Aaron.

"Awesome," shouted Benji. He inspected it further and saw that it extended into the trees above the rock. "It's huge!"

"It's actually several hundred yards long and sprinkled with twists and turns to keep you on your toes," said Yasha as he held out the swimsuits and towels. "I made it for your delight, which in turn brings me great joy."

Aaron, Benji, and Hannah found privacy behind some nearby bushes and changed into their swimsuits. They climbed up to the top of the rock and hiked back to the beginning of the water slide. They were a long way from the lake, looking down the immense slide to a tiny Yasha, Thomas, Sophia, and the animals below.

Aaron studied Benji and Hannah as they stared down the water slide. He said, "I'll go first to make sure it's safe." He felt the brisk water rushing down the slide and it only increased the nervous energy running through his body.

"I think I'll pass," said Hannah as she inched backward away from the slide. "It looks too big and too scary for me."

"You don't have to if you don't want to," said Aaron. He gripped the slide and jumped up to land in a sitting position at the start of the slide. "Once I get down, I'll yell to give you the green light."

"Geronimo," yelled Aaron as he let go to begin his descent. The rushing water made the slide slippery and fast. The upper portion of the slide traveled through the tree line, so Aaron was in a canopy of green flashing by as he whizzed downward. The sides were perfectly made to keep him safely in the slide, even with all the crazy twists and turns. As he zipped along, his eyes widened as he focused on a ginormous loop ahead. He closed his eyes and braced for the tumult. It felt like he was doing a summersault at high speed as his body did a 360-degree spin through the loop. His heart was beating fast as he hurtled down the slide toward the lake. The final section of the slide was open air with a grand view of the lake and surrounding countryside. The slope of the slide eased, which slowed his speed and gave him the opportunity to take in the majestic views. Suddenly, he reached the end of the slide and flew through the air the final five feet, landing in the deep clear lake water below. The water was cool, clean, and felt refreshing after the long hike from City of Light.

175

Aaron popped his head above the surface with a big grin on his face. "All clear," he shouted. "Let Hannah go next, and I'll wait for her in the lake."

"You go, Benji," said Hannah. "I'll walk down and jump in the lake down below."

Benji jumped on the slide and flew down the slide screaming all the way. He was half yelling and half laughing as his body zoomed down the slide ending with a big splash in the lake. "That's the most awesome water slide I've ever been on. Way more wild than any boogieboard ride," he yelled.

"I thought you'd like it," called out Yasha as he got to his feet and walked to the edge of the rock to get a look at the boys splashing in the water.

Hannah jumped off the rock next to the lake and began splashing her brothers. The animals had been watching the excitement of the children going down the water slide but were also hot and tired from the walk. They waded into the lake for a drink but didn't stray far from the shoreline. They all spent the next hour playing in the water to cool off. Afterward, they gathered back on the rock to have lunch.

Yasha pulled three apples from his backpack and handed one to each of the children. "See the city off to the west in the distance?" asked Yasha as he pointed westward.

"Yeah, what is it?" asked Aaron. He set his apple down and removed binoculars from his backpack to get a better look.

"Thornridge, the capital city of Shadowlands," replied Yasha. "Lake Enid is very close to the border of Shadowlands."

Aaron peered through his binoculars surveying the people and activity. "You said it's dangerous in Shadowlands."

"So, it is." Yasha took a bite of his apple and looked over the lake towards Thornridge. "Remember what I told you about Midnight Clover?"

"Yeah," replied Aaron as he lowered his binoculars and took a big bite out of his apple. "What about it?"

"There's more to the story." Yasha took a bite of his apple and hesitated before continuing. "It didn't come to Himmel on its own."

"Jack said it started in Shadowlands and spread to Highlands," said Aaron. He took another bite of his apple. "We saw some on the way to City of Light. Crazy Ian was lying in it."

"That's right. But it was created by someone very dangerous." Yasha peered into Aaron's eyes. "His name is Malby."

Aaron stopped chewing and swiveled his eyes to Yasha and then Jack. "Who's Malby?"

"He was once my gardener to help look after the gardens in the City of Light," said Yasha. He tossed his apple core into the nearby bushes as a present for the local critters and brought out small loaves of bread and blocks of cheese. "He maintained all the grounds in the city just as I designed them in my paintings."

Aaron perked his ears and leaned toward King Yasha. "What happened?"

"He thought he was a better gardener than me. He thought he was a better painter than me." Yasha shook his head with a disappointed expression as he handed each of the children a loaf of bread and block of cheese. "He started to change my paintings and the grounds of the City of Light."

"Sounds like he doesn't like rules either," chimed in Benji as he chewed on his apple. "I can relate to this Malby guy."

Aaron rolled his eyes at Benji, turned to Yasha, and said, "What a terrible thing to do." He tossed a small stone into the lake and watched the ripples expand across the water.

King Yasha continued, "His jealousy grew over time and eventually he was filled with hatred for me and my paintings." He peered into the lake watching the ripples move across the water. "I had to banish him from the City of Light and he fled to the far end of the kingdom."

"Is that Shadowlands?" asked Aaron. He pointed westward toward Thornridge. "Where Benji went?"

"I went to Dustmore, the District Office of the southern region of Shadowlands," chimed in Benji. "But it's all part of the same horrible Shadowlands."

"Yes, Shadowlands goes from Thornridge, its capital, in the north all the way down past Dustmore in the south. Anyway, that's how Shadowlands became Shadowlands." Yasha tossed a stone into the lake setting off another endless series of ripples. "Before Malby, it was a beautiful region of Himmel.

"Where did Midnight Clover come from?" Aaron was curious to find out every detail he could about Shadowlands and Malby. He kept thinking about what Papa had told him, *the vision to tell the difference.*

"Malby is very talented with plants. He started experimenting with various kinds of plants and eventually came up with Midnight Clover." Yasha paused to take a long drink of water. "He wanted to develop a plant that would blind people to the goodness and beauty of Himmel and turn them away from me."

"Why are you telling us?" asked Aaron. He ripped apart a piece of bread with his mouth.

"The Midnight Clover is spreading deeper into Highlands and more and more people are getting sick." Yasha stood up and brushed the dust off his pants. "The survival of Himmel is in jeopardy, and I want your help."

Aaron stopped chewing and stared at Yasha. "How can we possibly be of any help? You're the King."

"Let's continue our tour. I want to show you Mt. Superior." Yasha got to his feet and strapped his backpack on. "I'll tell you more when we get there."

***

The carefree hike through the scenic country had taken an abrupt turn. Aaron was uneasy about what he had heard. He was beginning to question whether they should even continue the tour. He thought maybe he could politely say they had to go and return to the redwood tree and leave all this behind. He was the oldest, and his mom and dad expected him to keep Benji and Hannah safe. He pulled out his compass and saw that the trail they were on was taking them south back in the general direction of Aspen Meadows and Lake Amari. He decided to keep his concerns to himself as they hiked along the trail, for he knew he might have to find a way to abandon this adventure.

"See that city off to the left," said Yasha. "That's Middling. You can find things you may need in the general store."

"What things might we need?" asked Aaron. Yasha's comment only made his concerns grow.

"It's hard to say right now," replied Yasha. He trekked along humming to himself like a man without a care in the world. "But good to keep in mind."

They continued hiking south until they got to the base of a large mountain. It was a steep climb up the narrow trail. The group had to go single file during most of the hike up Mt. Superior. Hannah was getting tired, so Piper Bear carried her on her back for the last part of the hike. Finally, they reached a small plateau overlooking a valley to the west.

"This is a good place to rest," said King Yasha. He took a seat on the large rock ledge. "Do you see that rock formation off to the west?"

"Yeah, what about it?" asked Aaron. He pulled out his binoculars for a closer look. "I don't see any activity."

"Those are called the Sariel Caves. There's something going on there. Something about a Project Raven."

"Why is the stream so dark?" asked Benji. He pointed to the steam in Shadowlands running past the caves.

"Malby built a water treatment plant at the border of Shadowlands." Yasha pointed further south. "All the fresh pure water gets mixed with Midnight Clover in the facility and then released back into the stream."

"One other thing; Malby has guards stationed along the border to Shadowlands." Yasha stood up and pointed to a group of guards with a menacing demeanor about them. "No one comes in or leaves without a crown or passport."

"I don't see how we can help," said Aaron. He was still weighing the situation carefully and leaned toward abandoning the entire trip. "Can't you just paint a new painting where all this goes away?"

"I wish it were that easy," replied Yasha. "They're blind and in full rebellion against my goodness and beauty. They're making unwise choices with the freedom they've been given."

Aaron stayed silent for a minute as he pondered the implications of what Yasha was saying. "But why us?"

Yasha looked at Aaron earnestly, glanced over to Benji and Hannah, and back to Aaron, garnering all of their attention. "I have known your family for many generations, ever since they first bought the Ranch. I warned your Papa that there would come a day when I would call on the Parsons family to do a very important job." Yasha paused, letting his words sink it. "That time has come. The three of you are here for such a time as this."

"So, what should we do?" asked Aaron. Papa's last words resonated in his head. *Take care of yourself and your brother and sister… Parsons Cord.*

"You'll need to find out what their plans are." Yasha moved close to the children and placed his hand on Aaron's shoulder. "And then come up with a way to defeat them."

Benji felt energized by the tour and King Yasha's faith in their ability to be his warriors in a battle against Malby. "Are there special tools or weapons you have for us?"

"I've given your family everything you need to defeat them." King Yasha smiled at Benji and tussled his curly blond hair. "But you must be wise and clever with what I've given you."

"I don't know if we're big enough to defeat them," said Hannah. She inched toward Aaron and reached out for his hand. "That Ian boy was huge and as ornery as a bull."

"Not to worry, Hannah." King Yasha glanced over to Thomas, Sophia, Jack and the other animals. "Your new friends from Himmel will help you."

"What about your guards, Mike and Gabe?" asked Aaron. His mind searched for ways to reduce the risk for himself and his brother and sister. "They'd scare them right away."

King Yasha paused for a moment to consider the suggestion. "They need to stay at the chateau with me. There's much to protect there."

King Yasha's face broke into a soft smile and a reassuring sparkle filled his eyes. "I know this is a very hard thing I have asked of you, but I've chosen your family especially for this job because I know you can do it and I trust that you will do it." King Yasha held up two crossed fingers. "Your family has lived on the Ranch for a long, long time… for such a time as this. I'll be watching over you every moment and you can call on me anytime."

Aaron, Benji, and Hannah hiked in silence back to the chateau. It had been a remarkable day in many ways, but they felt a great weight on their shoulders as they considered King Yasha's request. Aaron felt ill equipped to take on this challenge. He also had to consider the safety of Benji and Hannah. Papa had told him to weigh big decisions carefully and not rush. That's exactly what he intended to do.

Chapter Fifteen

A Secret War

———— ～◦◯◦～ ————

"He'll see you now," said the young woman sitting at the reception desk. Fister stood up and glided into the presidential office to speak with Malby.

Fister was a tall muscular man with long dark hair that he wrapped in a tight man bun atop his head, giving him the look of someone who'd been experimenting with hair gel that got very far out of hand. He wore a lime green custom-tailored suit. A bright yellow pocket square was meticulously shining from his breast pocket. He had expensive tastes and lived by the motto: *You need to project success to achieve success.*

"Your Most Royal Eminence, it's very unfortunate what happened to Troy," said Fister. He placed his hand on his cheek and grimaced at Malby. "Such a tragedy."

Malby glared at Fister. "Shadowlands can be a very dangerous place…" Malby flashed a menacing smirk before finishing. "…if you're not careful."

Fister began to sit in a stiff chair across from Malby's desk but froze momentarily at the evil oozing from Malby. Attempting to lighten the mood, he said, "Oh my goodness gracious, I can't imagine how such a robust man could meet his fate in a hiking accident."

"Perhaps your predecessor tried to ascend higher than his limits?" Malby stood up and walked to the window of his presidential office in the capitol building. "You come highly recommended, Fister."

Fister made a theatrical genuflection before Malby. "You're too kind, your Excellent Eminence."

"Troy's untimely demise has left a gaping hole in my media relations plan." Malby was already growing annoyed by Fister's overly dramatic mannerisms, but he appreciated the flattery. "Media relations is a crucial ingredient in my reign."

"And your masterful leadership of Shadowlands is truly awe-inspiring, your Exalted Eminence." Fister removed a notebook from his breast pocket.

"I am honored to contribute what meager skills I have for the benefit of your stunning vision."

"Let us hope so," Malby sneered, turning and glaring at Fister. "Discretion is another skill I highly value. Are you discreet?"

"Oh my, your Most Excellent Eminence." Fister giggled with a wry smile on his face. He raised his index finger to place it over his lips. "Secrets are too delicious to share with the world. They shall be our private oasis of merriment."

Malby was having a tough time interpreting Fister's odd personality. But he simply marinated in Fister's fawning adulation. He overlooked the pomp and moved on to more pressing matters. "We're in a war, Fister. Do you know that?"

Fister leaned back on his chair, raised his knee, and grabbed it with both hands. "War sounds so sinister. What kind of war doth thee wage, your Imperial Eminence."

"A secret war." Malby pounded his fist on his desk. "A war for all of Himmel."

"I don't see any armies or battles sir." Fister tilted his head with a coy smile. "Where's the war?"

"It's in the minds and hearts of the people, Fister." Malby glared at Fister. He had the urge to rip Fister's hair out of the tight little bun. The task at hand was too important, so he resisted the impulse and continued. "But still, it's a very real war. There will be a winner and a loser."

Fister leaned close to Malby, his face just inches away from his boss, revealing a disturbing smile. "Who has the unfortunate fate of being our enemy, your Supreme Eminence?"

Malby's pale complexion became fiery red as he hissed, "King Yasha and everything he stands for."

"I see." Fister drew his head back and cackled. He didn't have any personal grudge against King Yasha, but the great ship of his advancement was tied to Malby. The idea of waging war against the king was not an unpleasant thought, as long as Malby won. "What ingenious plan has your Unrivaled Eminence devised to conduct this war to bring about a magnificent victory?"

"We're already waging war. It's been going on for a long time." Malby's face relaxed and returned to its pasty color. "I'm bringing you on to take over where Troy failed."

Fister gulped as he stepped away from Malby. "Failed? Sir."

"He failed to appreciate the stakes and had a weak spine," Malby said. "Couldn't do what it takes." Malby stepped close to Fister and glared into his eyes. "Are you willing to do what it takes... Fister?"

Fister pursed his lips and shot a toothy grin at Malby. "Your one and only Eminence, I can be a very naughty boy."

"I have a top-secret plan that guarantees our victory," Malby said as he sat back at his desk and pulled a thick folder from his drawer. "It's a five-point plan. I call it the Road to Destruction. I must say, it's brilliant. If you want to turn the people against King Yasha, you must change their loyalty, their affections."

"It's absolutely sickening the way they fawn over King Yasha," said Fister. He was oblivious to his own tendencies in this area with regard to Malby. "Disgusting, your Regal Eminence."

"My plan takes them on a journey down a road that leads to destruction and chaos." Malby pounded his desk. "The first stop is doubt."

"Doubt, sir?" asked Fister as he stroked his glistening hair.

"Doubt is a powerful weapon." Malby grabbed a marble pen holder off his desk and tossed it in his hand. "It can do tremendous damage."

Fister stood behind his chair stretching his legs as if he were about to take a run. "Doubt what, sir?"

"Doubt anything, everything." Malby set down the pen holder and pointed out the window to the dark clouds in the sky. "What you see, hear, read. One small doubt leads to two, then three, ultimately everything is in doubt."

"I see, your Grand Eminence." Fister sat back down and started writing in his notebook. "To help me craft the media strategy for your ingenious plan, what would you say is the .... ultimate doubt?"

"King Yasha and his paintings. Their beauty, their goodness." Malby picked up a teapot, poured a cup of tea, and handed it to Fister. "On this first step, we have help."

Fister daintily held the saucer and picked up the teacup with his thumb and index finger. He pursed his lips as he tried to drink it. "Ooh, a tad hot...What help, your Excellence?"

"Midnight Clover." Malby pointed out the window toward the dark hillside in the distance. "We've developed a special hybrid that affects the mind to bring on a blindness to what is real."

"How enchanting, your Eminence." Fister puckered his lips and let out a gentle puff of air on his teacup. "How does Midnight Clover play into this Road to Destruction?"

"It's part of the plan but operates across all five points." Malby waved his hand. "Too much detail for today. It's called Project Raven. Middie is developing the Midnight Clover and Dusty is training the ravens. You'll get more on that later."

Fister set down his tea and scribbled a note: *More on Project Raven.* "Yes, of course your Resplendent Eminence."

Malby pounded his desk with two loud thumps. "The second stop on their journey is distrust and disbelief. As doubt grows, the mind travels to a place of distrust and disbelief."

Fister wrapped both arms around his chest flashing a smirk at Malby. "Enchanting, your Eminence...Distrust in what way?"

"Distrust is where doubt turns away from King Yasha." Malby said, stirring his tea for a moment. "King Yasha's paintings aren't beautiful or good. Maybe they're not even real. If they're not real, King Yasha can't be trusted. Maybe he's a liar."

Fister scribbled madly in his notebook. "I see the true genius of your mind, your Radiant Eminence. I can work with this. What else?"

"The third stop on the journey is to depart," Malby declared, delivering three booming thumps to the desk. "Being overcome with a sense of distrust, they will depart from King Yasha."

Fister began playing with his man bun, toying with the hair and rewrapping it. "Depart? You mean turn against King Yasha as king?"

"I mean turn against King Yasha in every way." Malby stared into his teacup and paid no attention to Fister's odd hair fetish. "As king, as artist, as the author of what is good and beautiful. Everything."

Fister finally gave his hair a rest and picked up his pencil. "Where will they depart to?"

"That's the beauty of this plan; it doesn't matter." Malby smiled into his teacup as he considered the prospect of all the citizens of Himmel departing from King Yasha. "We're going to make them wandering stars, Fister. Wandering stars."

Fister removed his yellow handkerchief and gently rubbed the beads of sweat on his forehead. "Wandering stars, sir?"

Malby stood up frustrated with Fister's obtuseness. "What are stars used for, Fister?"

Fister straightened his purple tie and puckered his lips in a strange circular motion. "I don't know, I guess navigation. We set direction by referencing them."

"Very good." A small smile emerged on Malby's face as he reassessed Fister. *Maybe this smarmy fashionista can be useful.* "So, what good is a wandering star that doesn't have a fixed location?"

"That's simply devilish, your Supreme Eminence." Fister muttered, nodding and scribbling more notes. "Once they depart from King Yasha, they'll be travelers lost on a journey . . . wandering stars that point away from King Yasha."

"Precisely. That brings us to the fourth stop on our journey." Malby landed four more blows to his desk. "Replacement."

Fister felt like he was playing a game of dodgeball as he tried to keep pace with Malby. "Replacement? Your most devious one."

"When they depart from King Yasha, they must replace the hole in their heart with something else." Malby looked at Fister to see if he understood. Fister felt the beads of sweat forming on his forehead as he battled to keep up with his sinister boss. He dabbed his forehead with his yellow handkerchief again as Malby continued, "You see my good Fister, the heart was made to have something at the center of it. If it's not King Yasha, then something else will fill the void."

"And what delicious morsel might that be, your Ingenious Eminence?" asked Fister. He broke into a coy smile.

"We don't care. It can be anything… fame, money, power, popularity, food, sports championships, good grades. The list is limitless." Malby stood and picked up a crown from the bookshelf next to his desk. "These crowns will be our replacement for King Yasha."

"I thought freedom was at the center of the crowns and kingships of Shadowlands." Fister crossed his legs and flapped his arms like a bird. "It's all about liberty… freedom to soar."

"And it is on the surface." Malby gave a sly look to Fister. "Each person is free to create their own kingdom – as long as King Yasha is not at the center of it."

Fister brought his hands down and stared at Malby with a quizzical look. "So, it is about liberty."

"Oh, on the contrary. You see, the final destination of our journey is prison." Malby held the crown over his head and laughed. "They believe they're kings and queens, but the reality is they will have voluntarily locked themselves into a prison of their own making."

Fister began nodding his head up and down with an exaggerated flair, causing his hair to slip and sway. "And we're the jailer."

"Exactly. They will have traveled along a road that leads them to a locked prison cell of their own making." Malby cackled as he glared at Fister. "There's no way out."

"Oh my, your Glorious Eminence. A plan of supreme brilliance." Fister held his pinky finger to his mouth and winked at Malby. "Besides Midnight Clover and the crowns, what other arrows are in our quiver?"

"Two very important weapons," Malby snickered to himself as he strolled back to the window gazing out at the courtyard below. "One held by us and the other by the people."

Fister leaned forward with his pencil to paper and his ear turned to Malby in a strange way. "What's our weapon?"

"Deception, Fister. I understand you're uniquely adept in that area." Malby sat back down in his chair, still fiddling with the crown. "Truth is what we make it. That's Yasha's Achilles heel. He will never move one inch off the truth."

"Excuse me, your Learned Eminence, but what's an Achilles and why does it have a heel? I beg you, enlighten me," asked Fister.

Malby rolled his eyes in frustration. "Not a fan of Greek mythology, I see. Achilles was the famous, mythical Greek warrior who attempted to conquer Troy. When their god Apollo stepped in and said Achilles would never succeed, Achilles ignored him. A Trojan archer named Paris, with Apollo's help, aimed a single arrow and shot Achilles here…" Malby said, raising his pant leg and pointing to the long tendon attaching his leg to his heel that controlled movement of the leg. "It put him down, immediately and made him an easy target for his enemy."

"Ah, I see. Deception is the sweet arrow of victory, your Most Dissembling Eminence." Fister puckered his lips and sipped his tea. "If deception is a weapon, where are we aiming it?"

"The easy things, Fister." Malby picked up a donut and took a bite. "These are good for you, right?" If we can tempt them to do the unimportant things, the easy things, through deception, they'll do the hard things without even being asked."

Fister struggled to draw the connection between eating donuts and deceiving the people. "Your Most Gracious Eminence, please elaborate on your delectable donut of deceit."

"If we deceive the people into believing they can be kings and queens and rule over their own kingdom," Malby said as he took a big bite out of his donut and slowly chewed it, "then they'll become our soldiers in this war against King Yasha without even knowing it."

"Brilliant, sir." Fister jumped to his feet and began applauding Malby with his back arched and his head held high. After an uncomfortably long time, he sat back down letting out a theatrical breath. "The second weapon?"

"Selfishness." Malby held up the crown again. "People have an insatiable love for themselves."

"How do we use that against them?" Fister didn't have the vaguest idea that he was particularly susceptible to this weapon.

"Selfishness is the fuel that drives the entire Road to Destruction, Fister." Malby repeated the five points pounding his fist on the table with each one. "Each stop along the journey, their own selfishness will push them to the next destination. It's the fuel that never runs out and will propel them to become wandering stars in our secret war."

"True genius, sir." Fister stood and saluted to Malby. His embellished hairstyle, lime-green suit and yellow handkerchief made the whole scene very unmilitary like.

"One final thing." Malby glared at Fister to impress upon him the importance of what he was about to say. "When I said top-secret, you and I are the only two people who know the full Road to Destruction plan. Others know parts related to their roles, but you need to see the big picture if you're going to run my media relations."

Fister sat back down and placed his finger to his lips. "Thank you for your confidence, your Most Trusting Eminence."

"Guard this with your life, Fister." Malby pointed to a mountain outside the window. "Shadowlands is a dangerous place as our friend Troy found out."

Fister gulped and placed his yellow pocket square back in his jacket. "Yes, sir, with my life."

"Consider this your orientation. Get me the media strategy ASAP." Malby stood up to shake hands with Fister signaling the meeting was over. "We have a lot to catch up on with Troy's unfortunate accident."

Fister left the presidential office exhilarated by his new role and the charter he had been given. Crafting the media strategy for his Eminence was the privilege of a lifetime. And the stakes couldn't be higher. Still, he had a sense of dread that he could easily meet the same fate as Troy. His Eminence was not a patient man and had exceptionally exacting standards.

Chapter Sixteen
Spy Craft

They were exhausted when they got to the chateau. Aaron asked Grace if they could have dinner served in the guest suite. He told Thomas, Sophia, and his animal friends to come to his guest suite at 7 o'clock. This would give him time to take a hot shower and do some planning... and talk to Benji and Hannah. The large suite had plenty of room for the group with a large sitting area away from the bedroom. The large sturdy table was plenty big for planning and the sofa and chairs would do nicely for the guests.

The sound of Gali Fountain trickled in the background as Aaron sat down to debrief with Benji and Hannah before the other guests arrived.

Aaron placed a notepad on the table and wrote out a chart of pros and cons. "What'd you think of today?"

"Lake Enid was awesome," replied Benji as he rubbed his freshly washed hair with a towel. "That water slide was epic."

"Yasha's so nice," said Hannah. Her hair was wrapped in a towel after a long relaxing shower. "He's simply glorious."

Aaron sighed. "I mean, what do you think about what King Yasha said about Midnight Clover and Project Raven?"

"I don't know. Part of me wants to help, but what's in it for us?" asked Benji. He set the towel down on the dresser and joined Aaron at the table.

"Seems like a lot of danger on account of their problem."

Aaron made a note on the con side of his chart, *not our problem*, and turned to Hannah who was fidgeting in a chair. "What about you, Hannah?"

"I'm scared." She placed a lovely purple flower in her hair that she had picked up on their tour. "I don't want to get sick, and everybody in Shadowlands sounds crazy."

Aaron scribbled another con on his chart, *dangerous*. "You both have good points. It's not really our fight and it is dangerous." Aaron spread the map on the table. "What would Dad tell us to do? He's always said to stand up for what's right."

Benji stared at the pros and cons chart Aaron was drawing and didn't see any pros. "What's right?"

"King Yasha said all of Himmel is in danger." Aaron jotted down, *save lots of good people*, in the pro side of the chart. "That's a lot of people."

"But why us?" asked Benji still staring at the chart.

"Yasha said our family has been in his plans for a long time, going all the way back to when even Papa was little." Aaron added, *Yasha's called us*, to the pro side of the chart. "We're being called by the king to do this."

"If King Yasha is so powerful, why can't he do this himself," said Benji as he stared at the map of Himmel. "It's Yasha's painting, not ours."

"I don't know, but he said we're here for such a time like this." Aaron saw the hesitation in Benji and Hannah. "Why don't we vote, majority decides."

Despite the inspiring conversation Benji had had with Yasha at the banquet, he resorted back to his old way of thinking and said, "I say we forget it and go back to the Ranch."

Aaron could see the fear in Benji's and Hannah's eyes. The mission involved a great risk for a world they were not part of. Going back to the redwood tree would free them from this great burden. Aaron searched his mind to see the path to take and recalled Papa's final words before they left to take up the adventure in Himmel: *Remember, the vision to tell the difference, and the courage to act.*

"Benji, remember when Papa was talking to us about wisdom while we were on the mountain looking for a Christmas tree?" asked Aaron as he tapped his pencil on the pad.

"Yeah, why?" asked Benji as he squirmed nervously in his seat.

"He said wisdom is the vision to see the difference between good and beautiful and evil and ugliness."

"I think we can see the difference, Aaron." Benji glared at Aaron. He was in no mood for a lecture from his brother. "After my day in Shadowlands, I definitely see the difference."

"But he said the second part was having the courage to act on what you see." A rush of energy filled Aaron as he realized what Papa had been telling him. "Papa was telling us to have the courage to accept the risk if it means protecting what is good and beautiful."

Benji was quiet for a moment as he considered what Aaron had said. As much as he hated to admit it, Aaron had a point. He replayed his conversation about loving others with King Yasha at the banquet. The decision became clear as day to him. "You're right, Aaron. We need to do this."

"I'm scared but I trust Yasha," said Hannah. "I don't want to see our new friends get hurt."

Aaron added several entries to the pro side of his chart, *love Yasha, love others - courage to act - save the good and beautiful.* "It's settled." Aaron stood and rubbed his hands together. "Now we need a plan and some help."

***

Thomas, Sophia, and the animals arrived at 7 o'clock sharp. Aaron was already busy reviewing the supplies on the table with Benji and Hannah.

Aaron stood and cleared his throat to start the meeting. "I don't know about you, but that was not what I was expecting from our tour."

"Yeah, I thought we were just going to have more fun and eat great food," said Piper Bear.

"We don't see Midnight Clover in the City of Light, and I've never seen Malby," said Thomas. "This was an eye-opening day. But I trust King Yasha. If he says it's time, I'm ready."

"I hadn't realized how bad it has gotten," said Sophia. "I trust King Yasha too."

Jack Deer stiffened his neck and his antlers looked even larger and more menacing. "Midnight Clover has been a growing problem for quite some time. I've seen people with Midnight Madness walking in Aspen Meadows more often lately. I agree with King Yasha. It's time to act," said Jack.

"I think I saw Malby in the Sane Forest when we were traveling here," said Jasper Lion. "He gives me the creeps and we need to stop him."

Piper Bear and Riley Raccoon were huddled next to each other whispering. Aaron nodded to them. "Jack speaks for us," said Piper. "Midnight Clover is getting worse, and something has to be done."

Aaron jotted more entries in his notepad. "It's unanimous. So, what's our first step?" mumbled Aaron to himself as he rubbed his chin, deep in thought. "We need to do some spy work to learn what they're planning."

"What do you suggest?" asked Jack as he maneuvered Enzo forward so he could see the table.

"We'll need to get fake passports or crowns. Sophia and I are set, but you three will need them," said Thomas. "I know someone who can help."

Aaron looked at Jack and Riley with a smile. "People need passports, but animals don't. We can get a small team into Shadowlands."

Aaron laid the map on the table and called them over. "We'll camp at Lake Enid. The capitol building is a short walk from there. Sophia, we'll try to get you inside the capitol. Jack and Riley can pick up some intelligence around the front of the building."

"I'm very good at blending in," said Jack trying to strike a nonchalant pose.

"Maybe in the forest, not the capital. You'll be as subtle as a rooster at sunrise," said Piper Bear. Piper patted Jack on the back of his neck in jest as the room filled with hoots of laughter.

Benji appreciated Piper adding levity to the meeting, "I have to remember that one."

Riley stepped on the table and said, "I'm a prowler spy by trade. Raccoon, Riley Raccoon." The room erupted in more screams as the diminutive raccoon tried to look stealthy.

They said their goodnights, and Aaron called Grace to ask her to bring a server's smock from the kitchen along with a small duster. He packed them with his supplies and turned in for some much-needed rest. Tomorrow would be a busy day.

***

The next morning, they set out for Lake Enid, except Thomas, who stayed behind to handle the passports. King Yasha was on his patio painting when Grace joined him to point out the departing spy team. He stopped and watched them as they marched along the stream toward Lake Enid.

Grace wore a look of concern as she watched them disappear into the distance. "Are you sure they can do this? They're just children."

"Yes, they are, but I know them, and I know the Parsons." King Yasha offered Grace a reassuring smile. "I've also given them our best team."

Grace stepped closer to Yasha and placed her hands on the patio railing. "Why didn't you tell them more of Malby's plan?"

"Sometimes a great challenge can help a lost person find their way." Yasha sat back on his stool and continued painting as he quietly hummed a tune. "These children came to Himmel lost, with a missing father and no hope."

The morning air was warm but not too hot. As they walked, Aaron went over the plan and supplies with each person. They passed animals along the stream and birds in the trees making their music. Aaron looked up and saw a raven on a tree watching them. It was distinctive because its eyes were deep red. There was something creepy about this raven, so Aaron picked up a rock and threw it at the bird. It flew off crowing loudly. They reached Lake Enid about 11 o'clock, and Aaron and Benji set up basecamp near the lake.

Aaron pulled some supplies from his backpack. "Sophia, take this radio; we'll use channel two. Your cover is going to be a janitor, so take this smock and duster. They'll help you blend in."

Aaron turned to Jack and Riley. "Try to get near the capitol building and listen for any conversations about Project Raven. Piper, go with them and loiter in the woods near the capitol as backup in case there's trouble."

Sophia, Jack Deer, Riley Raccoon, and Piper Bear headed off towards Thornridge. Aaron pulled out the binoculars and handed a pair each to Benji and Hannah. They positioned themselves on a hill with a clear view of the capitol. Jasper Lion, Ella Doe, and Enzo Fawn circled the hill and kept guard to spot any approaching strangers.

Sophia separated from the others as they approached the border. She sauntered up to the checkpoint and told the guard she was visiting her friend. The others calmly strolled across the border and appeared to graze when guards looked their way.

Once they got to Thornridge, Piper hung back at the tree line while Jack and Riley moved closer to the capitol building. Jack saw a teenage boy and girl sitting at a table outside the capitol building. He casually walked to a nearby tree and began nibbling. Riley crawled her way through the trees until she was close enough to hear them. Sophia put on the smock and took a seat on a nearby bench.

The boy and girl were fixated on their SIM screens as they talked. "Did you ever think we would be in this position?" said a boy with reddish tussled hair and wearing a blue jacket. His fair complexion and freckles looked like he was unaccustomed to the sun.

"No, I didn't, Dusty, but His Eminence is very determined," said a girl with wavy black hair and large brown eyes. "Hey, did you hear that? Is someone over in the trees? Dusty, check it out."

Riley froze as she saw Dusty walk toward her. She was hiding under the tree branches of a large pine tree, and she crept deeper into the branches hoping to disappear completely.

"Middie, you're paranoid," joked Dusty. "It's just a raccoon."

"Can't be too careful," replied Middie looking back at her screen. "I have to admit, Project Raven's a brilliant plan."

Dusty sat back down and picked up his SIM. "It better be."

"Let's head back in. We don't want to miss the final briefing."

Jack nodded to Sophia. She casually stood up, adjusted her smock, and followed Dusty and Middie into the capitol.

"I've got a lead, heading in," whispered Sophia into the radio Aaron had given her before slipping it into her smock. She stayed well behind Dusty and Middie and waved her duster along the walls and door handles. They went up a flight of stairs into a large conference room. Sophia carefully moved closer and peered through the small window set inside the door.

A large group of people was in the room and a tall man was at the front of a huge conference table. He had jet black hair with a pale white complexion. The contrast was striking. His black suit was loose on his thin skeletal frame. He had distinctive, sinister eyes. The whites of his eyes were severely bloodshot, crimson red. Sophia was horrified by his appearance. *He must be Malby*, she thought. There was a collection of others in the room including Dusty and Middie. Just to the right of Malby was a tall stylish man with dark hair wrapped in a man bun and wearing a garish purple suit with a bright pink pocket square. He was writing something in his notebook.

Sophia continued dusting the door and tried to get her head as close as possible. Just enough to make out what they were saying.

"Very soon, the revolution begins. Project Raven will bring us the power we have always deserved," said Malby. "Middie, give us an update on the new Midnight Clover."

"The new batch of seeds will be ready. The formula is over one hundred times stronger and will spread like wildfire," said Middie.

"His Eminence, are the ravens ready?" asked one of the men in the room.

"We've been preparing them for over a year. The last training test was a complete success. Dusty, give us a report on the ravens."

Dusty stood up, clicked his remote, and projected a picture on a large screen. It showed hundreds of large bird cages filled with ravens. "We have over a thousand ravens waiting at Sariel Caves."

"Are they ready?" asked Malby as he rubbed his hands together.

Dusty clicked to a new picture of a group of birds flying with pouches hanging from their beaks. "We've been using saliva from people infected with Midnight Madness to rewire their brains. At this point, they have avian Midnight Madness, but we're able to control it. We've filled their minds with two missions: First to spread Midnight Clover throughout Himmel.

"Pray tell, my trusty steed, Dusty. The second mission?" asked the man with the purple suit as he struck a strange pose like he was holding the reigns of a horse.

Dusty clicked to a third picture showing a group of ravens flying into a stuffed likeness of Yasha like kamikazes. "To kill the king if they see him."

"Outstanding, Dusty," said Malby with a loud cackle. "Once we seize Highlands, we'll make a water treatment plant out of Gali Fountain to control the entire kingdom forever."

Malby stood and began speaking in a rising oratory, rhythmically pounding his fist on the table. He looked crazed as though he were giving a speech to a stadium full of people. "Midnight Clover will spread all over Himmel. All will doubt King Yasha, and he will soon be forgotten. I will show everyone the lies about his goodness and beauty. A new era begins when the so-called beauty of Yasha's paintings will be burned and destroyed. The people will declare what is good... what is beautiful... what is real... what is true. We will bring liberty to Himmel!"

Everyone in the room stood and cheered with rabid enthusiasm. The glee in their expressions was unnerving to Sophia and caused her to drop her duster. She quickly left the capitol building and saw Jack and Riley waiting in the gardens nearby. She walked with haste and gave them a glare of urgency. They met up with Piper and made their way back into the woods and across the border to the basecamp at Lake Enid. Aaron had been watching their return through his binoculars and recognized the disturbing measure of their approach. The spies were greeted with hugs and gathered around the tent.

Sophia described everything she heard and saw in shocking detail. They sat back in silence. Their adventure had turned from exciting to downright terrifying. The entire kingdom of Himmel was in danger of being destroyed. To make matters worse, King Yasha's life was in danger. Malby wanted to kill the king, and they had very little time to do anything about it.

Chapter Seventeen

Counter Espionage

Aaron's mind whirled like a tornado as he tried to organize his thoughts to come up with a plan. He heard someone whistling and turned to see King Yasha strolling up the trail towards their tent near the lake.

"Such a beautiful day, if I do say so." Yasha admired the birds chirping in the trees along the lake and wore a "not a care in the world" smile on his face. "I heard Sophia's report on my way up."

Aaron turned to Yasha in disbelief. "It's worse than we thought." He wondered if Malby's evil aggression was getting to Yasha. *Is he cracking under the pressure? His very life is in peril!*

"I know, Aaron, not to worry. I'm not crazy." Yasha's face revealed a knowing smile and he winked as he glanced at Aaron. "This is serious, so let's get to work on a plan."

"The ravens are a big problem," Aaron said as he began pacing with his hands behind his back. "How're we going to stop a thousand ravens with Midnight Madness?"

"Water's the key, Aaron," replied Yasha as he pulled some Midnight Clover out of his pocket and handed it to Aaron. "We have a weapon on our side that will even the odds. Take a bite of this clover."

"Are you kidding?" Aaron shrunk back with surprise. *Is he crazy?* "Sir, it'll give me Midnight Madness."

Yasha smiled as he looked at the Midnight Clover. "Trust me, go ahead and take a bite."

Aaron looked at King Yasha with squinty eyes trying to see if King Yasha was going nuts. Yasha gave him a reassuring glance. "Here goes," said Aaron as he took a bite. Immediately his vision began to blur and forced him to sit down. "I can't see."

Yasha pulled a canteen from his backpack and offered it to Aaron. "Take a drink of this. It's fresh pure water from Lake Enid, just collected it a few minutes ago."

Aaron gulped the water, and his eyesight suddenly returned. "Hey, what just happened?"

"My water offers healing to all who drink it." King Yasha glanced down to the lake. "It's very powerful."

Aaron stood up with renewed hope. His eyes were opened wide as he took in Yasha's words. "So, if we can find a way to get your water to the ravens, they'll be healed from the Midnight Madness."

"Very good, Aaron." Yasha stood up and smiled at Aaron. He nodded his head and squeezed Aaron's arm. "I'm going to leave you to plan while Hannah and I take a walk down to the lake."

Benji studied Shadowlands through his binoculars as he listened to Aaron and King Yasha. "So, we have to find a way to get the water to the ravens in the caves."

Aaron grabbed his binoculars and locked his sights on Shadowlands. Their location on Lake Enid offered an ideal vantage point to see most of Shadowlands. He scanned from Thornridge in the north, down to Fallenbrook Pond, to the Sariel Caves, and finally, to the water treatment plant down south.

"Give me a minute to think," Aaron said, before he spent the next thirty minutes scanning back and forth, nodding and talking to himself in indecipherable chunks of words.

Benji went off with Piper Bear to look for fresh berries while they waited. They returned with a container full of berries to find Aaron still absorbed in his binoculars. "Well?" asked Benji, growing impatient.

Aaron lowered his binoculars and turned to Benji. "We need two teams. One for the caves and one for the water treatment plant."

Aaron stood up and waved his arms to gather everyone close. "Thomas, Sophia, Piper and Jasper, you're the Blue Team."

"OK, what's our mission?" asked Thomas as he rubbed his hands together.

"Blow up the water treatment plant." Aaron handed the binoculars to Thomas and pointed to the water treatment plant. "See how the color of the stream is clear blue as it enters the plant from the Highlands side?"

"Yeah," replied Thomas as he looked southward toward the plant. "Fresh, clean water."

Aaron positioned Thomas to see further north. "Look at it as it leaves the plant to flow into Shadowlands towards Fallenbrook Pond."

Thomas scanned the binoculars across the water treatment plant and downstream towards Fallenbrook Pond. "The water's dark purple blackish when it leaves the plant."

"That's how Malby's keeping everyone in Shadowlands sick." Aaron began pacing again staring at the ground. "He's contaminated the water."

"So, we clean up the stream and Fallenbrook Pond," replied Thomas. He looked again toward the Sariel Caves. "But how does that help us with the ravens?"

Aaron took the binoculars back and looked towards the Sariel Caves and then back to the water treatment plant. He spotted an old broken-down canoe by the stream a ways down from the plant. "There are a thousand ravens, way too many for us to lug water from Highlands. Once you blow up the plant, the stream will flow the pure clean water right up to the caves."

Benji was good at spotting angles, and he was impressed by his brother's angle. "So, all we'll have to do is get it to the raven cages," said Benji.

Aaron set his binoculars down and put his hand on Benji shoulder. "That's our mission. You, me, and Hannah are the Green Team."

Sophia had been listening quietly to the others discuss the plan. "A minor problem. All these areas are guarded. Malby has security

205

everywhere. We can't just waltz in there and destroy their water treatment plant and give water to a thousand ravens."

"We'll need a diversion… something to take the guards out. Let me think," said Aaron as he sat down and looked at the lake below where King Yasha and Hannah were walking along the shore.

***

"Have you ever skipped rocks?" Yasha picked up a flat rock and threw it across the lake. He watched it skim several times before it dropped beneath the surface.

Hannah picked up a rock and planted her feet on the shore. "Yeah, we do it back on the Ranch. I'm not very good." She threw the rock and it plopped into the lake without skimming at all.

"The key is choosing the right rock." Yasha picked up two rocks and showed them to Hannah. "This rock here is a flat rock made for skimming. This second rock is too round for skimming but would be good for marbles. Every rock is different, but all have a purpose."

"Hannah, do you know how special you are?" said Yasha as they continued to walk along the shore.

"I guess so." Hannah looked down and kicked the sand with her shoes. "Aaron is super smart and he's the fastest runner at school. Benji's funny and the best tree climber I know. They always seem to know things I don't know. I feel dumb sometimes."

"Remember when I said you're made like me?" Yasha stopped and looked at Hannah.

"Yeah." Hannah's demeanor lifted as she looked into Yasha's eyes.

"You have immeasurable value to me. You've been given amazing qualities that only you have." Yasha gently placed his hand on her shoulder and looked deeply into her eyes. "You're a treasure to me, Hannah, and I love you more than you can ever imagine."

Hannah's eyes began to tear up as she looked up at Yasha. "Thank you, Yasha."

"You're part of my family, royalty." Yasha wrapped his arms around Hannah. "That's your identity, who you are. Remember that, no matter what comes your way in life. No matter what anyone says about you, remember that."

Tears began to stream down Hannah's face. Yasha's words left her speechless, so she stayed in his arms relishing the warmth and love emanating from him.

"I think the way you see yourself sometimes makes you afraid." Yasha tossed the round rock in his hand as he considered his words. "Fear can be a good thing, but it can also become a prison."

Hannah's face crinkled, "Prison?"

"If it holds you back from what you're meant to do." Yasha knew his words would bring pain, but he also knew they were needed - for her. "Like being afraid of losing someone you love."

Hannah began to take deep breaths as she thought about her dad. She realized Yasha knew her deepest fears, maybe better than she did. "I'm afraid I'll never see him again. I love him so much. If I don't take chances, maybe I'll see him again."

Yasha sat down on the shoreline and motioned for Hannah to join him. "I met your dad when he was about your age. I see a lot of him in you, Hannah." Hannah's eyes brightened, "You do?"

"Yes, you're smart and I think you're very brave." Yasha wiped his hand across the sand to smooth out a small area on the beach. "How many girls your age would go on an adventure with their brothers like what you're doing now?"

"I don't know," said Hannah as she bashfully doodled in the sand with her finger.

"Not many. Your dad is smart, strong, and brave." Yasha gave her a reassuring look, like he knew something he wasn't saying. "Wherever he is, he's working as hard as he can to come home to you."

Hannah's spirits rose as she thought about how strong her dad was. *He'll find a way home.* She began to let go of the idea that she could hold on to her dad by avoiding the hazards of life.

"But in the meantime," Yasha continued, "he'd want you to go out in the world and do what you were meant to do." Yasha drew close to

Hannah. "Fear is such a strong emotion for people that when we allow it to take us over, it drives compassion right out of our hearts."

Hannah thought about the compassion she had for all her new friends in Himmel and the danger they were in. "I don't want to be afraid."

"Yasha placed the rock on the sand in the spot he had cleared. "People are like rocks. Every person is uniquely made for a special purpose. I want you to have confidence in yours."

Hannah stood up and looked out over the still water of the lake. "I am special. You know I'm the best handball player at my school. I beat everybody, even the teachers."

Yasha stood up and handed the flat rock to Hannah and showed her how to hold it in her fingers. He made a side-arm throwing motion to demonstrate how to throw. "Try it now."

Hannah imitated Yasha and threw the rock. It skimmed three times across the lake before it dipped below the surface. "Wow, three times, Yasha!"

"See you're very good. You just needed the right rock and a little help." Yasha put his arm around Hannah's shoulder as they walked back to join the others. "I think they could use our help."

"Yeah, I guess I am." Hannah walked with a spring in her step and a contagious smile on her face as she began to see herself in a whole new way.

"I'm royalty, made like the King."

***

As King Yasha and Hannah approached the basecamp, they heard the others debating the best way to get past the guards using a diversion. They hadn't made much progress. King Yasha and Hannah listened as they talked back and forth.

Aaron suggested starting a fire, Thomas wanted to pretend he was injured, Piper Bear wanted to unleash a beehive on the guards, and Riley Raccoon wanted to dump trash around the guards to make it too smelly to stay on duty.

King Yasha calmly lifted his arm. "May I offer a slightly different approach?" Everyone became silent at his voice. Aaron turned to him and said, "Sure."

"Why not put the guards to sleep?" said Yasha. He raised his two hands by the side of his head pretending to take a nap. "A sleeping guard is no guard at all."

Benji laughed when he heard King Yasha's suggestion. "That's great, but how do we put them to sleep, read them a bedtime story?" He flipped through imaginary pages with a big grin.

"I think your sister might have an idea." King Yasha smiled at Hannah and nodded for her to speak up. "Go ahead, Hannah."

Hannah walked into the middle of the group. They were all considerably taller than her. "Grandma showed me a recipe to make sleep tea. She uses it to make the raccoons fall asleep, but it'd work on people too."

Everyone looked at each other, surprised by this little girl's unusual idea. "Do you know how to make it?" asked Aaron.

"Yeah, we made a batch before we came here, and I know all the plants that go into it." Hannah started ticking off ingredients touching a different finger for each one. "Lavender, valerian, sage, chamomile, magnolia, passionflower, jasmine, rosemary, and lemongrass."

"All the plants can be found here around Lake Enid," said King Yasha as he placed his hand on Hannah's head.

Aaron began scribbling in his notepad. "How do we make them drink it?" He tapped his pencil on the pad as he considered the plan. "We can't force it down their throats."

"Perhaps a better question is how do we make them want to drink it?" replied King Yasha. He pulled a small mirror from his pocket and held it up to Aaron. "Vanity."

Aaron stared into the mirror only to see a bewildered expression gawking back at him. "Vanity?"

"Vanity – excessive pride in, or admiration of, oneself." King Yasha paused waiting for them to see the application. "What's the thing they value most?"

Aaron tapped his pencil on the pad as he thought. "Uhm, they think they're kings and queens. They believe something about themselves that's not true. Not real." He lifted his head with a grin. "They think too highly of themselves and would do anything to avoid having to face the truth about themselves."

"Yes... vanity," replied King Yasha with an approving smile. "Their pride will be their destruction."

"Yeah, I saw that when I was talking to Julia," said Benji. He grimaced as he recalled her crazed reaction to him when he didn't say she was the fiercest mountain lion in Shadowlands. "How do we create a diversion using their pride?"

"They think Shadowlands is better than Highlands," said Aaron. He began making notes on his pad. "We'll challenge them to an athletic competition – the Himmel Games."

"How does that help us?" asked Thomas as he rubbed his chin. "I love sports and all, but..."

"They can't stand to lose." Benji's eyes sparked up as the scheme crystallized in his head. "If we beat them in the Himmel Games and convince them that the sleep tea is the reason, they'll drink it by the gallon."

"Exactly. We have to pick some competitions we know we can win." Aaron looked at Benji and Hannah and scratched his head. "I know, I'll do a running race, and Benji you do tree climbing. You're the best."

"Yeah, I'll win that for sure," said Benji. He realized that taking on a mission for the king could be a blast. Scheming plans and angles with his brother – the best ever! "What about Hannah?"

"I know what I can do," said Hannah as she waved her hand to get their attention. "I'll play handball. I can beat any of them."

"That's great, Hannah." Aaron high-fived Hannah, pleased to see her assertiveness. "Now for the rest of you. We need to pick events where you have a big advantage."

"I can do boulder rolling," said Piper. She stood on her back legs and flexed her massive arm muscles. "None of them are as strong as I am."

"I'll do a race up the mountain." Jasper effortlessly leaped up on a rock. "That's kinda my specialty."

Jack looked at Ella and Enzo. "We can do a cross country race," He sprung into the air prancing a few paces. "We can run for hours."

Riley looked at the others uncertain what she could do. "I'm not sure what I'm good at." She rubbed her claws against the sides of her face. "I do like to scavenge for things around the forest."

"Excellent, we'll do a scavenger hunt for you Riley." Aaron looked at Sophia as he thought through his plan. "We need to distribute an announcement in Shadowlands, but not to everyone, just to the people we want to get the sleep tea."

"I can make flyers," said Sophia. "Where do you want to hold the Himmel Games and when?"

"How about in two days at Mt. Superior?" replied Aaron. He was madly scribbling in his notepad. "That'll give us time to prepare everything. And say there will be a great banquet after the Himmel Games."

"Hannah, make a big batch of sleep tea," said Aaron. He made more notes and then looked at the group with a determined expression. "Riley, you go with Hannah and help her collect the plants."

"We need to call it something else," said Benji. His scheming abilities were humming full speed. "What about royal tea, that'll make them want it."

Aaron assigned everyone else to various parts of the plan. Benji gathered wood for a fire to make pitch glue and royal tea. Piper and Jasper went down to the water treatment plant to scope out the area. Sophia prepared and distributed the flyers. Aaron went off to gather pine tree sap for the pitch glue to repair the canoe. Thomas, Jack, and his family left for Mt. Superior to prepare the site for the Himmel Games. They had a plan, but there was much to do.

***

King Yasha remained at the lake as the others separated to work on the plan. He sat on a rock near the water, deep in thought. He knew there would be challenging times ahead. Grace appeared on the trail and waved at Yasha as she approached.

"How did the planning go?" Grace asked as she took a seat next to him. "How did they do?"

"They've all done very well." Yasha nodded as he picked up a small stone from the shoreline. "Very well indeed."

"Splendid." Grace turned to him with a look of concern. "Will it fool Malby?"

"Malby's not stupid, in fact, he's quite clever," replied Yasha. He tossed the stone over the water skimming five times before it sank. "They can't beat Malby on their own, but they won't have to."

"Are they ready for such an important job?" Grace raked her fingers through the sand making a series of lines. "They're just children."

"I see them growing into the image I have for them right before my eyes." Yasha's smile revealed his delight as he reflected on the transformation he had seen in the children over their time in Himmel. "They'll do their part."

"They are a treasure, Yasha," Grace paused and peered into Yasha's eyes. "Are you ready for what lies ahead?"

"Yes, whatever my Father wishes." Yasha had a faraway look in his eye, staring into the sky at something only he could see. "Love is the fuel that conquers all things. There's nothing I wouldn't do to save them and everyone in Himmel."

Grace stood and gestured toward the trail leading to the City of Light. King Yasha gathered himself and joined her on the long walk back to the chateau.

"We should be on our way. I have a very important painting to complete."

Chapter Eighteen
The Himmel Games

Dusty and Middie sat enjoying lunch at a large table in the plaza in front of the capitol building; they were discussing the progress of Project Raven. The preparation was almost complete, and they were confident the plan would be a resounding success. As he took a bite of his sandwich, Dusty noticed a stack of flyers sitting on their table.

"Look at this, Middie, an athletic competition." Dusty picked up the flyer and showed it to Middie. "They're calling it the Himmel Games and they're looking for competitors."

"I've always wanted to be a national hero." Middie adjusted her crown as she read the details on the flyer. "What would we do? There are seven events."

"One of the things I declared in my kingdom is that I'm the fastest runner in Shadowlands," said Dusty as he pulled out his SIM and showed his settings to Middie. "I'm entering the running race."

"I spend a lot of time in the forest. I guess I could enter the tree climbing race." Middie pulled out her SIM and adjusted the settings. "There, now I'm the best tree climber in Shadowlands."

"This is going to be awesome." Dusty and Middie filled out their forms and dropped them in the box next to the stack of flyers. Dusty high-fived Middie, making a loud smacking sound that startled her. "Wow, someone's excited," joked Middie.

Dusty was almost jumping out of his shoes as they returned to the capitol. "I can't help it." His thoughts began building the monument he knew was rightfully his. *Champion of the Himmel Games. I'm going to be famous. A national hero.*

Sophia looked on from the tree line with a satisfied smile. After Dusty and Middie went back into the capitol, she picked up the flyers and began walking south toward the Sariel Caves. She had five other contestants to line up for the Himmel Games, contestants they had carefully chosen. There were three guards at the caves she wanted at the Himmel Games: Sable, Nyoka, and Birsha. Two guards from the water treatment plant were also on her list: Julia and Ian. She quickened her pace as there was still much to do and not much time left.

***

Holding a flyer, Fister rushed into the waiting area outside the presidential offices. "I have to see His Eminence right away."

His turquoise suit and violet pocket square confounded Malby's assistant. She had withstood more than a six act play of Fister's theatrics, and she was in no mood for them today. "May I tell him what it's about?"

"It's an emergency." Fister strutted around the waiting room like peacock waving the flyer in his hand. "He'll want to see this."

The assistant disappeared into the presidential office and returned a brief time later. "His Eminence will see you now." Fister marched into the presidential office to find Malby sitting at his desk going through sketches of statues of himself.

"Your Eminence, I'm sorry to interrupt, but we have an urgent matter." Fister slammed the flyer down on Malby's desk. "The Himmel Games event is taking place in two days. Did you know about this?"

"Let me see." Malby studied the flyer, then spun his chair to gaze out the window. "Where did you get this?"

"Downstairs in the plaza." Fister fiddled with his pocket square and tried to stay calm. "Some people have already seen it and signed up."

"We may turn this to our advantage." Malby swiveled his chair back and glared at Fister as his mind played out the scenarios. "We'll use this to show that Shadowlands is a force to be reckoned with... a great province."

"Your Most Wise Eminence," Fister said, his lungs heaving as he played out the possibilities in his mind. "I know you're a genius, but how can our people beat Highlands athletes?" Fister grimaced as he summoned the courage to continue. "They're real athletes.... our people pretend to be something they're not."

"The actual results don't mean anything," Malby chuckled as he envisioned slick videos of his athletes crushing the competition. "This will be a priceless PR event for us."

"Priceless PR?" Fister dabbed his forehead with his violet pocket square and wondered if he had misheard Malby. "What do you mean, sir?"

"Record the whole thing and get lots of extra footage of the events. The editing team will need lots of footage." Malby picked up the flyer and rolled it in his hand as he gazed out the window. "We're the storytellers so we say what is real, what is true." "Oh, how delicious, your Greatest Eminence." Fister's eyes lit up with a malicious eagerness. "We tell the story. We create the truth."

"Exactly. Like I said, the truth is what we make it." Malby stood up to dismiss Fister. "One thing, make sure no one from Shadowlands hears about or attends the Himmel Games except the seven athletes. Remember, we're the storytellers."

Fister puckered his lips, held his finger to his mouth, and imitated a shush motion. "Ooh... diabolical, your Supreme Eminence."

***

The Blue Team and the Green Team had moved their basecamp to Mt. Superior. Aaron had all the materials for the pitch glue and Hannah had gathered all the plants needed for the royal tea. They had two large buckets sitting over a blazing fire and were mixing in the ingredients just as Papa and Grandma had taught them. Aaron left the pitch glue to Benji and walked the event grounds to check on the preparations.

"How's the royal tea coming?" Aaron inspected the bucket of tea Hannah was mixing on the fire. "Do we have enough?"

"Plenty," Hannah said as she continued stirring in the ingredients. "We have seven canteens for the banquet. One for each of them."

"Great thinking, Hannah." Aaron walked over to Sophia and Thomas who were looking at a diagram of the water treatment plant. "Have all the flyers been distributed to our targets?"

"Yeah, all seven targets are signed up for the Himmel Games," Sophia said. She pulled out her list of registrations and went through each event and the Shadowlands competitors they had targeted to get the flyers. "I even made a Himmel Games Event Guide to make it seem more... you know, official."

"Excellent, Sophia." Aaron turned his attention to the diagram Sophia and Thomas had been looking at and waved for Piper and Jasper to come over.

"Feel good about your plan for the water treatment plant?"

"Absolutely," replied Sofia. "We have the explosives ready, entrance and exit routes, everything's set."

"What about a diversion?" asked Aaron as he scrutinized the plans. "If the royal tea doesn't work?"

"Jasper and I have that covered," replied Piper as she gave a pretend swipe at Jasper. "We've got a wild backup plan guaranteed to entertain... and divert."

"Thomas and Jack." Aaron waved for everyone to gather. "Give us a tour of the courses you've set up."

"They're ready to go," replied Thomas. "Let the games begin."

They spent the afternoon inspecting each of the event courses. Evening came quickly, and they enjoyed a delicious meal and songs by the fire. A calm suspense filled the air. Aaron reminded them of Mr. Wigglebottom's advice: *Success comes through clarity of mission and purpose. Clarity flows from the pursuit of the good and beautiful, what's real.*

They knew their mission and had done all they could to prepare. Tomorrow would bring danger, but they knew the battle to save Himmel was a noble one.

***

The day started far too early for Fister, and he had to put on his ensemble more hastily than usual. Adorned in an ivory white suit with royal blue pocket square, Fister hiked the arduous trail up Mt. Superior with his media crew. His freshly polished pointed-toe dress shoes were not the best choice for the rugged terrain. But to Fister, fashion came first.

"Simply a glorious day. Feel the fresh air. Feel the burn, my fragrant raconteurs." He bent over and gasped for breath, hopelessly trying to wipe the dirt off his suit and shoes. "Get every event and make sure you record extra footage of our brave combatants to this unrivaled test of mettle. We want to capture the sweet aroma of victory from our Herculean warriors."

"Whatever you say, sir," said one of the crew members as he fiddled with his camera equipment. "When are we broadcasting the event?"

"This production demands our finest editorial splendor to showcase these athletic artisans." Fister panted like a dog as they continued to climb the mountain. "I will personally oversee the editing process in our studio."

"So we're not going to broadcast the event?" asked the crew member.

"We'll be broadcasting an edited version to display the true story of these games," replied Fister. He was exhausted when they finally spotted the Himmel Games banner in the distance. Sweat dripped off his forehead and left wet spots on his suit, and strands of his over-gelled hair had slipped out of his bun and were hanging over his face. Splotches of dirt stains decorated his white suit, making him look more like a tuckered out dalmatian.

Fister gathered the camera crew over for a final word. His hands were on his knees as he gulped in air to regain his composure. After several minutes, he raised his head with a toothy grin. "Let's make some movie magic." He raised his finger to his lips and shot an unnerving smile at the crew. "Remember, hush hush my fragrant video cadets. His Grand Eminence has directed that nobody sees this footage until I'm done working my storytelling magic."

Aaron greeted Fister's team and showed them the course layout so they could position their cameras. The Shadowlands competitors arrived and Aaron welcomed each with an event guide and a special memento of the first Himmel Games. Sophia had picked up some Himmel pins while she was making flyers and buying supplies in Middling, the small town King Yasha had pointed out during their tour.

Inaugural Himmel Games
Official Event Guide

Event	Shadowlands	Highlands
Tree Climbing	Middie	Benji
100-yard Dash	Dusty	Aaron
Handball	Sable	Hannah
Boulder Roll	Ian	Piper Bear
Mountain Race	Julia	Jasper Lion
Scavenger Hunt	Nyoka	Riley Raccoon
Cross-country Race	Birsha	Jack Deer & Family

Aaron opened the Himmel Games with a short speech. "Our desire is to bring peace and goodwill to the kingdom of Himmel through the first ever Himmel Games," Thomas, who served as race official, rang a cowbell to formally open the games.

The first event was the tree climbing race which took place on two large pine trees at the edge of the forest. Benji walked up to the first tree and rubbed his hands. Middie sized up Benji and imagined the sweetness of her victory; he was several inches shorter and quite a bit younger. Thomas went over the rules: the first to climb up, pull the flag, and then climb back down was the winner. He rang the cowbell, and the race was on. Benji took an early lead, smoothly navigating up the branches. He looked across and saw Middie struggling on the second branch. Benji felt a surge of confidence and pressed on even faster. He grabbed the flag and started his descent. He glanced over and saw Middie caught in the branches about a quarter way up the tree.

Benji flew down the tree, jumped to the ground, and held the flag high in the air.

"First event goes to Highlands," Thomas announced, holding Benji's arm up in the air as Benji jumped up and down. "Benji is the tree climbing champion."

Middie was still up in the tree fighting like an insect stuck in a spider's web. "Somebody, help me down." Her hair had gotten tangled in several branches, so she was paralyzed, unable to move. Benji climbed up and unknotted her hair, strand by strand, as she shouted and complained. After untangling her hair, he guided her down the tree, and reached to shake her hand when they had made it safely back to the ground. Middie snatched her hand away and stalked off pouting.

Next up was the running race between Aaron and Dusty. Dusty was slightly distressed after watching Middie flame out in the tree climbing event. He began stretching, hoping it might calm his nerves. Thomas explained that the course was a 100-yard dash across the meadow. Jack, Ella, and Enzo had eaten and stomped on the flowers to make the two running lanes. Aaron and Dusty stepped up to the line and Thomas rang the cowbell. Aaron got off to a fast start and chewed up the yards with each stride. Dusty's feet slipped as he tried to fire off the line. He stumbled and lost ground to Aaron. The more agile Aaron glanced over and didn't even see Dusty, so he lowered his head and powered his legs like a steam engine pushing through the finish line at least twenty yards ahead of Dusty. Benji and Hannah high-fived Aaron as he held up his arms.

"The second event goes to Highlands." Thomas raised Aaron's arm signaling his victory. "Aaron is the fastest runner in Himmel."

Dusty coughed and shook his head as he slunk over to Middie, who was nursing her wounded ego under a nearby tree. Middie's hair looked like it had been run through the spin cycle of the washing machine one too many times. She had leaves, branches and a few mystery things crawling through her beehive of a hairdo. "Ouch," she cried as she pulled on a deeply embedded twig.

"Well, that was humiliating," muttered Dusty as he fell to the ground, still huffing and puffing like he'd run a marathon. "How'd that twerp run so fast? In Shadowlands he'd be arrested."

Middie laughed and gave Dusty a shot in the arm with her fist. "Tell me about it. I lost a tree climbing race to a squirt half my size."

Fister walked up with one of the camera crew. "Ooh Middie, I must have the name of your stylist." He let out an annoying cackle. "Simply divine."

"Don't want to hear it, Mr. La-de-da," shouted Middie as she rubbed her head. "You aren't looking so fine yourself."

"Not to worry, my brave warriors," said Fister as he tried in vain to twist strands of his long hair back into his bun. "We're making magic here. By the time we're done, you two will look like elite world beaters. Give the camera a big victory smile with your arms raised high."

Thomas drew everyone over to the handball court he'd made. Hannah was competing against a girl guard named Sable who was quite a bit older than Hannah and twice as tall. Thomas explained that the first player to get to ten points would be the winner. Hannah started the game and served two clean winners. Sable kept tripping over herself as she tried to get to the ball. Hannah realized competing against Sable was like playing against a first grader at her school, so she played easy on her and held back on her toughest shots. Even with that, Hannah won the game 10-2, without suspense. Hannah shook Sable's hand and congratulated her on a well-played match.

"I don't understand. I'm the best handball player in Shadowlands." Sable pulled her SIM out of her pocket and showed it to Hannah. "See, it says so right here."

"I don't know, Sable. I think you're pretty good." Hannah felt sorry for Sable as she watched her grapple with the fact she'd gotten crushed by a girl so much smaller and younger. "I probably just had a lucky day."

Thomas called Piper Bear and Ian for the boulder roll as the fourth event. There were two large boulders placed on a flat field, and the competitors had to roll the boulder twenty-five yards to the finish line.

Piper and Ian lined up behind their boulders, each one weighing about three hundred pounds. Piper was several times larger than Ian and didn't know what to make of Ian's unfounded optimism.

"This'll be a great race," Ian boasted, looking up at Piper as though they were equal combatants. "Two great bears proving their strength."

Thomas clanged the cowbell and Piper immediately began rolling her boulder. She used her massive paws to build a steady momentum with the boulder rolling over the course. Ian pushed his boulder with all his might but couldn't get it to budge. He lowered his shoulder and planted his feet and finally got it to make a partial turn. Piper quickly reached the finish line without even breathing hard and stopped the boulder to signal her victory. She looked back and saw Ian sitting by his boulder trying to get it to move. Piper sauntered back to Ian and helped him up, and together they rolled Ian's boulder across the finish line. Piper congratulated Ian on an earnest effort and Ian walked away shaking his head.

Jasper Lion and Julia were scheduled next for the race up the mountain. The course was about two hundred yards up a steep rocky mountain incline to a ledge as the finish line.

Julia approached Jasper as they stepped up to the starting line. "I'm the most fearless mountain lion in Shadowlands."

"I've heard. Benji told me how fearless you are. Nice to meet you, Julia." Jasper was baffled by her introduction. "Do you do much mountain racing?"

"I'm new at this," Julia told Jasper with a confident head nod as if she just might have to take it easy on the big cat. "But I'm the best in Shadowlands."

Thomas rang the cowbell and Jasper sprinted up the slope. His agile paws leaped from rock to rock as he made his way. His superior vision spotted the next moves like a chess master. Julia had made her way up the first rock and was surveying her next move. She crept over a crevice and successfully made it to a second rock up the slope. Meanwhile, Jasper had gotten all the way up the incline and was making his final ascent to the finish line on the ledge. He turned and saw Julia crawling up a rock not far from the starting line. Her knees were scraped, and she struggled to find a path she could navigate. With his powerful hind legs, Jasper leaped to the ledge and sat looking down below for all to witness his leisurely victory.

Riley Raccoon quickly dispatched Nyoka in the scavenger hunt. They had to find ten items hidden in random places on the course such as in caves and up in trees. Riley used her superior sense of smell, tree climbing skills, and knowledge of the forest to dominate the hunt. She found nine of the items while Nyoka was only able to find one.

The final event was the cross-country race between Jack Deer and his family and Birsha. The course was two miles through the forest. Birsha looked at Jack, Ella, and Enzo as they lined up at the starting line, and thought, *I don't know about Jack, but I'll definitely beat that runt, Enzo.*

Jack tried to make small talk as they waited to start the race, "Do you spend much time in the forest?"

"Yeah, I run in the forest all the time," said Birsha as he pawed the ground with his foot.

Thomas rang the cowbell, and they sprinted off the line. Jack leaped along the path darting from spot to spot as though he was floating. Ella was only one step behind with Enzo working to keep up. Birsha got a fast start, as well, and sprinted through the woods, but his two legs were no match for the fleet-of-foot deer. He tried to run faster, but after about a quarter mile, he had to stop to catch his breath. Jack and Ella were making fast work of the course and reached the mile and a half mark without strain. They waited for a minute and Enzo soon caught up with them. Birsha reached the half mile mark and decided he needed to pace himself, so he slowed down to a medium jog hoping Jack, Ella, and Enzo stopped to graze along the way. Jack and his family decided to finish the race together and set a pace Enzo could keep up with. The three of them effortlessly pranced the last half mile and crossed the finish line at the same time. It took Birsha another twenty minutes to finish the race, but he finally crossed the finish line, exhausted and beaten.

***

While Jack Deer and his family were dominating Birsha, Aaron and the others prepared the banquet. All the competitors gathered, and a meal of fruits, nuts, fresh grilled fish, and rolls was served. The Shadowlands team was downtrodden, having been thoroughly humiliated in all seven events. Fister was there filming it all, trying to find something positive to say to his team. Notwithstanding the lopsided results, the athletes had a marvelous evening sharing stories and eating delicious food together.

Benji was sitting next to crazy Ian as they enjoyed the feast. "I got a crown in Shadowlands. I didn't want anything difficult, so I just said I get to eat a lot of sweets."

"That's a pretty good thing to have in your kingdom," replied Ian as he took a bite of grilled fish. "I should do that."

Benji took a bite of fish and sized up Ian. "I know the rules in Shadowlands about doubting someone's kingdom, but I have a question. Is it OK if I ask a question?"

"Sure," replied Ian as he scooped another mouthful of grilled fish.

"What's it like being a bear?" Benji creased his lip into a tiny smile. "I mean, how's it different than being a boy?"

Ian thought for a moment and pondered the question. "I guess the biggest thing is that I get to act like a bear, and nobody can complain," he said.

Hannah and Julia were sitting next to them listening. "People like me more because I'm a mountain lion," said Julia jumping into the conversation. "I'm more popular. Being just a girl in Shadowlands isn't very exciting."

Hannah looked at Ian and Julia with a caring smile. "We learned from King Yasha that people are very special. Animals are special, but we're very special because we're made like him."

"I didn't feel very special as a boy," replied Ian with a furrowed brow. He set his food down and held out his SIM. "As a bear, everybody looks up to me."

"You're special because you're a boy who was made like the King of all of Himmel. I think that's more special than a bear." Benji turned to Julia and paused as he chose his words carefully. He remembered how his last encounter with her had gone. "Julia, King Yasha loves you very much. You don't have to be something different than the girl you were made to be. You don't need a crown and you don't need to be something else."

"That all sounds fine for you," Julia said. She nodded and began eating her food again. She pulled her SIM out and showed it to Benji and Hannah. "But I like being a mountain lion, and that's what makes me special."

Hannah's eyes teared up as she listened to Julia and Ian. She stared off into space caught in her own thoughts. *These pitiful blind people. They're missing out on the goodness and beauty King Yasha offers to everyone in Himmel. They're sick and need help.* She knew what she had to do. Their plan was aimed at helping people like Julia and Ian. Hannah excused herself and picked up the seven canteens from behind a tree. She set them on the table in front of Aaron.

"Here you go."

The dinner was winding down, so Aaron stood up to give a toast. "We established the Himmel Games in the spirit of peace and friendship." Aaron lifted his glass to toast. "To our friends in Shadowlands, may you experience the goodness and beauty of the kingdom."

"Here, here," said Thomas. He stood and lifted his cup. "To our friends from Shadowlands."

"The Highland athletes performed wonderfully today." Aaron looked down the table at the members of his team and then glanced at the Shadowlands competitors. "We had some help, and we offer it to you."

The Shadowlands team looked up from their food with intense curiosity. "What kind of help did they have?" asked Dusty.

"We made a special blend of tea that will bring clear vision and allow you to reach your full potential." Aaron lifted up the canteens. "We call it royal tea. You can take this back to your home and start training with it tomorrow morning."

Aaron walked around the table and handed a canteen to each member of the Shadowlands team. The entire Highlands team stood and walked around the table. They thanked the Shadowlands team and congratulated them on a successful Himmel Games. The Shadowlands team exited in haste after their drubbing, canteens in hand.

"That was an odious day; they clobbered us," said Dusty. He was holding his canteen and talking to Middie. "We can take this to the caves. Training in the morning."

"Royal tea, I like the sound of that," replied Middie. "Definitely more fitting for us than that vagabond band of misfits."

"I have a feeling this is the last time they humiliate us at the Himmel Games." Dusty quickened his pace with a renewed sense of optimism. "The future is ours."

The Highlands team gathered around the campsite on Mt. Superior and celebrated the historic victory at the Himmel Games. They went back through each event and savored the lopsided triumph. They chuckled at the bizarre sight of the Shadowlands team floundering in races for which they were completely ill-equipped.

"This was all fun, but the real victory belongs to Hannah." Aaron lifted Hannah in his arms so everyone could see her. "Thanks to her, they will be taking some unexpected naps tomorrow morning."

Chapter Nineteen
The Battle Begins

Aaron woke up before sunrise and started a fire to heat up the pitch glue. Slowly the others began to gather around the fire and welcome the new day. They ate a quick breakfast and discussed plans and contingencies if things went south.

Aaron looked out across Shadowlands. "If all goes well, the peril to Himmel should be over by the end of today."

"A lot can happen in a day," Thomas said. He looked up at the sky and added, "King Yasha painted this day for us, so we look to him as our guide."

Aaron pulled a radio out of his backpack and handed it to Thomas. "Take this and try to stay in touch."

The Blue Team of Thomas, Sophia, Piper Bear, and Jasper Lion packed their supplies and headed south toward the water treatment plant. The Green Team of Aaron, Benji, Hannah, Jack Deer, Ella Doe, Enzo Fawn, and Riley Raccoon headed west toward a canoe lying by the stream just across the border of Shadowlands. Aaron got out his binoculars and saw the canoe in the distance. He directed his team on a westward path. He and Benji traded carrying the bucket of pitch glue since it was heavy. They were able to cross the border to Shadowlands without being noticed by crawling on the ground between two guard posts and arrived at the canoe after about an hour.

"Just as I thought, it needs a patch right here." Aaron started to apply the hot pitch glue to the side of the canoe. "It should harden in about thirty minutes, so we can investigate the stream while we wait. Jack, you, Ella, Enzo, and Riley make your way up to the caves and wait for us there. We'll meet you at the edge of the stream."

***

The Blue Team made good time to the water treatment plant. They settled into a patch of bamboo reeds Piper Bear and Jasper Lion had found during their reconnaissance trip.

Thomas took out his binoculars and surveyed the plant. "The guards are walking around, so let's give them some time."

"Do you see them drinking the royal tea?" Sophia was anxiously examining the explosives in her bag. "I'd like to relieve us of these as soon as possible."

Thomas' eyes remained fixed on the guards at the entrance to the plant. "There are two guards pacing on different sides of the plant. I see the canteens with them; no drinking yet."

"We've got our contingency plan if we need it," said Piper. She poked Jasper with her giant paw.

"Wait, he's picking up a canteen, just took a big swig." Thomas pointed toward the left side of the plant. "It's Ian, the guy who did the boulder roll against Piper."

"Hannah said it only takes about fifteen minutes to work," said Sophia. "Hopefully Julia will drink up too."

"She's talking to Ian; she just took a big drink from her canteen." Thomas pulled down the binoculars and looked at the team. "Get everything ready; we have to move like lightning. In and out."

They waited about fifteen minutes until Thomas could see Ian and Julia lying on the ground. They weren't moving. Thomas picked up the radio. "The targets put to bed. We're moving in."

"Sophia and I will plant the explosives." Thomas stood and motioned for the Blue Team to advance toward the plant. "You two stand guard by the door, and don't let those two guards get in our way."

"If Hannah's royal tea works, they'll sleep through the whole thing," said Sophia as she hoisted her backpack of explosives. "Time to redecorate that water treatment plant."

Thomas and Sophia worked with speed and precision as they placed the explosives in critical areas of the facility. They had studied the blueprints of the building to identify the locations they needed to hit to take the whole thing down. Sophia and Thomas set the timer for two minutes, ran out of the building, and gave a thumbs up to Piper and Jasper.

"What do we do about these two?" asked Sophia. She stopped next to Ian and Julia who had fallen asleep right near the entrance to the plant. "They'll be caught in the blast."

Thomas grimaced at the thought of what the blast would do to them. "Piper, drag Ian away from the building." He reached down and grabbed Julia's arms.

"I'll get Julia."

They ran back to the bamboo reeds and Thomas checked his watch. It read thirty seconds. They sat silently as the clock ticked down... 5-4-3-2-1. A thunderous explosion filled the air and the sky lit up with fire. Debris flew in all directions. The plant had been completely destroyed in the blast. They looked at the stream on the Shadowlands side of the plant and the water was slowly changing from dark purple to clear blue. Soon the pure blue water was flowing downstream. Thomas radioed Aaron and they quickly secured their backpacks and started off toward Mt. Superior.

***

Fister strutted into the presidential office with his arms full of video disks from the Himmel Games. His bright yellow and black striped suit made him look like a giant bumble bee.

Malby had been anxiously waiting for word all day. "How did we do in the Himmel Games?"

"Your Most Excellent Eminence, it was a tad less fruitful than we wanted." Fister placed the video disks on a table and sat in front of Malby's desk. "Our athletes were..." Fister struck a pose of exaggerated contemplation. "Obliterated in devastating fashion."

"Don't sugarcoat it Fister," Malby laughed at the sight of Fister's distress. "It can't be that bad."

231

"Oh contraire, your Supreme One. I'm quite serious. We lost every race by a margin I didn't think was even possible." Fister shook his head. He removed his white pocket square and waved it in grand motions like a flag of surrender. "None of our athletes had the foggiest idea how to compete in their event. We got mugged by reality. By children and animals, no less!"

Malby glared at Fister, imposing his force of nature on him. "Who are the storytellers, Fister?"

Fister picked up one of the video disks and gave a sinister smirk to Malby. "We are, your Most Artistic One."

"Exactly. I have full confidence in your team's editing skills to make the first ever Himmel Games a total Shadowlands rout and show the entire kingdom our superiority."

Fister sat down and crossed his legs, which made his newly pressed garish suit even more prominent. "The only good news is that they gave us a drink that is supposed to dramatically improve our performance in the future. It's called royal tea."

"Tell me more about this royal tea; I'm intrigued," said Malby. He stood up and gazed out the window rubbing his chin. "To whom did they give this royal tea?"

Fister thought for a moment. "Seven canteens, one for each competitor. Dusty, Middie, Ian, Julia, Birsha, Sable, and Nyoka."

"Interesting list of people, wouldn't you say?" Malby pressed the button on his desk to page his assistant. "I think it's time for a tour of the Sariel Caves and the water treatment plant."

***

The Green Team waited for word from the Blue Team while they gave the canoe time to dry. Suddenly, they heard a loud explosion in the distance.

Aaron's radio crackled, so he picked it up. "Plant destroyed, heading back to base." The Blue Team had completed their mission.

"Green Team is up," called out Aaron. He and Benji picked up the canoe and set it in the water. They all climbed in and started paddling down the stream. The water was still purplish black, so they were careful not to touch it. The current was swift, and they made good time to the caves. By the time they got there, the water was almost perfectly clear blue. They hid the canoe behind some river grass and met up with Jack Deer and the others on a small hill overlooking the caves.

Aaron pulled out his binoculars and surveyed the entrance to the caves. He saw Dusty and Middie talking by the cave entrance and three guards positioned to the left, right, and center of the entrance. He recognized them as Sable, Nyoka, and Birsha from the Himmel Games.

"Are they drinking?" Hannah was eager to see if her royal tea would work the way she planned. "It must have worked on Ian and Julia."

"Not yet, but I see the canteens next to Dusty and Middie." Aaron scanned back and forth to keep an eye on the three guards. "Dusty's picking up his canteen; he just took a drink. Middie just drank from hers." "What about the guards?" asked Jack Deer.

"OK, Sable is coming over; she just gulped from her canteen." Aaron scanned over to the other two guards. "Nyoka and Birsha are talking and walking over to Sable. That's it, they just swigged from their canteens."

"I'd give it fifteen minutes," said Hannah as she looked down at her watch.

"Then, night, night time."

While they waited, Aaron reiterated the plan and checked all the supplies to make sure everyone knew their part. They had a long hose and pump to flow water from the stream to the raven cages in the cave. Benji was ready to man the hose and foot pump at the stream with Jack serving as lookout. Aaron would handle the hose in the cave and spray the ravens with pure clean water. Hannah was lookout at the entrance to the cave with Riley, Ella, and Enzo maintaining a perimeter security watch.

"It's been fifteen minutes," Hannah said, pointing to her watch and hoping her tea had done its job. "Are they down?"

"Let's see." Aaron looked at the entrance of the cave and saw all five people on the ground sleeping, none of them making a move. He ordered, "Move in, Green Team."

Benji and Aaron each had an end of the hose. Benji ran to the stream, and Aaron ran to the cave entrance. All the other members of the Green Team moved to their designated positions. Benji positioned the end of the hose in the stream and began pumping water to Aaron. By this time, the water was clear fresh water with no signs of purple. Water started to flow up the hose and Aaron was positioned right in front of the first raven cages. Suddenly an ear-piercing squeal came from Riley's direction.

"Drop the hose and lay on the ground." A large guard appeared from nowhere. He tackled Benji and ripped the hose out of his hand.

Jack heard Riley's call and immediately knew something was wrong. He told Ella to take Enzo back to Mt. Superior and wait for them there. He then rushed toward the cave to protect the children. He saw Benji already on the ground surrounded by guards with a large group of guards charging toward the cave.

Hannah was cowering on the ground near the entrance to the cave. "Aaron!" she screamed.

Jack charged at the guards in an attempt to rescue Hannah, but two of the guards turned and swung their batons at him and struck his side. He collapsed to the ground, wounded from the blows.

The guards rushed into the cave, dragged Aaron out, and threw him to the ground next to Benji. Another guard grabbed Hannah's arm and forced her to lie next to her brothers. Aaron saw Jack lying on the ground and knew he had to get to him. He tried to wrestle away from the guards, but it was no use. Their grasp was too tight.

After subduing Aaron, Benji, and Hannah, two of the guards turned and walked toward Jack slapping their batons into the palms of their hands, practicing blows. They had wicked glee in their eyes. Jack was still on the ground, dazed by the assault. Suddenly, Riley appeared from under a tree and rose up on her hind legs, snarling at the two guards. Stunned by the oddity of an attacking raccoon, they froze in their tracks. It was just enough of a diversion to give Jack time to get to his legs and hobble into the forest. Riley turned and scuttled after Jack to escape.

Malby walked around the corner and looked at the children lying on the ground. "What do we have here?" Malby kicked the hose away from the stream. "You didn't offer me any royal tea. I'm hurt." He cackled as he surveyed the scene with the culprits on the ground and guards securing the area.

Aaron was crushed. He had worked so hard on the plan and at the eleventhhour Malby destroyed it all. His mind was spiraling into a flood of recriminations. *What did I miss? What did I do wrong? Himmel, King Yasha...*

"Take them to the prison," Malby commanded, glaring at the prisoners as the guards hauled them away. "I've got to check on the water treatment plant." He sneered at Aaron as he swaggered away. "You and I have much to discuss."

Chapter Twenty

Prisoners in Enemy Territory

―――――∽∝∾―――――

Aaron sat slumped in the prison cell and looked over his body. He was sore all over and had bruises and scratches on his arms and legs from being dragged by the guards. Benji was next to him talking to himself about how close they had been to spraying the ravens with water. Hannah had her head on Aaron's shoulder and was softly weeping. The prison was made of cold, hard brick and had one small table and two dirty pads on the floor to sit on. The door was made of thick steel bars and the only light came through a small window with bars on it.

Birsha stood guard outside the door. He swept his baton against the bars and made a head-splitting noise that caused the children to recoil in fear. "You three are pretty nasty, giving us sleeping potion; you could have hurt us."

"We didn't want to hurt you," replied Aaron. "It was the saftest way for us to get clean water to the ravens."

"Well, we caught you," Birsha bragged and continued to bang his baton on the bars reveling in their misery. "So you won't be doing that."

Fister sauntered in with a bag in his hand and asked Birsha to let him in the prison cell. He was still wearing his bumblebee suit and had an out of place gleeful look on his face as he surveyed the children.

"Oh my. The agony of defeat is not worn well on you. Are you enjoying our five-star accommodations?" He let out a loud cackle as he flashed his phony-baloney grin at them.

"What do you want?" Aaron was in no mood to entertain Fister. He had concluded that Fister's main gift was irritating others, just by his presence.

Fister set the bag on the table. "You three are facing some absolutely scrumptious charges. Destruction of government property, drugging government officials, and terrorism. And Benji, there's already a warrant for your earlier unceremonious treatment of Queen Julia." Fister paused long enough to showcase his phony smile again. "But we are compassionate."

"Compassionate?" muttered Aaron. He was too sore to stand up, so he nudged Hannah to move behind him on the floor. "Huh!"

"Yes, my young rebels, compassionate. We want all the citizens of Shadowlands to find the freedom and liberty we offer." Fister pulled three crowns and three water bottles out of the bag. "His Eminence is prepared to offer you leniency if you drink the Midnight Clover water and take a crown to declare your allegiance to Shadowlands and His Eminence."

"May we have a minute to discuss it?" replied Aaron. He crawled to a corner of the prison cell with Benji and Hannah and whispered, "We saw what it did to crazy Ian and the rest of them."

Hannah put her hands to her mouth to shield her words. "I don't like Fister or Shadowlands. I only want King Yasha."

"Me too," said Benji. "Tell Mr. Flimflam Man to forget it."

Aaron turned and glared at Fister with determination in his eyes. "We're loyal to King Yasha and only King Yasha." He nodded to Benji and Hannah. "We won't drink your water and we won't wear your crowns."

"My young renegades, these charges have a life sentence." Fister puckered his lips and dramatically swiveled his head back and forth. He cupped his hands over his mouth as if to convey a deep secret. "Trials in Shadowlands are not like other places. His Eminence is the judge and jury, and he alone will pronounce your verdict. You'll have no chance to defend yourselves."

"You can tell Malby to forget it," snapped Aaron. "It will never happen."

Fister picked up his bag and strutted away, shaking his head in disbelief. "I'll report this to His Eminence. I'm sure he'll want to talk to you." He was mystified why the children would turn down freedom and accept life in prison, all to remain loyal to some painter in the Highlands.

Fister's visit boosted their spirits in unexpected ways. They felt more powerful, freer by following their convictions. They were standing up for goodness, beauty, and truth. By doing so, Malby had no power over them. The events had also brought them closer to their dad. He had emphasized standing up for what's right many times. Knowing they were following in his footsteps made him almost present with them in their prison cell.

Aaron thought back to Papa's parting words, *the vision to see the difference, and the courage to act.* Even though their plan was foiled, he had clarity in the mission and was resolute in their purpose.

"This is what Dad and Papa would have done," said Aaron. Still, he and his brother and sister were facing life in prison, so he was not entirely without worry. It had been his responsibility to keep them safe and he had failed. Spending life in a prison cell was no small matter.

"King Yasha makes a new painting every day. He can make a painting where we aren't in prison." Hannah pointed out the window towards the sky. "I trust King Yasha. He said he loves us more than we can ever imagine."

"You're right, Hannah, he does." Aaron was trying to be optimistic, but he realized the grave circumstances facing all of Himmel. Their plan to prevent Project Raven had failed, and soon, a thousand ravens would be spreading terror across Himmel. "But King Yasha might be busy with more important things right now."

"He won't forget us. I've got an idea; let's sing." Hannah started humming to get them in the mood. "We can't do anything else in here, so let's sing. It'll cheer us up."

"What do you want to sing?" asked Benji. He fluffed the dirty pad and sat back with his head against the wall.

Hannah stood next to Aaron holding onto his shoulder. "The song Enzo taught us, *My King*."

"That's a great idea," replied Aaron. He grimaced as he struggled to his feet.

Hannah started and soon they were all singing *My King* over and over, filling the air with their music.

You've made the day for my delight.
You bring us warmth and light.
And keep us safe at night.
You guard our lives with your love and might.
Oh, what a good and beautiful King.

The sound of the music was irritating to Birsha, so he moved down the hall where he could no longer torment them with his baton. They heard a couple of prisoners in adjoining cells join in to form a chorus throughout the prison. With each verse, their mood lightened, and the terror of their situation was transformed to an unexplainable peace.

***

King Yasha was on the patio at the chateau working on his painting. He gazed across the countryside toward Shadowlands. "The children have done well; they've taken great risks for our sake."

Dio was at the other end of the patio in front of his own canvas. "Yes, they did, for the sake of all Himmel." He set his brush down and turned to Yasha. "Are you holding onto them, Yasha?"

"With all my might." Yasha raised a clenched fist. "I'll never let go."

Yasha turned his attention back to his painting. "This is my most important painting so far." He gazed at the canvas considering his next brush stroke.

"Yes, it is," said Dio. He walked over to Yasha and admired his painting.

"It'll have everlasting impact on Himmel."

"Must it include this scene?" Yasha pointed his brush at a section of his painting. "Is that beauty?"

"There's no other way." Dio gently rubbed Yasha's back. "Sometimes great beauty flows out of great pain."

"Each stroke I paint brings me anguish." Beads of sweat trickled down Yasha's forehead as he studied his painting. "If it must be so, that is the scene I'll paint. Your will be done, Abba, Father."

Dio wrapped his arms around Yasha, and they enjoyed a long embrace. "I love you, Yasha. Our love for Himmel and the people demand this."

Yasha held on to his Father seeking the strength to finish his painting. "There's no end to the road I would travel for the people of Himmel."

"I know, Son."

Grace strolled out to the patio to find Dio and Yasha embracing. "I thought I'd check on how the painting is going."

Dio looked at Yasha with admiration. "Yasha is almost done with his most exquisite painting."

Grace examined Yasha's painting and nodded in agreement. "I see what you mean. This painting will bring unrivaled beauty to all of Himmel."

"Grace, I may be busy later, so can you look after the children?" Yasha pointed to an area of his painting. "They're a treasure."

"Yes, they are," replied Grace as she gave him a long embrace.

***

Aaron, Benji, and Hannah were still singing *My King* when they heard Malby's voice down the corridor. Malby screamed, "What is that hideous song?" Aaron had been able to climb to his feet and was standing with his hand on the prison door for balance.

Hannah stepped away from the cell door. "It's *My King*," she said.

"It's a revolting song and it won't help you." Malby pressed his face against the bars. "Fister tells me you've declined my generous offer to become kings in Shadowlands." He turned to Hannah with a phony smile, and whispered, "and a queen for you missy."

"That's right." Aaron stumbled away from the door, almost falling down. He wanted to put as much distance as possible between him and Malby.

"We're not interested."

Malby picked up a baton and pressed it into the bruise on Aaron's leg causing him to cry out in pain. "It's not an option," shouted Malby in a fit of anger. He pulled a crown from his bag and showed it to the children. "I have the power to sentence you to life in prison."

"We trust King Yasha," replied Hannah as she stepped toward Malby.

"Your threats don't scare us."

Malby laughed at Hannah. "You think King Yasha can save you?"

"He's probably making a painting right now," replied Benji. "You'll see."

"His paintings have very little impact in Shadowlands." Malby reached into their cell with the crown and temped them to take it. "He's going to be extraordinarily occupied later – you like that word, don't you?" Malby was taunting them and enjoying every minute of it. Anything King Yasha loved, he despised. Especially, these three troublemaking children.

"King Yasha can rescue us from you," Hannah declared. She poked her finger in the air towards Malby, and her bravado startled him. "But even if he doesn't rescue us, we won't drink your stupid water and we won't wear your stupid crown."

Malby saw their unflinching conviction and put the crown back in his bag. "Have it your way. I sentence you to life imprisonment. You'll regret this the rest of your life. Get used to your new home."

Malby stormed out of the prison and headed back to the capitol building. Fister was pulling gigantic tarps off a statue in the plaza when he saw Malby walking by.

"Follow me to my office; we have much to discuss." Malby's face appeared bloodless as he obsessed over the children's insubordination.

Fister had to jog to keep up with Malby. His pointy-toed dress shoes went clickety clack the whole time. "Your Speedy Eminence, how did it go with the children?"

"They'll be spending the rest of their lives in a dark prison cell," Malby said, looking like he was about to explode. "They'll soon learn who I am and what I can do."

"Your Most Just Eminence, I have something to show you that I think will please you." Fister was shaking inside. He had seen Malby angry on other occasions, and everyone in his sight was in danger when he got in these moods. "Feast your eyes on the celebration of your greatness, oh Mighty One."

Malby looked out his window to find a twenty-foot-high granite statue of himself. It depicted him standing with one arm pointing in the distance and his face looking upward, casting a vision into the future. Fister knew the statue was unrealistically flattering of Malby and made him look more handsome and impressive than he truly was, but that was Fister's gift, and a valuable gift at that, with a boss like Malby.

"Outstanding, Fister." Malby was now smiling as he fixated on the statue. "This is the respect the future leader of Himmel deserves. After our victory, everyone will bow to my statue."

Fister was relieved to have calmed Malby down. "Sir, Project Raven is ready for launch."

"Excellent, this day is getting better every minute." Malby grabbed a pair of binoculars from his desk drawer and looked out the window in the direction of the Sariel Caves. "Get Dusty on the phone."

Fister rang the number. "Are they ready? His Eminence wants to talk to you." He handed the phone to Malby.

"Everything ready?" Malby impatiently waited for Dusty's reply. "Good, let them all out, every last raven." Malby hung up the phone and picked up his binoculars.

Fister stood and pressed his suit with his hands. "We're close, your Supreme Eminence."

Malby stared out the window at his statue. "Fister, tomorrow at this time, Himmel will have a new ruler."

"Your Patient Eminence, I have a question. It's about the Road to Destruction plan." Fister was sheepish as he considered how to ask, not wanting to trigger Malby's wrath. "I understand that we're using deception and selfishness to accomplish our Road to Destruction plan, but to what end? What are you trying to create?"

"Create? We're not creating anything, Fister." Malby was miffed that Fister could so fundamentally misunderstand his plan. "We're transforming the minds of the people. We scatter seeds of doubt, carefully nurture distrust and disbelief, inspire them to depart from King Yasha, replace him with anything else, and ultimately lead them to a prison of their own making."

"I understand all that, your Most Eloquent Eminence, and it is a brilliant plan." Fister paused. He knew he was tempting Malby's patience. "If you destroy King Yasha and his paintings, what'll you create in its place?"

"Nothing." Malby's voice was filled with anger as he glared at Fister. "I destroy King Yasha and all he stands for and leave only chaos. What's the End? Destruction and chaos, nothing more."

Fister was terrified by the desolation of Malby's plan, but he was tied to him for better or worse. He hoped he'd picked the right side in this war and that victory was near.

Malby peered through his binoculars towards Mt. Superior. The entire skyline was filled with ravens flying eastward toward Highlands. He was particularly pleased with himself. *King Yasha will soon be bowing before me. I'm the King of Kings.* Project Raven had started and all of Himmel would soon be his.

***

Aaron looked out the cell window. The sky was painted black with ravens. "It's started; they released the ravens."

"Let's sing," said Hannah. She stared at Aaron searching for something in his eyes that would give her hope.

"I don't feel very sing-ee," replied Benji as he sat on the dirty pad tending to his scrapes and bruises.

"Signing is exactly what we should do right now," said Aaron. He gathered Benji and Hannah next to him to lift their spirits. "The sky is dark with ravens, but Yasha is the master artist. Nothing's impossible for him."

You've made the day for my delight.
You bring us warmth and light.
And keep us safe at night.
You guard our lives with your love and might.
Oh, what a good and beautiful King.

Chapter Twenty-One

Attack Against the King

Dusty and his team had been working around the clock preparing the ravens. Small pouches were made to carry Midnight Clover seeds, which were strapped to each of the thousand ravens. He and Middie watched in awe as all the cages were opened, and the ravens flew eastward toward their targets.

"There's no way to stop them. They cover the sky." Dusty traced their flight east using his binoculars. "Midnight Clover will be growing all through Himmel."

Middie brimmed with excitement as she marveled at the blackened sky above. They had spent more than a year preparing for this day. "I think we're going to be getting promotions. We'll be standing next to the ruler of Himmel."

"Their flight path is right on track," Dusty said. He peered through his binoculars and scanned the skyline. "Fly over Mt. Superior and onto the eastern side of Highlands with the ultimate destination of the City of Light."

***

Aaron, Benji, and Hannah continued to sing as they watched the ravens fly by their cell window. It was a terrifying sight, a thousand ravens speeding across the horizon as weapons of war. The situation looked bleak, and the more ravens they saw fly by, the greater their sense of doom. Their singing had only temporarily buoyed their spirits, and the attack seemed daunting.

"Get used to this cell. You're going to be here a long time," Birsha sneered through the cell door banging on the bars with his baton. "See those ravens? They're going to make all of Himmel like Shadowlands."

Benji's face was red with rage as he felt the oppression of being totally subject to the control of Malby and his mad henchmen. "Don't count your ravens before they're hatched," he sneered at Birsha.

"That doesn't even make sense," Birsha replied in a mocking tone as he banged his baton right in front of Benji to deliver an extra dose of degradation. "The ravens are already hatched."

"Yeah, we see that, Captain Obvious," sniped Benji.

As Benji and Birsha bickered about the ravens, Aaron heard a commotion coming from the corridor. It sounded like a woman's voice, and then oddly enough, somebody snoring. Aaron craned his neck down the corridor and saw Grace strolling toward them. She approached Birsha and whispered something in his ear. Suddenly, and without saying a word, Birsha lay down on the ground and began snoring, fast asleep. A strange light shined into their cell and the chains on the door fell away.

"Quick, get up," Grace said as she opened the door and handed a hooded cloak to each of them. "Follow me."

They put on the cloaks and lifted the hoods over their heads in disguise. Grace led them past Birsha and several other guards, all sleeping soundly. They stepped out of the prison complex and Grace pointed to the path eastward without saying a word. The scene outside the prison was pure chaos. People scurried about in every direction. The ravens had aroused all of Shadowlands. Everyone was staring at the sky and chattering about what might be the cause.

"We have to get to Mt. Superior." Grace ran effortlessly along the path and guided Aaron, Benji, and Hannah to safety across the border. "That's where King Yasha is waiting."

***

King Yasha had left the chateau in the morning and was making his way to Mr. Superior as Dusty released the ravens. He climbed the steep slope and pulled himself up on the ledge near the top of the mountain.

It was on the western side of the mountain and had a clear view of Shadowlands. He watched as the thousand ravens entered the sky and flew toward him on their journey to destroy Himmel. He sat on the ledge reflecting on the depth of his love for the people of Himmel. He was saddened that the war had turned so ruthless, so many lives at stake. But he was also overwhelmed with the joy that accompanies fulfilling one's purpose. That moment had come.

When the lead ravens were about a hundred yards away, he stood to his feet and raised his arms. "Here, I AM."

The leading ravens saw King Yasha and immediately began to fly with increased fervor. They had been trained for only two things: distribute Midnight Clover and kill King Yasha. The second was an overriding command that turned them into a frenzy. The ravens in front began to crow madly, alerting all thousand ravens of the new target – King Yasha.

***

Malby strained to see the ravens' flight as they made their way towards Mt. Superior. Fister was by his side hoping the day went according to plan for many reasons, not least of which was the desire to keep Malby from exploding in a fit of rage like an errant missile. He also knew that a victory for Malby would be a victory for him and a promotion to elite status in the new kingdom's ruling class. He had adorned himself in a ruby-red suit to celebrate what he believed would be a day of victory in the battle over the kingdom of Himmel.

"They're almost to Mt. Superior." Malby was so anxious his hands were shaking as he held the binoculars. "I can't see, bring that telescope over."

Fister quickly picked up the telescope and positioned it by the window pointing toward Mt. Superior. "All set, your Supreme Eminence."

"Much better." Malby turned the nobs to bring the telescope into focus. "What's this?"

"What's what, your Visionary One?" Fister had picked up the binoculars, but he couldn't see the details of Mt. Superior. "What's happening?"

"A particularly fortunate turn of events, Fister." Malby had an oversized grin on his face and was snickering as he peered through the telescope. "King Yasha has magnanimously presented himself for us on Mt. Superior."

Fister was shocked by the news. *Why would King Yasha put himself in the center of the battle? He should be hidden away in the chateau.* Fister realized this would be even better for him. With King Yasha's death, the revolution would be over much faster and his ascent to the top would be swift indeed.

"The ravens see him. They see him, Fister." Malby's lungs were heaving as he tried to contain his zeal over this turn of events. The lead ravens were changing their flight path towards King Yasha on the ledge. "He's put himself on a silver platter and laid it before us. What a fortuitous turn."

Fister had his feet together and was hopping up and down like a child in need of a bathroom. "What are they doing?"

"All thousand ravens are heading toward him. This will be over quickly; they'll devour him in minutes." Malby looked on with delight; he had waited a long time to experience this. The death of King Yasha and his ascent to ruler of Himmel was moments away.

***

King Yasha watched as the ravens adjusted their route toward him. He continued to stand tall with his arms raised and shouted, "here, I AM."

The first raven nosedived toward him, plunging its beak into his forehead. After that they came in droves, by the tens and then the hundreds. Each raven thrust its beak into his body piercing him with painful wounds.

As the ravens continued their assault, his body became weak, and he fought to remain standing. "Father, give me strength to finish."

Miraculously, he braced himself, lifted his arms and again shouted, "here, I AM."

***

Malby was absolutely giddy as he peered through the telescope. "They're attacking him. There must be hundreds, no all thousand ravens are hitting him. I can't believe he's still standing."

Fister strutted back and forth across the room like a peacock in his ruby red suit. He wore an oversized grin on his face as he cackled with an unsettling gaiety. "Oh, your Dastardly Mastermind Eminence. This is entirely delicious. A fallen king by the hand of our ravens. Ravens made mad by the saliva of the king's own citizens. The poetry of this sweet moment is simply sublime."

***

Grace, Aaron, Benji, and Hannah finally reached the basecamp on Mt. Superior to meet the others. Everyone had managed to make it safely back to the basecamp after their mission at the water treatment plant and Sariel Caves. The joy and relief of reuniting was interrupted by the horrible sound of the ravens crowing further up the mountain.

Mr. Wigglebottom had heard of Jack Deer's injury through the animal network and had hiked to Mt. Superior with his supplies. Jack was lying on the ground and Mr. Wigglebottom was tending to his wounds.

Aaron strained his eyes up the mountain to the ledge where King Yasha was facing a barrage of ravens ruthlessly flying into him. "Yasha's being attacked. We've got to get to him."

Grace was already running up the trail toward King Yasha. "Follow me, we don't have much time."

***

The attack on King Yasha was brutal and merciless. Every raven was torpedoing him from above and many were making second runs. The onslaught seemed to be without end.

Yasha's head throbbed, and excruciating pain pulsed through his entire body. He fell to his knees, but somehow continued to raise his hands. Again, he declared, "here, I AM."

He looked at the ravens and saw them as he had painted them. Beautiful creatures flying from tree to tree, building nests and caring for their young. "I love all the creatures in my kingdom, even these ravens. They're blind and don't know what they're doing. Father, forgive them."

Using all the might he could muster as life seeped from him, Yasha staggered to his feet one last time. His body was battered and beaten by the relentless attack of the ravens, covered with puncture wounds. He gazed upward with his hands raised and declared, "It is finished." Then, his lifeless body fell to the ground.

***

Malby saw King Yasha's body fall, and he raised his hands in celebration, "It's done. He's gone." He turned the telescope upward to locate the ravens. They needed to move on to their next assignment. Deposit Midnight Clover throughout Highlands bringing all of Himmel under his control.

Fister stared out the window primping his tightly wrapped hair. His mind wandered to a future that seemed inevitable. He imagined a statue of the heroic Fister next to Malby's. A great liberator of the people. "Our day has come."

***

When King Yasha fell, the air above Mt. Superior immediately became tranquil. For several minutes everything stood still, motionless, soundless, as though time had stopped.

Without warning, ominous dark clouds filled the sky, and loud cracks of thunder could be heard over Mt. Superior.

Yasha's body lay on the ledge at the top of Mt. Superior. Suddenly, hundreds of streams of water gushed out of Yasha and shot upward into the dark clouds above. It was a miraculous sight. Each stream of water looked like a brilliant ray of light beaming skyward into the heavens. This continued for several minutes and then abruptly stopped.

The clouds above were saturated with water and quickly spread across the entire kingdom of Himmel. Droplets of rain began to fall, and soon the entire kingdom was engulfed in a torrent of rain. There wasn't a living creature that could escape the deluge.

The rain blanketed the sky and washed over the ravens still enroute to release their Midnight Clover seeds. Their red eyes immediately cleared, and they all reversed course and began flying back to the Sariel Caves in Shadowlands.

The citizens of Shadowlands had been chaotically running around screaming about the commotion that had visited them when the ravens were released. The rain caused everyone to stop and stand in silence with their heads tilted upward. The falling water rushed over their faces and their eyes immediately cleared.

Julia and Ian were standing by the destroyed water treatment plant rummaging through the carnage. They looked up and the fresh clean water rushed over their faces.

"This is amazing." Julia held up her arms and let the water cover her entire body. "I can see the real world. I feel ... Renewed. Alive. Refreshed."

Ian threw down his crown as he looked skyward and let the water wash over his face. "I can see. The real world, it's beautiful."

***

Aaron and the others finally reached the top of Mt. Superior to find Yasha's lifeless body sprawled across the ledge. Aaron, Benji, and Hannah ran and knelt next to him, clinging to his battered body as they cried out in anguish. His face had a serene peaceful expression. Aaron wondered; *how could he look so calm in the wake of such a brutal death?*

Everyone gathered around his body and sobbed at the realization that King Yasha was gone. His goodness, his beautiful paintings, everything he was to Himmel had been cruelly ripped away from them.

"But look what he accomplished." Grace stood on the ledge looking out over Shadowlands. The ravens were flying westward landing peacefully back at the Sariel Caves. "His death brings life."

Aaron pulled out his binoculars to take a closer look. "They didn't drop the Midnight Clover. Their eyes aren't red anymore; the rainwater healed them."

"Julia and Ian are dancing and stomping on their crowns," shouted Benji as he looked through his binoculars towards the rubble that used to be the water treatment plant. "They're healed."

They all stood on the ledge and watched as Shadowlands was transformed, renewed, before their eyes. The streets were swarming with people. They trampled their crowns, sang, and danced as they looked skyward. They were seeing the goodness and beauty of Himmel for the first time in a very long time. The cleansing rain also killed the Midnight Clover throughout Shadowlands ridding the kingdom of that horrible weed.

Aaron walked back to look over Yasha's tattered remains. "He did this for us." He began to sob with the realization of the depth of Yasha's loved for him. "He was willing to face this vicious end to save me, to save all of us, and everyone in Himmel."

"He wanted this end." Hannah replayed the last hour in her mind. "I saw him standing on the ledge shouting, 'here, I AM.' He drew the ravens to himself to save us."

Mr. Wigglebottom climbed up to the ledge holding Jack Deer, who limped by his side. He whispered to Jack, "Will you give honor to our king?"

Jack called all the animals to give tribute to their fallen king. Grace, Aaron, Benji, and Hannah stepped back to give them space, respecting this solemn moment for their friends. One by one the animals slowly walked up to King Yasha's body and formed a circle around him. Jack, Ella, Enzo, Piper, Jasper, and Riley stoically guarded his body and bowed their heads to honor their fallen king. Thomas, Sophia, and Mr. Wigglebottom stood alongside them, still weeping as they tried to grasp the hard truth of this moment. Their king was gone. Their faces were contorted with pain and tears streamed down their cheeks as they took in the horrendous punishment King Yasha had absorbed to save them.

Enzo wept uncontrollably and rubbed his nose in King Yasha's face hoping he might somehow still be alive. Death was foreign to Yasha's kingdom. After several moments of silence, Ella pulled Enzo away from King Yasha's body. In a whimpering voice, he asked the animals to sing *My King* to honor King Yasha. Their voices cracked with emotion as they sang out the lyrics,

You've made the day for my delight.
You bring us warmth and light.
And keep us safe at night.
You guard our lives with your love and might.
Oh, what a good and beautiful King.

***

Malby remained in his office fixated by the events occurring on Mt. Superior. He had seen King Yasha fall to the ground assuring him that victory had arrived. His euphoria turned to horror when he saw the water gushing out of King Yasha into the sky and the resulting torrent of healing rain.

"What's happening?" Malby squinted through the telescope. "The rain is flooding all the Midnight Clover. It's destroyed."

Fister's heart began to beat faster as he heard the turn of events. "Sir, King Yasha is dead, right?" He was desperately searching for any bright spot to soothe Malby's volatile temper.

"Yeah but look what he's brought about." Malby stepped away from the telescope and picked up the binoculars which were better for scanning the horizon. "The ravens are turning around. They're going back to the caves."

Fister stopped his strutting, sat down in a chair, and placed his head in his hands. "With King Yasha dead, we can produce a new plan. Destruction and chaos, right, your Most Victorious One?"

"Look at the plaza," screamed Malby. He glared outside in shock at what he was witnessing. "They're destroying my statue." He picked up the marble pen holder off his desk and hurled it as hard as he could. It flew by Fister, missed his head by an inch, and crashed into the wall leaving a deep hole.

"Your Magnificent Eminence, perhaps we should lock down the presidential offices." Fister was on the phone directing staff to secure the building. "We'll wait this out and come back stronger than ever."

Malby put down the binoculars and the tension in his face eased. "King Yasha is dead, and that's all that really matters. I'll find a way to rule Himmel now that he's gone."

Chapter Twenty-Two

Kingdom Restored

———— ⟋⟍⟍ ————

Aaron woke up startled by his dream of falling on the mountain. His head still throbbed from the beating the guards delighted in giving him. Recent days had created a fog in his mind. He couldn't tell if he was having his familiar mountain dream or if his mind was simply replaying the traumatic events of the past several days.

The morning light was just beginning to peek over the horizon with beautiful shades of orange dressing the skyline. This was the morning of the third day since Yasha's death, and Aaron was confused and lost in a sea of sorrow and recrimination. *How could I have let this happen to King Yasha? To Himmel?*

Mr. Wigglebottom had wrapped King Yasha's body in a linen cloth that Grace provided and Thomas and Sophia gathered fresh sweet-smelling flowers and fresh smelling spices to spread over his body. King Yasha had been the focus of the past two days. They shared stories about him and all he meant to the kingdom. All he meant to each of them personally. The only safe place to sleep was in a small field below the ledge, so they spent the nights nestled together.

Aaron surveyed the area and saw the others still fast asleep. A perplexing aroma wafting from the mountain top drew him to investigate. He hiked up to the ledge and his eyes feasted on the most astonishing sight he could ever imagine. King Yasha was sitting by a fire cooking breakfast. Aaron was stunned and speechless. He rubbed his eyes with thoughts swirling in his head. *I saw him dead, gone. Dead people don't come back to life. Did I catch Midnight Madness? Did the recent terror drive me insane? Wait, both my nose and eyes can't be daft.*

He cautiously crept toward the sitting king, his mouth agape. "King Yasha, are … are… you really here?"

"Aaron, it's so good to see you." Yasha gently stirred the frying pan. "Would you like breakfast?"

"But I saw you yesterday. You're… you're dead." Aaron rubbed his hands through his hair trying to clear his head of the doubts that streamed to the surface. *Maybe Malby is playing a cruel joke on me.*

Yasha stood up, took a small step toward Aaron, and reached out his hand. He was wearing a loose-fitting cotton robe that covered his entire body except his hands and feet. "That was yesterday's painting. Today's painting brings life, not just to me, but to all of Himmel."

Aaron glared at the scars on Yasha's hands and feet and stopped in his tracks as he reflected on the painful death Yasha had suffered for him. After this moment in his own thoughts, he ran to Yasha and wrapped his arms around him. A wave of comfort pulsed through Aaron when he felt Yasha's warm, strong body. "I saw the ravens attack you. I thought I had killed you and failed everyone in Himmel."

"You, your brother and sister are so courageous," Yasha reassured Aaron and looked him in the eye. "You did exactly what I needed you to do."

As Aaron held on tight to Yasha, he replayed in his head the calamity at the caves and the brutal raven attack on Yasha. "But my plan failed. We didn't get to spray the ravens with cleansing water."

"That was your plan as far as you could do on your own," replied Yasha. "You try so hard to be perfect, but that's impossible for you, Aaron. You don't have to be perfect. You were not made to conquer all of life's problems by yourself."

Aaron stepped back peering into Yasha's eyes. "But it was my job to come up with a plan to save Himmel. Save you. Benji, Hannah."

"You're not alone, Aaron. You never have been and never will be alone." Yasha placed his hand on Aaron's shoulder. "I think you've accepted burdens that weren't meant for you. The burden of saving Himmel and the burden of keeping your family safe."

Yasha's words pierced Aaron's heart. His dad was missing, and he had put all his effort into keeping his family safe. "I have to make sure everyone's safe while my dad's away."

"You're a very brave boy, Aaron." Yasha looked deeply into Aaron's eyes. "I'm watching over your family and so are your mom and your Papa and Grandma.

You can let go of the burden and rest in me."

"How?" Aaron's face revealed his bewilderment. "How can I?"

"Trust, Aaron. Trust me and trust those you love to help you in life." Yasha smiled at Aaron. "You have help in ways you don't even realize."

Aaron hesitated as he searched to see what King Yasha saw. "What do you mean?"

"Think of all the ways our team supported the mission we can now celebrate. How each member did so many little things to bring about our victory."

As Yasha described all the members of their team and all they had done to contribute to the mission, Aaron began to see that he really wasn't alone. They had all been in it together. Like a family.

"Even dreams can be used to help a plan along," said King Yasha. He tussled Aaron's hair with his hand and winked at him. "You know."

Aaron gasped. "My mountain dream?" He stepped back in shock staring at Yasha.

"Yes, Aaron. I said I'm everywhere, even in your thoughts. Even when you sleep." King Yasha stepped toward the fire and waved at Aaron to follow. "You're never alone."

"So, did you give me the mountain dream?" Aaron sat down next to King Yasha cautiously studying every move he made. "Why would you give me that dream?"

"Trust, Aaron, to show you what trust looks like, even when circumstances are dire." King Yasha paused to let his words sink it. "I needed you to take great risks for the kingdom. Overcoming Malby and the evil he planned required more than any one boy could do by himself. Even a very talented boy like you."

"So, it was your plan to have the ravens attack you?" asked Aaron. "You're the man in the dream I've been trying to save. The man who saved me."

"Yes, Aaron." Yasha broke into a wide smile. "You were very courageous to do your part, but more was required."

Aaron rubbed his chin as he reconsidered so much of what he thought he knew. "Why didn't you tell me about the ravens attacking you?"

"That was the only way, Aaron." Yasha flipped the fish in his pan. "If I had told you, would you have let me face the ravens the way I did?"

"Probably not," Aaron admitted. "I see what you mean." Aaron paused to let Yasha's words sink in. "What Malby planned for evil against us, you used for good to save us all."

Yasha dished up several plates of fresh grilled fish from the frying pan. "I was the only one who could save you."

Aaron listened intently. He was stunned by Yasha's ability to convey deep thoughts by a simple look. Yasha's eyes comforted Aaron without words and told him he had willingly, even joyfully, faced the ravens, and would do it again a million times over. "I love you, Aaron, more than you can ever imagine. Nothing can separate you from my love. Now run and get the others; I've worked up a healthy appetite."

***

Malby stewed in his presidential office revisiting yesterday's calamitous events. *How could my plan have gone so far off course?* He hadn't gotten much sleep and glared out the window as the sun rose. His statue was a pile of rubble in the plaza and the people of Shadowlands had destroyed their crowns and were drinking freely from the pure fresh water of the streams now that the water treatment plant was destroyed. Their sight had been restored and they could see the goodness and beauty of the kingdom and its king.

"At least King Yasha is dead," Malby assured himself. He looked through the telescope towards Mt. Superior to gaze upon King Yasha's dead body as a way to cheer himself up.

"Nooo!"

Malby's scream woke up Fister who had spent the night on the couch in Malby's office. He jumped to his feet still wearing his now rumpled ruby red suit. His heavily gelled hair had fallen out of its bun. It was hanging down his face and gave him the look of a decrepit old rock star. "What is it, your Most Vicious…I mean Victorious One?"

"King Yasha's alive!" Malby slumped in his chair in disbelief. "Check the telescope. Am I crazy?"

Fister peered through the telescope and saw King Yasha calmly enjoying breakfast, surrounded by Aaron and the others. "He looks very much alive, your Most Honorable Eminence."

"Time to hunker down, Fister," Malby declared. He rose from his chair and paced his office like a caged animal trying to find a way out of this nightmare that would not end. His rage was bursting out as he realized his reign over Shadowlands had been destroyed by King Yasha. "Go to code red lockdown. Nobody in or out, including us."

"Yes, sir. Right away." Fister's heart sank with the realization that he had tied his fate to the supremacy of Malby. Now that bond had become handcuffs. This office had become a prison. He let out a muffled chilling laugh as he grasped the devilish irony of his situation. Malby's plan was supposed to place everyone else in a prison of their own making. Now, he and Malby found themselves in a prison of their own making.

***

King Yasha led Aaron and the others on their hike back to the chateau. Hannah was so overwhelmed with joy at seeing King Yasha alive that she was singing repeated rounds of *My King*. It was a beautiful day in Himmel. The sky was blue, and the birds were chirping and singing their songs. The townspeople cheered and joined in the singing as the group passed. The animals were frolicking, playing games, and leaping in the air. The whole kingdom was in a festive mood.

"Tonight, we'll have a great banquet," said King Yasha. "We have much to celebrate."

Grace was captivated by the grandeur of the countryside and all the people and animals celebrating. "Himmel is showing even greater shades of beauty today," she said.

"Yes, it is," said Aaron. He grinned ear to ear as he quietly discovered the abundant joy radiating out of every creature in Himmel. "The king is alive."

When they arrived at the chateau, Grace arranged for everyone to have spa treatments to help them recover from the past few days. Aaron, Benji and Hannah were lavished with care and attention and were soon relaxed and refreshed. Upon returning to their room, they were surprised with brand new clothes that Grace had picked out, suitable for the grand celebration.

As they walked toward the banquet hall, Aaron saw Yasha at his easel. He nudged Benji and Hannah to follow him out to the patio.

"It's nice to see you back at your painting," said Aaron. "I hope deadly ravens won't be in your paintings again."

"No, I don't expect they will," Yasha chuckled and gestured for the children to look toward the other end of the patio as he stepped over to join them. "I'd like you to meet my Father, Dio."

Aaron was startled to see another man sitting by the second easel on the patio. He had wondered about this. The man looked quite a bit older than Yasha. He had long flowing white hair and piercing blue eyes that were both kind and penetrating at the same time – just like Yasha's. His features were chiseled, making him appear both impressive and intimidating.

"Thank you for your heroic work these past few days," said Dio as he set down his brush. "These have been difficult days in Himmel."

"You're welcome, sir," replied Aaron. He couldn't take his eyes off Dio. There was something so alluring about him that Aaron simply couldn't resist. "We were ready to do anything for Yasha."

"Your faith and loyalty are well noted, Aaron." Dio looked at Hannah to invite her closer. "How are you holding up with all this, Hannah?"

"Fine, sir," she said. "Yasha helped me see my special gifts and gave me the courage to use them to protect Himmel." Hannah leaned in close to Dio and examined his face. "Are you Yasha's dad?"

"Yes, I am, his Abba" Dio smiled at Yasha and placed a hand on his shoulder. "He's my Son and I love him very much."

"Do you remember when we talked about my Father, Abba?" said Yasha. He clasped Dio's hand as it rested on his shoulder. "You're part of our family."

"Are you like my father?" asked Hannah. The conversation reminded her of how much she missed her dad and brought tears to her eyes. "I miss my dad."

"Hannah, that saddens me to no end." Dio crouched down so his face was even with Hannah's. "We're both your father, but in different ways."

"What do you mean?" asked Hannah as she inched closer to Dio.

"Your father is your earthly father, and a very good one at that." Dio reached out his hand to Hannah. "I'm a father of a different kind. Think of me as your father from another world, your Himmel father."

"I trust my dad to protect me," said Hannah as she stared at Dio's extended hand. "Are you like that?"

"Yes, Hannah, I'm like that." Dio waved his hand pointing out the vast kingdom beyond the patio. "But my power to protect goes even farther."

"Can we call you Father?" asked Hannah, moving still closer to Dio. "Yasha said I could."

"You can call me Father if you like, Hannah," replied Dio. He gave her a gentle embrace. "Some call me Abba for short, and you can call me that too."

"So, you two are our king and our father?" asked Benji. He swiveled his head between Yasha and Dio with a confounded expression.

"That's a good way to think about it, Benji," Dio chuckled as he watched Benji's gaze pivoting between him and Yasha. "You're not the first to be confused by this. To those who see my Son as king, I'm also their Father."

Grace glided out to the patio and motioned for them to make their way to the banquet hall. "The guests have arrived, and the banquet awaits you."

The banquet hall was adorned with bright colors and festive decorations. There were balloons floating, garlands hanging, and large banners throughout the room. The same large rectangular wooden table sat in the middle of the room and ten smaller round tables circled the room. All the animals sat on one side of the main table, and Thomas, Sophia, and Mr. Wigglebottom sat on the other side. Dio sat at the head of the table with Yasha on one side and Grace on the other side. Aaron, Benji, and Hannah sat at the other end. The smaller tables were filled with people from all over the kingdom of Himmel who had participated in the plan to defeat Malby.

The dinner was a feast that surpassed all others. The servers brought out broiled fish, mashed potatoes, grilled carrots, and freshly baked biscuits. There were as many other side dishes as you could imagine. Jack Deer, Ella Doe, and Enzo Fawn had fresh flowers brought in from Aspen Meadows, grass picked just today from Asha Grasslands, and leaves from Sane Forest. Piper Bear was served a large platter of fresh fish caught at Lake Enid. Riley Raccoon was served fresh fruit and vegetables, and Jasper Lion was served his favorite meal, too.

Dio stood to offer thanks. "I want to thank everyone who has faithfully served the kingdom and helped bring victory over Malby. May the kingdom of Himmel be everlasting."

Aaron's face blushed when he noticed that the people in the room were smiling at him with their glasses raised in appreciation. He lowered his head as he tried to shift the attention back to Dio.

Dio smiled at Aaron, but then his face grew serious "We have won this battle, but make no mistake, Malby will not concede. He's plotting his next attack as we speak." Dio paused for a moment and surveyed the room looking at each person. "Be vigilant, for he prowls like a roaring lion, seeking to destroy the good and transform the beautiful to chaos."

King Yasha stood and raised a glass of water. "But tonight, we have much to celebrate. We have washed all of Himmel with rainwater that cleanses and heals the blindness of Midnight Madness." He gazed across the room at the faces of people and creatures he knew who had come from all areas of Himmel. "You have been invited to share our joy this evening. Now all can see the good and beautiful kingdom of Himmel."

Dio nudged Yasha on the side and suggested, "Shouldn't we provide a little entertainment?"

"Rightly so," Yasha chuckled and waved his arm across the room. "Tonight, the most splendid show in Himmel… You."

Suddenly, the gorgeous landscape murals on the walls transformed into moving real-life portraits. It was like a video, but not a video. It was a real window into the kingdom of Himmel. The trees swayed in the gentle wind; the animals roamed the lush fields.

Aaron gazed up to the ceiling and the birds soared across the blue skyscape above. "Wow." He turned his head around the room watching the majestic scenes of Himmel unfolding right in front of him.

Yasha and Dio sat back in their chairs imbibing with delight the beauty of their creation. They seemed to be enjoying the show even more than the guests, if that were possible. The two chuckled and oohed and aahed as the scenery shifted to new wonderous places within the kingdom. All the other guests were in awe as well. They had never seen their kingdom in this way and were staggered by its majesty. The animals were particularly keen in pointing out their appearance in the scenes, like fledgling actors seeing themselves on the big screen for the first time.

The rest of the evening was full of tasty food, fascinating stories, and heaps of fun. They reminisced on the past few days with a sense of unrivaled jubilation. So many incredible things had occurred, and the dangers had been great. As the evening was winding down, Yasha and Dio quietly invited Aaron, Benji, and Hannah back to the patio. They said their goodnights and slipped out.

***

"We want to share something with you before you return to the Ranch," Dio said. He was sitting on his stool at his easel and lifted the tarp off his canvas. "This is a painting Yasha and I have been working on for a long, long time."

The children stepped closer to the painting with expressions of wonder. It was even more beautiful than Yasha's paintings, if such a thing were possible. It was only partially completed, but depicted all of Himmel in the finest detail with brilliant colors, shades, and landscapes.

"Do you like it?" Dio admired the painting as he drew the children into its detail. "We call it, *All in All.*"

"It's even more beautiful than the other paintings we've seen," said Aaron. He craned his neck to get a closer look at the miniscule details of the painting. "But why is it unfinished?"

"Because the story of the kingdom is not complete." Dio gathered his thoughts to form words the children could understand. "This painting shows all people and living creatures, in all places, over all time. It's a very complicated painting and takes much thought and time to fully create."

"If it's not finished yet, how can you be certain it will be good and beautiful when you do finish?" asked Benji. "I mean, what if something like Malby happens again?"

"Oh, but the painting is complete in my mind," said Dio. He gazed up to the ceiling with a far-off look in his eye. "I have every last brush stroke complete in my mind."

"Then why isn't the painting finished?" asked Hannah. She moved closer to get a better look at the painting. "It is beautiful...so far."

Yasha stepped over to the canvas to help them understand. "I continue to make paintings every day that become real. Each of my paintings becomes part of this *All in All* painting." Yasha pointed across the patio to his painting and gestured back to Dio's painting. "So, day by day this *All in All* painting is being completed."

"You see the new scenes just added include all that happened in Shadowlands and on Mt. Superior." Dio pointed to the section of the painting that showed the children in prison, Yasha on Mt. Superior, and the raven attack. "The pain of those days has become part of the beauty of the *All in All* painting."

Yasha directed their attention to his easel and the painting resting on it. "There will come a day when the *All in All* painting is complete, but it isn't today. We have many more days to paint."

Aaron scrutinized the painting, and a quizzical look came over his face. "But I see the Ranch in this painting and my mom, Papa and Grandma." He stepped back from the painting with his mouth wide open. "How can that be?"

"I said my kingdom is very big and includes everything," Yasha chucked, as Aaron's eyes widened at the revelation. Yasha smiled and continued, "Everything is a very big word."

Aaron was perplexed by Dio and Yasha's discussion of the *All in All* painting. He pulled out the map that Yasha had given him and held it out for Yasha to see. "The map you gave me has some regions that we didn't see."

Yasha glanced at the map and smiled at Aaron. "You mean, the Mysterious Everlasting Pathway, Land of the Great Unveiling, and the Abyss to Outer Darkness?"

"Yeah, why didn't you take us there on our tour?" Aaron stared at the map trying to figure out any other parts of Himmel he didn't know about. "I want to see the whole kingdom."

"Our kingdom is vast and bigger than you can ever imagine," Yasha said, gently taking the map from Aaron. "I showed you the parts of the kingdom you needed to know about for the mission I gave you – defeat Malby and help me restore Shadowlands."

Aaron's curiosity was piqued, and he asked, "So what are these other areas?"

"Those places are not for today, Aaron." Yasha folded the map and placed it in his pocket. "Perhaps you'll learn of these areas in the years ahead as you spend time with us in Himmel."

Hannah moved close to Yasha. "Can we stay here in Himmel with you?"

Yasha stroked her head gently and knelt down to gaze into her eyes. "We would love to have you stay with us, but you have much to do in your world. I have seen each of you grow more like me during your time here, and you will use that back in your world."

Hannah was sad at the thought of leaving Yasha, but excited by the idea of being used by him back in her world. "How?"

"You're a strong and courageous young lady, and your heart is pure." Yasha hugged her tightly. "There are important things for you down there. You're time in Himmel has made you strong and courageous to persist and endure, whatever may come."

Benji wanted to understand too and asked, "Yasha, what do you have for me?"

"When you came to me, you thought mostly about your wants, and you were angry with the world." Yasha placed his hand on Benji's shoulder. "I have seen you learn the joy of loving others and placing their needs before your own. You've replaced your anger with love and the picture is quite beautiful. You will use this to help many people."

Aaron smiled at Yasha and reflected on their discussion on the mountain.

"Aaron, you came to me carrying the weight of your family, and the weight of the world on your shoulders. You don't have to carry that burden. I'm the artist of all kingdoms and you can rest in me. There are many in your world who need to learn this same lesson."

Grace gathered the children and escorted them back to their guest suite. "It's been a long day; you should get some sleep. Tomorrow, we'll see you to the redwoods."

Chapter Twenty-Three
Christmas at the Ranch

It was a beautiful day in Himmel as Aaron, Benji, and Hannah set off for Aspen Meadows and their return to the Ranch. Yasha, with Aaron and Benji at his sides, led the procession. Piper Bear insisted that Hannah ride on her back, and Hannah was glowing as she waved goodbye to the people. Jack Deer and Ella Doe had a regal look and were on either side of Piper. The townspeople of the City of Light lined the plaza and waved and cheered as they walked past. Enzo Fawn nuzzled close to Piper Bear so he could chat with Hannah. They laughed and joked about all the attention they were receiving. Jasper Lion and Riley Raccoon were at the rear of the procession scanning the scene for any dangers.

They reached the orchards and saw Thomas and Sophia waving from the side of the road. "You're courageous children. Thank you for all you've done for Himmel," said Thomas.

Aaron stepped over to embrace Thomas, then Sophia. "Thank you, but we simply did what was right."

"Thanks for showing us the way in Himmel." Benji hugged Sophia and Thomas. He smirked at Thomas, "How do you make an apple turnover?"

Thomas rolled his eyes waiting for Benji's punchline. "Roll it down a hill," cried Benji.

"Never lose that, young comedian," said Thomas. "We hope you come back soon." Thomas patted Hannah on her head as she sat comfortably on Piper.

Hank waved his arm and ran toward them as they passed by his farm. "Goodbye, children." He handed Aaron a bunch of carrots and a small basket of strawberries. "In case you're hungry." They paused for a minute to share their terrifying adventure with Hank and gladly accepted his wonderful gift before saying their farewells.

The rest of the trip down to Aspen Meadows was splendid. The warm fresh air filled their lungs and people and animals waved all along the way. They had become celebrities in Himmel for their bravery in facing Malby.

When they arrived at Lake Amari, Yasha picked an idyllic meadow next to the lake to rest. "This looks like a grand place for farewells."

Piper lowered herself to the ground and Hannah stepped off. Hannah gave her a big squeeze barely reaching halfway around her neck. "You're a special girl, Hannah," said the bear. "Come back soon."

"I will," replied Hannah. "We need to play hide-and-seek soon."

Yasha placed his arm around Benji and said, "I want you to keep painting.

"You like my painting?" Benji smiled at Yasha. "What should I paint?"

"Your imagination has no limits," replied Yasha. "Remind yourself of the Razzle-Dazzle Den."

Benji recalled the extraordinary splendor of the cave. "That's beyond what I could even imagine."

"I've made you like me, so there's a little of my creativity inside you." Yasha patted Benji's chest. "Find that artist inside you, Benji. Use it to reveal my goodness and beauty to the world."

Mr. Wigglebottom waddled out of his cottage to say goodbye. He gave a long embrace to Benji and Hannah, then stepped aside with Aaron for a private moment. "Sir Aaron, I'd say you had a very successful journey."

Aaron laughed as he remembered Mr. Wigglebottom's parting words at the beginning of their journey. "Yeah, kept my eyes on the goodness and beauty of King Yasha and ignored all the bad and ugly things coming from Malby."

Mr. Wigglebottom wrapped his arms around Aaron and gently patted him on the back of the head. "Yes, you did, my boy. Goodbye, Sir Aaron."

Benji stroked Jasper and Riley on their backs. "Thank you for taking care of us." His heart was full as he reflected on their bravery and the risks they had taken to protect them. "I love all of you."

"I'm going to miss you," Enzo began to whimper, and tears streamed down his face. "When are you coming back?"

"We're going to miss you, too." Hannah rubbed his back and kissed his head. "We'll come back and you can teach us more songs."

"We live far away from the Ranch and don't visit very often." Aaron realized they may not see their friends in Himmel anytime soon. "We're not sure when we'll be back."

Aaron gave a personal farewell to each of the animals and saved Jack and Ella for last. "You cared for us like family. I'll never forget you."

"We're all part of the family in the kingdom of Himmel," said Jack, rubbing his neck on Aaron's shoulder. "That's what families do."

"I have a gift for you to take back," Yasha said as he stood by the lakeshore and picked up two round pebbles. He placed one in each of Benji's and Hannah's hands. He then took a fine woven scarf from around his neck and handed it to Aaron. "I have a feeling you may have a need for these on the Ranch. These will remind you of us."

"Thank you, Yasha," replied Benji and Hannah. They put the pebbles in their pockets and wrapped their arms around his neck. "I'm so glad I got to know you," said Benji.

"May our friendship be lifelong and ever deepening," replied Yasha. He looked into Aaron's eyes. "When you see goodness, beauty, and truth in the world, you will see me."

"By your actions and words," said Aaron as he wrapped the scarf around his neck and gazed at the picturesque scenery surrounding them. "And what you've made."

Yasha acknowledged Aaron's wisdom with a nod and a smile. "I have a feeling we'll be seeing each other again." Yasha gave Aaron a long embrace. "No matter what comes today, be hopeful. The artwork of tomorrow may bring even greater goodness and beauty."

They slowly walked off toward the redwood with tears in their eyes. They had not only seen how extraordinary the kingdom of Himmel was, but they had also undertaken a great adventure to save it. Benji stepped out onto the tree first. These were new friendships they cherished, and they didn't want to let them go. Aaron helped Hannah, and then he turned and gave a final wave before disappearing into the fog.

***

The climb down the tree seemed faster than they remembered. They were soon through the fog and making their way to the ground below. Rocky was parked where they'd left it with fresh snow covering its roof. Aaron and Benji brushed off the snow and shoveled track lines.

Aaron handed the keys to Benji. "Why don't you drive, Benji?"

"You mean it, Aaron?" Benji stepped back with a shocked expression. "Awesome."

"Sorry, I should trust you more, Benji." Aaron broke into a wide smile. "Drive us home."

They climbed in and headed back to the lodge. Their mood was both gloomy and exhilarated. They were saying goodbye to an adventure of a lifetime and many new friends they may never see again. At the same time, they were happy to be back on the Ranch and eager to share their incredible adventure in the kingdom of Himmel.

"They're not going to believe us," said Benji. His eyes were laser focused on the trail to avoid any pitfalls along the way. "I barely believe it."

"Now I see why Papa says the Ranch is extraordinary," replied Aaron. He gazed out the window at the snow-covered trees in the forest. "Not like Himmel, but still spectacularly beautiful."

The winter beauty of the Ranch was captivating. Their time in Himmel had given them new eyes to appreciate the goodness and beauty in fresh ways. Untouched powdery snow blanketed the hills, and the scent of pine filled the air. Aaron pointed out a snowy white owl on a tree for Hannah as it craned its neck and welcomed them with a loud, "Hoo... Hoo."

The beauty that surrounded him made Aaron reminisce about his meeting with Dio and the *All in All* painting. The newly gained knowledge that their world was the handiwork of Yasha's loving creative mastery was both stunning and almost too much to take in. *I see Yasha in everything around me. The snow, the trees, the owl. Everything.*

They reached the lodge just as the sun was setting. Papa saw them from the woodshop window and ran out to greet them.

"Welcome home," yelled Papa. He gave Hannah a big bear hug as he inspected Aaron and Benji to make sure they were all right. "We were beginning to worry."

Sarah and Grandma ran out from the lodge and clenched them like found treasure. "Is everybody OK? We didn't know if you were going to make it back tonight."

Bailey bounded out of the lodge and jumped up on Aaron, knocking him into the snow. "Hi boy, you miss us?" said Aaron as he rubbed Bailey's head. Bailey's tail was whirling like a helicopter as he licked Aaron's face. Suddenly, he started sniffing Aaron, then moved on to Benji and Hannah. He had a serious look of a detective following a clue.

Benji fell back in the snow laughing as Bailey smelled his pants and jacket.

"I bet you smell our new friends."

Aaron got to his feet and squeezed his mom to reassure her, "We're all fine." He hoped that news had arrived during their time in Himmel. "Did you hear anything from Dad?"

"Not much, Aaron. He's still missing." Sarah stroked his head and smiled. She didn't want to spoil this moment with troubling thoughts about Peter. "I can fill you in later."

"It's getting cold. Let's go inside," said Grandma as she ushered them toward the lodge. "You're just in time for Christmas Eve dinner."

Aaron, Benji, and Hannah dropped their backpacks off upstairs and washed up for dinner. Everyone gathered around the table and Grandma and Papa brought out large platters for the Christmas Eve feast. One platter had a whole turkey that Papa had carved. There were bowls of mashed potatoes, stuffing, gravy, cranberry sauce, grilled vegetables, and fresh biscuits with Grandma's homemade honey-butter. The tasty aroma of Grandma's cooking filled their hearts with gladness. They were home.

Sarah's face glowed as she gazed at the children. They were home safe, and she was spending Christmas Eve with her beloved family, even if Peter couldn't be there. Grandma was smiling and Papa was laughing as they joked about having so many side dishes for such a small group.

Aaron noticed his mom's radiance as she helped dish out the food, and he was happy for her. Still, he was melancholy. He missed his dad so much and this would be another Christmas without him.

As they were about to pray, there was a knock at the door. "Who could be all the way out here on Christmas Eve?" Papa excused himself and strode into the entryway to open the door. "Well, I'll be. What a Christmas surprise!"

What sounded like Peter's voice could be heard saying, "Merry Christmas." Everyone ran to the entryway to find Peter standing in the doorway in his Navy uniform with a large duffel bag over his shoulder. Sarah ran to him and wrapped her arms around his neck. Tears of joy streamed down her cheeks.

Aaron, Benji, and Hannah wrapped their arms around him, clasping any part of him they could get their hands on. Bailey could only jump and bark nearby. There was no room for him to join the joyous reunion.

"Let me take your bag," Papa grabbed the large duffel bag and set it in the entryway.

"We're just sitting down for dinner," said Grandma. "Let me fix you a plate."

The lodge was filled with noise as they shared stories and oohed and aahed about the food to Grandma.

Grandma looked at Peter with glistening eyes. "Did everything go well?"

Peter put down his fork and paused for a moment considering the question. "I can't say much, operational security and all. The mission was a success, and we got the children to safety."

"I understand, Peter," replied Grandma. "I'm just glad you're home."

Peter's mind returned to the terror of his mission and the utter darkness he had faced. He looked at Aaron, Benji, and Hannah to anchor himself to something beautiful. "I want to hear about all you've been doing."

"We've been exploring the Ranch, and we've got stories." Aaron was chewing as he spoke and was so excited, some of the words came out garbled. "Boy, do we have stories."

Peter chuckled at Aaron's excitement. "Do tell, but slow down. We have all night."

"Papa took us to Redwood Grove," started Aaron as he smiled at Papa. "And we climbed the tree named *The Way*."

"Oh…" Peter grinned at Aaron. "And what did you find?"

Benji was getting antsy just listening to the story and burst out, "We found a place called Himmel. We talked to animals, met the king, and all kinds of stuff."

Peter glanced at Papa and smiled. "Sounds like a pretty amazing adventure," replied Peter.

"But it got super dangerous." Aaron sheepishly looked at his mom and dad. He was nervous about describing exactly what they had done in Himmel. His parents expected him to protect Benji and Hannah and he'd taken some mighty big risks. "A man named Malby wanted to destroy the kingdom and King Yasha asked us to help."

Peter said, "Seems serious, Aaron." He stared at his firstborn son with concern. "Tell me about it."

Aaron told them everything. Yasha and his paintings and their visit to the chateau. Shadowlands and Malby's plan to spread Midnight Madness all over Himmel. Yasha's tour of the kingdom and their counterplan to stop Malby. The spy mission to the capital, the Himmel Games, and the sabotage and explosion of the water treatment plant. Getting caught by Malby, going to prison, and the miraculous escape orchestrated by Grace. The ravens killing Yasha, water gushing from him into the clouds, and the rain that washed away the Midnight Clover and healed the sick. Yasha's miraculous return to life. Benji described the enormous banquet at the chateau. Hannah filled in many of the stories about their new friends along the way, such as Jack Deer trying to save their lives. Peter, Sarah, Papa, and Grandma intently listened, riveted by the unfolding drama.

"Wow, that's simply incredible," Peter said, as he sat back stunned. "While I was away on my mission, you've had your own mission."

"It was scary, Dad." Aaron looked at his dad for any sign of approval. "I tried my hardest to protect Benji and Hannah."

Benji felt Aaron's anxiousness as he tried to show he'd done everything possible to protect his brother and sister. He realized the burden of responsibility Aaron had to carry as the oldest, and he had a newfound compassion for his brother. "Aaron was super brave, Dad. He came up with an awesome plan and risked a lot to keep us safe. We also had Yasha, Grace, Dio and all the others on our side. They all risked their lives for us."

"That's good to hear." Peter smiled affectionately to ease the tension. "Aaron, thank you for looking after your brother and sister. You all were very brave. So, are Yasha and Himmel safe?"

"Yeah...for now," replied Aaron as he recalled Dio's warning about Malby's persistence. "Yasha said he remembers you."

"I spent a lot of time in Himmel when I was your age." Peter tilted his head back as he recalled his adventures in Himmel. "Yasha changed my life. I wouldn't be the person I am today without him."

Papa took a sip of water and cleared his throat. That was his way of saying he had something to say. "Your dad and I both have many stories about our time in Himmel when we were young."

"Can we hear your stories?" replied Benji. He sat up in his chair excited to hear more about Yasha and Himmel.

"That's for another day." Papa looked at his watch and noticed it was getting late. "Your adventures in Himmel are quite enough for one day, not to mention your dad's return."

Peter noticed Papa's effort to move off Himmel for now. "Aaron, how'd your football season end up?"

"We lost the championship game." Aaron reflected back on the game with pain. "I didn't trust Jason on the last play, and it cost us. The last few days showed me there's a better way."

"That's the most important thing, Aaron. Learning and growing." Peter reached across the table to give Aaron a high-five. "Do we have any pictures?" Aaron turned to Sarah with a wide smile. "Yeah, Mom has some great ones."

Sarah opened her phone and shared the photos of the game. Everyone gathered around the phone, oohing and aahing at the action pics and videos of Aaron catching the screen pass.

Peter knew Benji didn't like being in Aaron's shadow, so he tried to think of something to ask him. "Benji, how'd school go for you?"

Benji turned to his dad with a serious expression on his face. "Well, I have something to tell you and Mom." Ever since his conversation with Yasha, he had been racked with guilt.

"What's that, Benji?" replied Peter. He spoke slowly not knowing what to expect from his oh so clever son.

"I cheated on a math test and lied about it to Mr. Jacobson. I did it to get chocolate bars, and I feel terrible about it." Benji's guilt released from him as he openly talked about what he had done. "It wasn't loving to the other students or the teacher, and it was disrespectful to

Yasha and our family. I'm going to tell Mr. Jacobson on Monday and repay him for the chocolate bars."

Peter and Sarah sat back astonished by Benji's admission. They knew Benji was capable of such shenanigans, but his confession and desire to make amends was remarkable.

"Benji, I'm really proud of you for admitting this," said Sarah. She reached out and combed her fingers through his hair.

"It's hard to always make wise choices, Benji." Peter stepped around the table to clasp Benji. "It shows real character to admit you didn't do the right thing, and to take steps to correct it."

Papa grinned affectionately at Benji and said, "A very wise man wrote, 'A man does not call a line crooked unless he has some idea of a straight line.' Benji, I think you met the truly straight line in Himmel, so spotting the crooked line will be much easier."

Grandma was pleasantly surprised to see the transformation in Benji's character, but not too surprised. She knew Yasha had this effect on children because Peter had a similar transformation when he was Benji's age. In her wisdom, she saw the work had been done, and it was best to move on. "Anyone for pecan pie and ice cream?"

They spent the rest of the evening by the fire eating pie, telling stories, and playing board games. The fire had burnt itself into tiny glowing embers by the time the night ended. Peter and Sarah escorted the children upstairs and said their goodnights. As the children lay in bed, they marveled at the miracle of Christmas they were witnessing. The whole family was together on the Ranch. This was the picture of Christmas they had so wanted but had little reason to expect. Just yesterday, they had been in Himmel battling the evil Malby, and their dad was missing and facing danger in a far-off land.

"Do you think it'll snow tomorrow?" asked Hannah. "I'd love a white Christmas."

"It just might, Hannah. We have much to be hopeful for." Aaron recalled what Yasha had said to him: "No matter what comes today, be hopeful. The artwork of tomorrow may bring even greater goodness and beauty."

***

Peter and Sarah were in their bedroom holding each other. Sarah was comforted to have Peter back after fearing she'd never see him again. She shared some of the challenges of the past month but held back just how broken she had been at times while he was away. She thought there was no use putting that weight on his shoulders. They talked about the children, their future, and their dreams for their family — what really mattered in life.

Peter excused himself to prepare a lastminute Christmas present for the children. "I hope they'll like it."

"They will Peter, believe me," replied Sarah. "I think we all will."

Once Peter went off to work on his gift for the children, Sarah scrolled through the news on her phone to catch up on the day. One of the top breaking stories had a headline, "87 Children Rescued in Nigeria." She hesitated for a second, nervous to read on, but she had to know. The article reported that eighty-seven young boys and girls had been kidnapped by notorious Fulani militants from a school near the Gongola River in Nigeria. The children were going to be forced to fight or turned into slaves. If they refused, execution would have been their likely fate. The article claimed an elite military unit of Navy Seals had successfully breached the compound where the children were being held and escorted them to helicopters waiting about a mile from the compound. The article didn't go into any more detail, but Sarah knew there was a lot more to the mission than the bare bones press account.

Sarah was aghast by the evil Peter had confronted on this mission. He was always so kind, patient, and loving. How could he turn off the horrors of what he had seen and be the kind of husband and father he was to their family? What could she possibly do to honor such a man?

Peter returned with a small box and announced it was ready for Christmas morning. "Peter, did I ever tell you how wonderful and amazing you are?" said Sarah. "And how much I love you?"

"Not since about an hour ago," Peter chuckled and an odd look passed over his face. "Did you read something in the news?"

"Yeah, but I won't ask any questions." Sarah smiled coyly at Peter. "Well, maybe just one. How can you erase such evil from your mind when you get home?"

"I don't erase it, can't erase it. It becomes part of me, for the rest of my life." Peter sat on the bed considering the heaviness of the question. "I learned a long time ago, living on this Ranch in fact, that the world is full of good and beautiful things. That's what I choose to fill my mind with."

Sarah wrapped her arms around Peter and squeezed as tight as she could. "Let's go peek in on three little good and beautiful people in the next bedroom."

They opened the door a crack and gazed at the angelic faces of Aaron, Benji, and Hannah. Peter and Sarah were filled with a peace that surpassed understanding as they watched them sleep. Seeing their own children safe and secure made them think about the eighty-seven children a world away. They too, would be safely sleeping tonight. Perhaps Peter had not saved the entire world, but he had courageously saved the world for those children.

Chapter Twenty-Four
White Christmas

R omeo's crowing came early on Christmas day, and it was a welcome reminder to Aaron that he was home. "Wow, he's really excited about Christmas," joked Aaron. He rubbed his eyes as he looked out the window and down on the barn.

"It's snowing! Everything's white," said Benji amazed by the heavy snow falling.

"Hannah, wake up," whispered Aaron gently shaking Hannah's shoulder. "It's Christmas."

The three of them gathered around the window and stared at the snow-covered mountain. "Let's build a snowman today," said Hannah.

"Sure, maybe later," replied Aaron. "I'm heading downstairs to see what's in our stockings."

Benji and Hannah rushed after him. "Wait for me," they said. Bailey was not far behind as he bounded after them.

They ran into the family room to see three bulging stockings hanging on the mantle in front of the fireplace. Each stocking had one of their names stitched on it. They emptied their stockings and surveyed the gifts: small puzzles, stickers, candy, and other fun things. They set aside the new toothbrushes and toothpaste as an afterthought.

"Oh boy," shouted Aaron as he combed through his treats. "Chocolate covered caramels," he squealed as he opened the pack and plopped one into his mouth.

"I got a chocolate and peanut cluster bar," yelled Benji. "It's the humongous theater size."

"Fruit gummies," shouted Hannah, "my favorite."

"Good morning," said Grandma from the kitchen. The scrumptious aroma of her famous breakfast on the griddle filled the lodge. "Merry Christmas!"

"Did you see the snow coming down?" asked Papa. He was sitting in the kitchen sipping his coffee. "Quite a flurry out there."

"Come sit down, breakfast is ready," called out Grandma. She balanced two large platters in her hands and placed them on the table. One platter had eggs, bacon, and hashbrowns, and the other had homemade cranberry muffins.

"Papa, do you think the animals are OK in the snow?" asked Hannah. She grabbed a cranberry muffin and took a big bite.

"They're all in the barn, safe and warm," replied Papa as he scooped up a serving of eggs, bacon, and hashbrowns. "Enjoy your breakfast and we'll deal with them after that."

Sarah gazed fondly at the children. "How did you sleep?" she asked. Sarah's smile announced her joy over the return of the children and Peter. "Nice to have you back in the lodge."

"Good, but Romeo woke us up so early," replied Aaron. He smacked his lips as he finished off one of his chocolate caramels. "This is our snowiest Christmas ever."

"That's Romeo," added Papa with a chuckle. "I don't recall many whiter Christmases on the Ranch."

"After breakfast, we can open presents," said Peter. "There might be something under the tree."

The breakfast was so delicious they scraped every last bit off their plates. The family room had an inviting glow with the glimmer of the fire reflecting throughout the room. The Christmas tree was sparkling with lights and ornaments radiating the spirit of Christmas. A large picture window displayed the breathtaking snow-covered mountain as nature's magnificent portrait. Under the tree were presents of all sizes and shapes wrapped in bright shades of green, red, and white.

"We didn't have time to get a lot this year with Dad being gone and all," Sarah said as she reached under the tree to retrieve one of the presents. "Hannah, why don't you open this one." Sarah handed her a large box wrapped in bright green paper with a candy cane tied to a red ribbon.

"It's such a big box," said Hannah as she pulled the wrapping off the present. She opened the box and squealed with delight, "It's a handball!" She held up the large red inflated rubber ball for all to see and exclaimed, "It's just what I wanted. Thanks, I love it."

Hannah bounced the ball as she eyed Aaron and Benji. "Anyone brave enough to take on the champion of Himmel?"

Aaron and Benji quickly shook their heads shutting down the possibility of losing to their little sister. "Not a chance," said Aaron with a chuckle.

"Aaron and Benji, here's a little something for each of you," said Sarah. She handed the boys small rectangular boxes wrapped in red and white striped paper with matching candy canes on top. "Open them at the same time… you know why."

Aaron and Benji opened their gifts keeping one eye on each other. Benji got his wrapping off a second sooner and yelled, "An army knife, awesome." They began to examine all the tools including multiple blades, screw drivers, scissors, and a can opener.

"It has twelve tools; I hope you like it," said Sarah. "It's a must have now that you're adventurers." Sarah chuckled as she enjoyed the boy's delight.

"I love it," exclaimed Benji. He fidgeted with all the tools testing them out, one by one. "It would have come in handy in Himmel."

"Me too," said Aaron. "Just being here on the Ranch with everyone, that's the best gift."

The handball and army knives were very nice, but Peter being home with them was the most precious Christmas gift, and an unexpected one at that. He had been gone for what seemed like an eternity, and they hadn't been sure when or if he would return. Their hearts were full just being with the entire family for Christmas. Nothing else was needed. Their time in Himmel with Yasha had changed what they cared about.

Peter reached down and pulled a small flat box from under the tree. It was not covered with fancy gift wrap and seemed like it might have been a lastminute recycled box used in the past. "This is for all three of you from your mom and me."

Aaron and Benji used their new knives to cut the scotch tape holding the box together and the three of them carefully lifted the top. They pulled out a large piece of paper, unfolded it, and held it out to examine it more closely. It was a pencil sketch of a building of some sort.

"What is it?" asked Aaron with a quizzical expression on his face. "It's a nice drawing."

"It's a cabin," replied Peter. "Sorry it's not better. I drew it last night after everyone went to bed."

Benji turned his head sideways and strained to understand the sketch. "Do we put this on the wall like art?" He didn't want to be rude to his dad, but the sketch was definitely not wall art quality.

"You can, but this isn't the real gift," said Sarah. She saw that Peter needed a little help explaining it to them. "You know how much you love coming to the Ranch to visit Papa and Grandma?"

"Yeah, it's great," replied Hannah. "Now that we know about Himmel, it's even more awesome."

"I retired from the Navy Seals," said Peter. "This was my last mission. So, we can live anywhere we want." Peter was about to burst as he watched the children try to grasp what he was saying. "How would you like to live at the Ranch all the time?"

"Are you serious?" asked Aaron. His eyes lit up and he jumped to his feet.

"I'd love it."

Benji ran up to Peter and leaped into his arms. "When can we move?"

"Papa and Grandma said we can stay with them in the lodge until we finish building the cabin." Peter smiled at Papa and Grandma as he shared the news with the children. "We can move our stuff next month."

"That's right," said Papa. He picked up the drawing and held it up for everyone to see. "We can start building the cabin as soon as the snow melts. It should be ready to move in by next fall.

"But if you retire from the Seals, what will you do?" asked Aaron. "The Seals is your job."

"I'm starting up the wood crafting business again," said Peter as he glanced at Papa, who was smiling ear to ear. "I'm getting into the family business."

"And I'll move my veterinary practice," said Sarah. "There are plenty of animals in need of care here in the mountains."

Peter pulled out a map of the Ranch and laid it out on the table. "There's a nice spot next to the greenhouse with a beautiful view of the valley and the forest."

"Can we see it?" asked Hannah. She squeezed her handball so hard; it looked like it was about to pop. "We're going to live on the Ranch!"

"Yeah, let's go there now," shouted Benji. He stuffed his new knife into his pocket and ran to put on his winter jacket. "I think the snow is easing up."

The whole family dressed in their warm clothes, put on their scarves and hats, and headed out to the plot of land they had chosen for the cabin.

"Dad, can I go on your shoulders?" asked Hannah. She held her hands up in the air with a look that melted Peter's heart. "The snow's pretty high."

"Love to, Hannah," he said, and picked her up and placed her on his shoulders. The view from her dad's strong shoulders was especially delightful today. She could see the whole family walking together through the snow with a large forest on one side and a beautiful valley below on the other side.

Aaron and Benji walked alongside Peter as they trudged through the snow. "We didn't want to leave the Ranch, but I was afraid to tell you," said Aaron.

"I grew up on the Ranch and I want you three to have the same experience. Now that I'm done with the Seals, I'll have a lot more time with you." He grinned at Aaron and gave him a friendly slap on the back. "Plenty of time to work on our football game."

They arrived at the plot of land and Peter gave them a tour of where everything would be. He walked through the imaginary front door and escorted them through each future room. He pointed out the views from each room and where their bedrooms would be. Aaron, Benji, and Hannah ran around the parcel of land and pretended to enter each room. Their laughter filled this imaginary home.

Papa nudged Grandma and then reached into his pocket and pulled out three small boxes. "Hey kids, come on over for a minute."

Aaron, Benji, and Hannah rushed over and slid into the snowbank next to Papa and Grandma causing snow to spray all over them. "What's up, Papa?" replied Aaron still panting from his roughhousing with Benji and Hannah.

"Grandma and I have a small gift for each of you." Papa handed the boxes wrapped in shiny silver paper to the children. "It's part of our family."

They ripped off the paper and opened the boxes to find a beautiful cord bracelet in each. The bracelets were made of colored strands of twine that were intricately braided into a single cord. The white, red and green strands shimmered in the light.

"It's beautiful," said Hannah. She held it up to Sarah to help her put it on her wrist.

Aaron fidgeted with his bracelet, trying to fasten it to his wrist, but eventually gave up and handed it to Peter to help. "Thank you, Papa and Grandma. This is cool."

"Very slick, Papa," said Benji. He twirled the bracelet in his hand admiring the colors.

Papa smiled as he collected the wrapping paper and stuffed it in his pocket. "This will be a reminder of the Parsons Cord."

Aaron moved up close to Papa as Peter worked on his wrist. "Tell us the story of the Parsons Cord, Papa."

"It's been a tradition of our family for many generations." Papa pulled more cord bracelets from his pocket and handed them to Grandma, Peter, and Sarah. "Every Parsons child is added to the Parsons Cord, making it stronger and stronger with each generation."

Aaron's eyes were as big as the moon as he listened to Papa. "What's it mean, Papa?"

"It's a symbol. An unbreakable cord that overcomes every sort of challenge that life may bring." Papa fiddled with his bracelet trying to attach it to his wrist. "The white strand represents Yasha. The unbreakable center of the cord."

"What's after that?" asked Benji, still admiring the colors now on his wrist.

"The red strand represents Yasha's truth and love radiating from the center." Papa twisted his wrist to highlight the red strand. "Truth and love are the bright lights to guide our path in wisdom."

"Yasha told us about love and truth, Papa," said Hannah as she examined her wrist. "What's after that?"

Papa was still fussing with his bracelet grimacing as he vainly tried to attach it. "Here let me help you," said Grandma. She snatched his wrist and began working on the bracelet.

Papa smiled at Grandma, then continued. "The green represents the goodness and beauty that flow out of Yasha's truth and love. The green also represents goodness and beauty of our family. This stream of goodness and beauty nourishes us with an abundant life," said Papa.

"The past few days have given me a whole new understanding of that," replied Aaron with a wry smile. He held his wrist up to Papa's and compared the two identical bracelets. "And what's after that, Papa?"

Papa looked deeply into the eyes of Aaron, Benji, and Hannah. "With each new child this strand grows thicker, making the Parsons Cord an ever-stronger bond."

"Hey, Papa," called out Aaron with a curious expression. "Since Yasha is the center of the cord, shouldn't we call it Yasha's Cord?"

"I suppose we should," replied Papa as he admired his new bracelet. "That's where the power and strength come from."

After they finally secured their new bracelets, they waved their wrists to show off the colors to each other. Peter held up his hand extending his two crossed fingers, and yelled, "Long live the Parsons' Cord... I mean Yasha's Cord."

Without warning, the former Navy Seal wrestled Papa into a snowbank that quickly escalated into a dog pile. Sarah wasn't going to miss the opportunity, so she leaped on top of Peter, stuffing handfuls of snow down his shirt. Aaron nodded at Benji, and they both jumped on top, grabbing whatever appendage they could get their hands on. Hannah climbed up the mountain of humanity screaming, "Yasha's Cord." Grandma, being more refined, simply laid her hand on top of the pile of jumbled arms, legs, and other assorted body parts. Bailey barked, running circles and kicking up snow around the mayhem, not sure what to make of his animal-like family. The mixture of groans and laughter emanating from the pile mystified Bailey as he weighed his conflicted sense of duty to protect and desire to play.

As they slowly unraveled the knot of Parsons, Aaron had an idea. He didn't want this moment to end. This time with family swelled his heart with the same contentment he had experienced when he was with Yasha. "Hey, let's build a snowman here to mark where our cabin will be."

"That's a wonderful idea," said Papa. "Aaron, why don't you make the bottom snowball, and make it big."

"Benji, you make the middle snowball, a little smaller than Aaron's." Peter was overjoyed to be back with his family savoring the simple gifts that life brings. Compared to the world he had just left, this was paradise. "Hannah, sweetie, you make the head a little smaller than Benji's snowball."

Papa and Grandma receded several steps, happy to take in this family time from the background. They wanted Peter and Sarah to relish this moment with the children, and it gave them immeasurable joy to see Peter reunited with his family. "Such a precious time," whispered Grandma. Papa squeezed her shoulder gently and smiled as they watched their family play on Christmas day.

The children gathered the three snowballs and carefully assembled them with Aaron's first, then Benji's and finally Hannah's on top.

"Now we need to create the face for our snowman," said Sarah as she stepped back to admire the new frozen member of the family. "What can we use?"

They looked around for small things to create the snowman's face. Aaron paused and something struck him. "Hey, I've got an idea." He motioned for Benji and Hannah to gather around him. The three of them whispered out of earshot of the adults. Aaron pulled on his scarf and Benji and Hannah checked their pockets and nodded as they talked.

They turned and rushed over to the snowman and began working on him. Benji pulled a pebble from his pocket and set it in the face of the snowman for one eye. Hannah pulled a similar pebble from her pocket and did the same. Aaron then took his scarf off and carefully wrapped it around the snowman's neck. They scavenged the area for a few more small pebbles or bits of wood and soon had a smiling snowman.

"What do you think?" asked Aaron. He stood next to the snowman with his arm extended like he was introducing a good friend. "The doorman to our new cabin."

"It's wonderful," said Peter. "He'll make a fine doorman."

"I haven't seen that scarf," said Sarah. She ran the scarf through her fingers examining it. "Where'd you get it?"

"Yasha gave it to us as a gift when we left Himmel," replied Aaron. He held a corner of the scarf in his hand admiring its beauty. "He gave Benji and Hannah the pebbles we used for the eyes. Yasha said he thought we would need them."

"He's very wise," said Peter as he stepped closer to admire the snowman. "I guess this is Yasha's way of telling us he'll be watching over us and providing for our needs."

"Well, it's a fine-looking snowman," said Papa as he scraped off some extra snow from the snowman's head. "A doorman for the new cabin, indeed. At least as long as the snow lasts."

They all stood in a semi-circle surrounding the snowman and admired both it and the beautiful view of the valley below.

"We learned a new song from Enzo Fawn in Himmel," said Hannah. "It's about Yasha." Hannah had an overflowing feeling of delight as she cuddled with her family. It reminded her of the warmth and peace she had experienced with Yasha, especially on their walk on the lake shore. "It's called, *My King.* Let's sing it."

"That's a wonderful idea," said Sarah. She reached over and grasped Hannah's hand bringing her close to her. "How does it go?"

Hannah spoke the lyrics once and then hummed the tune. Peter's eyes glistened as he silently reminisced about the song's impact in his life. *Mr. Wigglebottom taught me this song so very long ago. Reminds me of who Yasha is. Funny thing, I taught it to the African children during my last mission.*

Papa smiled as he heard the lyrics. "A wonderful song, Hannah. It's been my favorite for many years. Helped me through some very dark days."

Hannah started singing, and Aaron and Benji quickly joined in. After a verse, Peter and Papa began, and soon they were all singing the song with joy in their hearts. King Yasha was with them. As were the many good and beautiful things in their life that they now could see clearly.

> *You've made the day for my delight.*
> *You bring us warmth and light.*
> *And keep us safe at night.*
> *You guard our lives with your love and might.*
> *Oh, what a good and beautiful King.*

Epilogue
The War is not Over

Malby and Fister were still in the lockdown of the presidential office that Malby had ordered when King Yasha's cleansing rain wiped out his reign over the people of Shadowlands. Fister paced back and forth as he watched Malby stew in the corner of the presidential office. The air system had been shut down during the lockdown for security reasons, so the office had taken on an overwhelming stench from a toxic blend of stale air, bad breath, and body odor.

Fister had given up on his man bun, so long greasy strands of hair rested on his jacket. The stains from his oily hair along with a flood of flop sweat transformed his ruby red suit into a menacing blood-red tone. His gaunt face revealed the stress of spending the last several days confined with the unhinged Malby. Fister summoned the courage to approach his psychopathic boss, stopping several feet away. He was still leery after the flying marble pen holder incident. "Your Most Wise Eminence. What's next?"

Malby sneered at Fister with the fire of a thousand torches. "I blame you for this, Fister. If you hadn't gone to those infernal Himmel Games, none of this would have happened."

Fister recoiled into the far corner of the room calculating his reply in his head. *Me! He's the fool who insisted we're the storytellers. Go, we'll make movie magic. The truth doesn't matter. Blah, blah, blah. This man is certifiable, but oh so dangerous. How do I manipulate ... manage such a lunatic. Ah... redirect.* He crept toward Malby and moved the strands of hair stuck to his face. "Oh your Unsurpassed Eminence, if I may beg your indulgence. There may be another culprit to this most heinous of outcomes."

Malby's pale complexion had been replaced by burning cheeks so it resembled a big red balloon ready to pop. "What do you mean... and don't give me any of your flowery poetry."

"The children, sir." Fister slunk to the window and stared out at the pile of rubble that was formerly Malby's monument to himself. "It seems our plan went astray when those children entered the picture."

"Those children," hissed Malby. "With their sweet, innocent, little faces. Disgusting."

Fister could see Malby's vision taking a favorable turn. "I oh so humbly suggest we address the real enemy. King Yasha seemed to place quite a bit of faith in those children."

A slithering smile emerged on Malby's face. "Yes, the plan was good... but those children."

Fister removed his stained sweaty jacket and laid it on the chair. He strolled over to the sink and splashed water on his face and began combing his hair back into a bun. This relief from Malby's rage was welcome, but he knew the winds could shift any moment with the storm called Malby. Fister was a storyteller. Like every good story, this new one would have villains: King Yasha and the children. Of course he planned a leading role for himself, but it certainly wouldn't be that of a villain. "Most Magnificent Eminence, isn't it time to rebuild the Road to Destruction?"

"We've been thinking too small, Fister." Malby glared down at the rubble imagining a rebuilt statue of himself for all to worship. He let out a foreboding cackle, "It's time to expand, indeed. The Road to Destruction never ends."

Attribution

In Chapter 23, Papa refers to a wise man comparing a crooked line to a straight line as an illustration of objective morality. "A man does not call a line crooked unless he has some idea of a straight line." This quote is from C.S. Lewis in his book, Mere Christianity.

Continue the Adventure

Congratulations on finishing *Kingdom in the Redwoods*. I hope you enjoyed the story and that it left you wanting more. If you do, I've got good news. I'm working on a sequel that takes Aaron, Benji, and Hannah on an even greater adventure. If you want to see the latest news on upcoming books, sign up for my free newsletter at: www.kevenbaxter.com.

But you don't have to wait until the next book is released. You can continue the journey with *Kingdom in the Redwoods Bible Study*. This study is a fun way to explore the theological themes presented in *Kingdom in the Redwoods*. This resource is fantastic for Bible study groups, youth ministries, homeschool use, families, or individual study and reflection. **You can request a free copy of the *Kingdom in the Redwoods Bible Study* at: www.kevenbaxter.com.**

Thank you for joining me on the adventure, *Kingdom in the Redwoods*. I am dedicated to creating captivating stories for you that deliver light and hope, so I would love to hear from you. I value your feedback and want to hear from you. You can email me at: **bax@kevenbaxter.com.**

Thank you,
Keven Baxter

Other Awards Won by the Author

About Kharis Publishing

Kharis Publishing, an imprint of Kharis Media LLC, is a leading Christian and inspirational book publisher based in Aurora, Chicago metropolitan area, Illinois. Kharis' dual mission is to give voice to under-represented writers (including women and first-time authors) and equip orphans in developing countries with literacy tools. That is why, for each book sold, the publisher channels some of the proceeds into providing books and computers for orphanages in developing countries so that these kids may learn to read, dream, and grow. For a limited time, Kharis Publishing is accepting unsolicited queries for nonfiction (Christian, self-help, memoirs, business, health and wellness) from qualified leaders, professionals, pastors, and ministers. Learn more at:
 https://kharispublishing.com/

www.ingramcontent.com/pod-product-compliance
Lightning Source LLC
Chambersburg PA
CBHW030645020726
47493CB00006B/1883